AAIDA

All the kinswomen #2

Amal Ibrahim

AAIDA

AMAL IBRAHIM

AMAL IBRAHIM

PART 1 : 1988 - 1998

TRADITION

Tradition: the transmission of customs or beliefs from generation to generation

Once upon a time, a long long time ago, in a land far far away, an unknown person came up with the idea of tradition.

Hundreds of traditions were created over time, put into place and passed down from generation to generation, and each culture had its own set of traditions. At times, these traditions crossed over, and some were so outlandish, they would defy belief in the modern world.

Long before newspapers and television and the internet, there was a tradition called "word of mouth." If you wanted something, or someone, you could find said article by asking someone who knew someone who knew someone's cousin/ neighbour/friend who was in possession of said item.

And that's how one particular tradition came to be. *The arranged marriage.* However, not so arranged, because at the end of the day, both parties would meet, get to know one another in the company of their families, find they had a lot in common, and voila! They would be married. So it may have started out arranged, but really, it's a combination of minds coming together to create an invisible algorithm that matches two people who are perfectly compatible with one another.

For a more diverse explanation, I'll put it to you this way. The age old tradition of an "arranged marriage" mirrors exactly today's practise of a "blind date." Tina thinks Jodie would make a good match with her friend Steve, who Jodie has never met. So she sets them up on a "blind date". When they do meet, they realise they have a lot in common, are attracted to one another, and this could possibly go somewhere. A series of dates/ meetings/outings ensues, culminating in a union.

The same can be said for dating apps. Based on your age, race, hobbies and gender, a computerised algorithm will match you up with several choices that will either pan out, or they won't. In most cases, you will see a digitally enhanced photo of said match, and based on what you see, you make a choice whether or not to meet this person. Granted, once you meet, you may realise the person in the photo looks nothing like they actually do in real life, but the option for a "blind date" is there anyway. So your first impression of this person, quite literally, is a superficial one. And it's also an "arranged meeting".

In Arab cultural tradition, the concept of the arranged marriage is one that can be traced back thousands of years and is also based somewhat on the concept of a "blind date", however its core algorithm is a referral system of humans making recommendations to one another about prospective matches they believe would work well. This tradition is still widely practised, with a majority of arranged marriages resulting in long and happy unions.

The arranged marriage (explanation above) is not to be confused with the forced marriage (explanation below). This practise has been widely exploited in various parts of the world since the advent of time, and reports indicate it still happens globally on a wide scale to this day.

A forced marriage, much unlike an arranged marriage, is one where either or both of those involved in the union had no say in the matter, specifically where one (or both, sometimes) had no desire to be united with said partner. It is defined as a union where informed consent has not been given by one or more parties involved.

My mother Aujene was the subject of a forced marriage.

My grandmother Tala before her was also forced into a marriage to a man not of her choosing.

And my aunt Farida agreed to an arranged marriage to save herself from certain death.

Me, I was determined to do my own thing on my own terms.

AAIDA

My relationship with my mother is a special one.

Most likely because I'm an only child.

So when I'm in my 40's, I find that my mother is practically my best friend.

For a long time, I was almost an endangered species. Being an only child, mother practically smothered me, until all her women friends rose up in my defence and told her to just let me be.

My parent's divorce when I was 15 years old was the best thing to happen to me. And to my mum. My dad...meh...maybe not so much. I think he lost the comfort he had known all his life in having someone look after him. For my mother played more the role of subservient and housemaid, rather than wife and lover. And I swore to myself that I would never become that person.

Shortly after their split, my father moved to Lebanon and remarried, then proceeded to have many children back to back with his new wife. When I couldn't understand why I was an only child when my father so obviously was able to have- and care for- so many children, my mother would look at me sadly, blinking back tears as she told me it was not written for her to bear more than one child. I never really understood what she meant until I was older and sitting with my *tayta* Tala, who explained, in simple terms, the reality of my parent's marriage.

"Your father was...is...," she corrected, "a very selfish man. Well, at least he was when your mother was married to him."

This from tayta Tala, who never lowered herself to speak ill of *anyone*. And this was as bad as it would ever get, for she never stooped to a lower station to paint anyone in a bad light.

Contrary, she would always be making excuses and concessions for a person's misgivings.

I take tayta's hand and smooth over it with my own, committing every ridge and valley of her hands to memory. I love tayta Tala more than life itself. Ever since that first trip I'd made to Lebanon years ago, when I was still young and carefree and she could still see me in shadow. A mere outline. But she could still see, no matter how fuzzy. Now, years later, she has lost her eyesight completely and sees things merely as movement. Blurs that move. But more than any other sense a human could possess, tayta Tala possesses an uncanny ability to identify people by mannerisms and touch.

She knows me by the click clack of my heels on her concrete walkway before I enter her beautiful *dhar,* a magnificent garden of fruit and olive trees peppered with the fragrant scent of basil, parsley and oregano.

"*Ahhh, ijjit Aaida! Ejjitee ya binti?*" and she would guess right every single time. When I tried to fool her by walking in with sneakers, she merely smirked and told me I couldn't fool her, stopping me dead in my tracks.

"But how could you possibly know it was me, tayta!?!" I squealed in surprise.

"Because aside from the click clack of your heels, you have a very distinct pitter patter when you walk," she explained. "And the air..." she jutted out her chin and sniffed the cool Spring air, then slowly shook her head left right left, telling me that the air shifted anytime I was around. The only thing she could compare my presence to, she explained, was the earthquake that tore through their village many years ago.

"So I remind you of an earthquake?" I laughed.

"You remind me of the ground shifting. For I feel your presence Aaida, as though the earth is moving."

AUJENE

It's 1991, I'm 36 years old and I'm a divorced woman. I've been divorced for 2 years. It's funny how society's perception of a woman changes once a woman gets divorced. As a married woman, I was popular with everyone and well respected in my community. As a divorcee, I became a pariah. It was 1991. It may as well have been 1951.

All of my friends who knew me, those who had frequented my home and spent many an hour at the kitchen bench with me stood by and supported me, offering a sympathetic ear whenever I had a meltdown. For there were many meltdowns as I second guessed myself and wondered whether or not I was doing the right thing. But every time I looked at Aaida and remembered that Samer had practically not contributed anything of substance to her life, I pushed through and willed myself to muster all my strength to keep going.

Of course, there were those in our community who literally crossed the road with their husbands whenever they saw me walking down the street, as though fearful that the mere interloping of our lives would rub off on them and they would also end up divorced. For many could not understand why Samer and I had divorced, and this was obvious in the whispers I overheard here and there all over the neighbourhood. "He's such a good husband, hard worker, bought her a beautiful house, working hard to support his wife who doesn't work..."

On and on it went, anywhere I went, constant whispers from those that knew me and those that did not - it was all people were talking about. And eventually, I realised this was because even in 1991, I was one of the first in our tight-knit Lebanese community to be divorced. I was definitely the only woman I knew about that was divorced.

Where at first I conditioned myself to ignore the rumours and the whispers, eventually they started to grate on my nerves as I realised most of the gossips had sided with my husband and were blaming me for the divorce. It struck me as odd how people were so quick to judge others and draw conclusions, especially when no-one really knew what went on behind closed doors. I wondered, had the women known how I'd been treated over the years, would they have been more forgiving? Or would they still have laid the blame squarely on my shoulders?

So it came to be that I was the talk of the town for many months after my divorce, by those that knew me, and those that did not. It was on one such occasion that I came to be standing in the local butcher's shop right behind two women I didn't know, but who obviously knew each other. I looked down at the meat display, mentally prepping my order in my head. The butcher looked up at me nervously, announcing he wouldn't be long, then cast his eyes down as he continued to pack the other women's orders.

The whole conversation being played out in front of me would have flown right over my head had it not been for my name being uttered by one of the women.

"An unusual name for an unusual woman," one of the ladies said, my name rolling off her tongue like a lullaby. "Aujene. She's beautiful, I hear."

"Beauty didn't prevent her getting divorced!" the other woman scoffed. "I hear she was a terrible wife and an even terrible mother. Refused to give him more than one child."

I stood still and unmoving, not knowing whether I should just leave the store or stand my ground. I suddenly understood the butcher's nervous greeting had been because the conversation had started even before I'd stepped foot in the store.

"Nonsense!" The first woman denounced. "No-one could possibly know what went on in that house except the husband and wife. All these rumours people keep spurting!"

"Not rumours," the second woman defended. "I have it on good authority he left her because she was having an affair!"

And that's when I felt the heat rise up my neck and flush through my face as I felt myself burning up. I realised they hadn't heard me come in and held my breath as their conversation unfolded and the second woman continued her attack on me.

"You shouldn't talk such rubbish, Samah!" the first woman admonished, and the second woman went on to explain how I had been caught in the act and that was the reason I had been divorced.

I exhaled the breath I'd been holding and pursed my lips, trying to hold my tongue but failing miserably as anger and rage surged through my core.

"And you know all this HOW?!?" I bellowed.

Both women turned in surprise and saw me standing there enraged. The first woman, the one who had been defending me, lowered her eyes in embarrassment, while the second lady's face turned crimson as her bottom lip started to tremble.

"I am Aujene, and here I stand before you!" I screamed. "I'm not afraid of anything you say, but prove to me that what you're saying is true! To my FACE!!"

The woman sputtered as she tried to form words to explain herself, but I saw so clearly that she was a silly, misguided fool who liked to gossip and didn't understand the consequences of her rumours. Overwhelmed with grief and anger, I came up close to her face and almost whispered, asking her if she had daughters. She nodded her head quickly in answer and tried to step backward, but stepped right into her friend.

"Remember that one day your daughter will be married. One day she may go through trials. She may not be blessed with children. Her husband may not be a good match for her. But remember this," I hissed. "The good you put out there today is the reward you reap tomorrow. Don't you *ever* forget that you wronged me today, and karma will get you one way or another."

"*Ekhti...*" the first woman began, but she was cut off by the slanderer.

"I'm only repeating what others are saying!" she defended herself.

"Exactly!" I hissed. "This is how rumours are started and reputations are ruined. You know nothing, NOTHING about me! You don't even KNOW me! And here you are, one woman tearing down another! You disgust me!"

By the time I was finished, I was visibly shaken and tears were streaming down my cheeks as my life played in reverse like a movie reel. All the sacrifices I'd had to make. All the losses. Coming to a foreign country where I had no family and no support. An absent husband. A dead son. The pain was overwhelming as I clutched with trembling fingers at my chest and pulled at my dress.

"You know nothing. Nothing," I whispered indignantly, reaching for the door and taking flight out of the shop.

AAIDA

We're driving from the airport to our family home in Tul Ghosn, a small village in Lebanon's North. The country is in ruins. It has been decimated after 15 years of civil war and internal conflict arising from sectarian violence.

When we near our village, after driving hours on potholed roads and witnessing first hand the destruction of a once beautiful country, I see an old advertising board for Lipton on the side of the road. It is faded and ripped, and I marvel that the board is actually still standing.

There is a quaint charm to the way Lebanon has been sent back in time to an era of pre-modernisation. Life is simple, and there is an authenticity to the Arab way of life that has not yet been touched by westernisation.

In the first week we are in Lebanon, there is the heavy thumping of artillery and bombs in the distance, and when I run out in my pyjamas, shocked and terrified, my grandmother laughs and tells me it is the Israelis shooting off rounds at a nearby Palestinian camp. As though this is the norm, the Lebanese have become accustomed to such incidents. After 15 years of war and conflict, this is tame compared to what they've seen and lived through, my tayta tells me.

I walk back into the house and hold a pillow to my head to drown out the sound of the violence. This is my first trip to Lebanon, and already I'm questioning the wisdom of having come here to this. It was my understanding that the war was over and we'd be safe here.

It becomes a common occurrence. I see the night sky awash with the vibrant hues of yellow and orange and grey as I stand on the balcony and look out toward the sea. A huge ship comes in close to the port and starts firing at the refugee camp backing on to the seabed. The next morning, we hear the rapid firing of machine guns and the wailing of alarms in the distance as the dead are honoured and laid to rest.

On one occasion, we are travelling on the single road not destroyed during the war to get to the city, which cuts through a Palestinian refugee camp. The traffic is backed up and we are forced to stop as a mass of people converges on the street by foot, carrying three dead bodies cloaked in burial shrouds. I can see the faces of three youthful men peeking out from the shrouds, and my heart stutters as my tongue goes numb with grief and tears form in my eyes. This is my first taste of death, and the zeal and fervour of the death march tugs at something deep within me.

The national news plays out on the little black and white TV set that tayta has when the generator is switched on so we have electricity to do the washing. The TV is barely 30cm and the antenna is a makeshift coat hanger stuck in a back socket. Tayta Tala loves her little television set, even though she rarely switches it on. We have tried to replace it with a newer model on numerous occasions, but she insists on keeping this one. Obviously, it holds some sort of sentimental value for her, otherwise why would she hold on to it, I wonder?

I have a certain patriotic hunger for my country. I love Lebanon, but I hate what the war has done to its people. It's understandable, after so many years of instability, yet still, there has to be some measure of change in order for the country, a tiny dot on the world map which is sandwiched between warring neighbours, to flourish.

AUJENE

Precisely two and a half years after I left Samer, I travelled to Lebanon with Aaida to see my family for the first time in almost 15 years. By now, Samer had remarried and his wife had given him two sons, who he apparently doted on. If I were a lesser person, I may have been jealous, but I actually found myself quietly pleased that he was now someone else's problem.

He came to see us merely days after we arrived, but to my surprise, he didn't bring his wife with him. Rather, he brought his mother. We sat awkwardly in my mother's lounge room, making small talk. My ex mother in law had never really taken to me, and I could see that nothing had changed as she explained that she had only come to check on her grand-daughter, saying it in a way that minimised my existence to a speck of dirt beneath her shoe.

I turned around to pour the *ahwi* and rolled my eyes, realising some things were bound to never change.

"You must still be exhausted from the flight," Samer said, looking at my hand as I stretched it to pass him his cup. His eyes lingered a little too long on my chest, and I wrapped my shawl closer against my dress, hiding beneath the layers where his eyes could not penetrate. Ex-husband or not, he no longer had any rights over me, and he definitely shouldn't have been looking at me that way.

"Why don't we go for a walk, my dear," Samer's mother suggested, turning to Aaida, who stood and took her grandmother's hand in hers before she led her outside to the *dhar*.

"How long will you stay for?" Samer asked.

"We're only here for a few weeks; feel free to use this time with your daughter wisely, as it is very limited."

"What about you?" he asked. "Will you be supervising the visits?"

"Have I ever?" I asked him. "Aaida's 17, she doesn't need a babysitter."

"I just thought you might like to spend some time with us as a family," he corrected, setting his cup down and leaning forward so he was closer to me.

"We're no longer a family, Samer," I reminded him. "You have a new family now. But as I said, feel free to spend time with Aaida and introduce her to her half-brothers."

Samer clicked his tongue and continued to stare at me for the longest time without saying anything, making me uncomfortable.

"We can still be a family."

I shook my head and looked away, pursing my lips. I know he probably thought I was upset, but I just had an overwhelming urge to laugh, so I chose to look away instead. When he threw out his next sentence, I almost choked on the laughter I'd been suppressing. I didn't know if he was suggesting or offering.

"What did you say?" I asked, because I was sure I'd heard wrong.

"I'll marry you again." Like he was doing me a favour; he was definitely offering.

"You're already married," I explained to him. He moved further forward, somewhat eagerly, as though what I'd said gave him hope.

"I can marry four wives. You know that, Aujene." Explaining to me as though what I'd said was the stupidest thing he'd ever heard.

"I'm not remarrying you," I gasped, when I realised that he was serious.

"Well, why ever not? We divorced over something so inconsequential, but that's over now. We could start anew. We haven't lost a lot of time," he reminded me.

"Samer," I started, letting out an exasperated breath. "There is nothing on this earth that could compel me to marry you again. I'm not the same girl you married."

"Yes," he murmured. "However, I can see some things haven't changed. You're still as stuck up as you ever were."

I shook my head in regret as I looked at his eager face. God only knew I had tried my hardest to muster some feelings for Samer, but in all the years I'd been married to him, I'd not so much as grown to even like him. What person stays with someone they don't even like for the better half of a generation?

"Our divorce is not what your father *Allah yerhamou* would have wanted, Aujene. He's probably turning over in his grave right now."

I scoffed.

"And I feel like I've let him down," he continued. "I never should have signed those divorce papers."

"Well, you did," I reminded him. "You signed and I signed, and we're divorced. There's no going back now."

"There's always second chances if you're just willing to give it a go," he urged.

"But I'm not, Samer. I don't want to go back to you, nor the life we had. I'm happier where I'm at now."

He narrowed his eyes at me and silently asked the question he'd been dying to get out of his mouth since the moment he'd arrived. Of course, he'd noticed the changes in me. My hair was shorter, stylish. I wore colour instead of the dark shades he'd always insisted I wear. I had even lost some weight and my overall demeanour was happier.

"Are you *with* someone?" He asked, a note of accusation ringing in his voice.

"Not that it's any of your business," I said, crossing my arms across my chest defiantly "but no, I'm not. I just don't want to be with you."

He looked at me wearily, as though he didn't believe me. In truth, he probably genuinely couldn't understand why I didn't want to be with him. In his mind, my life began and ended with him.

"Aaida loves it here," I told him, in an attempt to change the subject.

"We're not talking about Aaida right now," he reminded me.

"Then what are we talking about, Samer?"

"Us. We're talking about *us*!" He hissed at me.

I smiled at him sweetly. "Without Aaida, there is no *us*."

Samer left my mother's home shortly thereafter, and that was the last I saw of him the whole time we were in Lebanon. He did not make any effort to visit with his daughter, or ask about her, or even invite her to his own home to meet his sons. I could taste Aaida's heartbreak every time there was a knock at the door or someone mentioned her father.

Her grandmother continued to visit her sporadically, but even then, she spent the majority of her time talking me down while Aaida tried to guide her grandmother away from the subject of me. She still, after all these years, carried me like a thorn in her side wherever she went and would trash my name to anyone who would listen.

There came a day when Aaida finally reached her threshold, and felt like she could no longer tolerate the abuse her grandmother hurled at me and my name. Aaida gave her an ultimatum-that if she was to maintain ties with her grand-daughter, she was not to mention me in any way, shape or form. And although I advised Aaida that her grandmother was elderly and prone to bouts of mania and she shouldn't shut her out, Aaida was finally fed up and didn't want to be surrounded by so much negative energy and toxicity.

Samer's mother, now losing her control over Aaida in her attempts to brainwash her against me, eventually also stopped coming around and left us to enjoy the rest of our visit in peace.

KHALED

Aaida never knew her grandfather Amjad, my mother's father. She was only three years old when she left for Australia, and she didn't return until after his passing. It's been just over two years since he died, and I know that aunt Aujene never would've come back to Lebanon had he still been alive.

I remember my grandfather and everything about him. He had been a grumpy old man with a mean streak and a hardened heart. I also heard stories here and there about how he'd mistreated aunt Aujene to such an extent that she hadn't spoken to him in the years prior to his death. Although I didn't know all the details, I did know some things, and one of those things was that he had his regrets on his deathbed. He had been too proud a man to voice his regrets, or make amends, or right old wrongs. But he did have regrets, and I know this because he voiced them to me when he was falling in and out of delirium and on one such occasion, he mistook me for my father.

He told me he missed his daughter Aujene, and understood why she had shut him out of her life. It had hurt him tremendously, especially later on in life, after she had been gone for years and he realised that her bitterness toward him had not waned.

Aunt Aujene was a textbook example of an Arab woman who had fallen prey to the cultural norms that dictated her life and environment. She had a heartbreaking childhood which ended in a loveless marriage that almost destroyed her. All this, from bits and pieces gathered here and there over the years.

No-one really wanted to talk about aunt Aujene's past, except to say they missed her presence in their lives and worried about her immensely because she was on her own in that strange country that spoke a different tongue. No-one wanted to open the can of worms that was aunt Aujene's existence before she left Lebanon. Her childhood, I gathered, was a bleak one, riddled with horrifying experiences no one should ever have to go through. The entire family was reluctant to talk about her past, and I know that many things that happened within the family over the years were most likely better left in the past.

When aunt Aujene announces that she is divorcing uncle Samer, I can't say that anyone is upset. Surprised, maybe, but no-one voices their disagreement with her decision. The reason, I soon came to realise, is that no-one particularly liked Samer, and most people believed aunt Aujene had been dealt a bad hand and deserved better. So, while not altogether saddened by the news, most were surprised that my aunt had finally mustered up the courage to leave him. My mother, for one, was over the moon when she heard the news. Not for her sister's misfortune, but rather, for her sister's newfound freedom. My father had looked at my mother, somewhat intensely, in that way he often did, and reminded her that Aujene should never have been married off to Samer in the first place, and what a travesty it was that they had all allowed it to happen.

"I should have been a bigger man and done more," my father had said to my mother, to which she scoffed and reminded him that there had been no swaying her father once he had made up his mind.

And that's when I learnt that aunt Aujene had basically been forced to marry her husband. And apparently, by all accounts, it was not a good marriage.

So when she surprises everyone with an announcement that she and her daughter Aaida are coming to Lebanon for a visit, it's as though you told the family it would be raining liquid gold for the next month. That's how excited everyone was. And I, having never met my aunt Aujene, my mother's younger sister, was infected by my mother's happiness that she would finally be reunited with her younger sister.

"So, what's she like, this cousin of mine?" I asked, a few days before they were due to arrive. I leaned against the kitchen counter and watched as my mother sat folding vine leaves.

"Aaida? I haven't seen her since she was 3. But I'm told she's just as intelligent as she was back then. She's a happy, well adjusted teenager, Aujene tells me."

"Who does she look like?"

My mother purses her lips and smiles as she looks down at the vine leaves. It's like she has a secret that only she is entitled to know. Aaida is the only cousin I have not living in Lebanon, and I've never so much as seen a picture of her, so I'm a little curious to know what she's like.

"Why don't you wait and see?" my mother throws at me.

"I'm curious," I tell her.

"Well, she doesn't look like her bum of a father, that's for sure. You'll know her when you see her; apparently she's not the kind of girl people don't notice."

I shrug my shoulders indifferently and fold my legs at the ankles, leaning back into the bench top as I ask how long they'll be staying.

"8 or 9 weeks, I believe. Aaida has to be back in time to start university."

"Wow. She's *that* old?"

"17. A few years younger than you. That's not old," my mother argues, her eyebrows creasing.

"What is she studying?"

"My, you're full of questions," my mother says, looking at me out of the corner of her eyes. "Why don't you save them for when Aaida comes so you actually have something to talk about?"

FARIDA

God didn't bless me with a daughter. No matter how much I longed for one, it was not to be. Ironic, though, that I came from a family of only girls, then bore my husband only boys. Of course, Hassan was so proud of our boys, as was I, and so grateful that our family line would continue on, but I know he had wished for at least one girl, if only to name her Farida after me.

Khaled was the eldest, my first born, the one who most resembled his father, with his scruff of light brown curls bouncing on his head and his stormy grey eyes. We had all been so certain his eyes would revert to brown after a few weeks, but months passed and his beautiful grey eyes had remained just that – grey and beautiful and mesmerising, confounding us all.

Turan was born two years after Khaled, and was a miniature version of myself, dark hair and dark eyes, while possessing the same masculine features as his father.

The twins, Jude and Yousef, kept us on our toes with their mischievous ways, ensuring there was never a dull moment in the house.

And then there came Aaida.

Aaida, who bore such a striking resemblance to me that Hassan could not help but love her as he would his own flesh and blood. My sister Aujene's daughter, Aaida tumbled into our lives like a whirlwind, unwittingly turned our lives upside down, and had every boy in the village vying for her attention, including my sons.

The first time we met Aaida, she was 17 and had come to Lebanon to visit with her mother Aujene. They stayed with my mother, and I spent most of my time in the village to maximise our time together before they flew back to Australia.

Aujene was now divorced; she was the first woman in our family, and even in our tiny village, to ever be divorced. This fact in itself ensured that Aujene would be met with curious eyes and wagging tongues. Most of the women, who no longer had anything else to gossip about except the "Australian girls" who had come to visit, surmised that Aujene's migration to Australia and subsequent exposure to a foreign way of life had resulted in her demise. No-one really cared what the true story was; they just wanted something to talk about. Never mind that her ex-husband Samer had made his way back to Lebanon, remarried, and already had two boys since his divorce; no-one concerned themselves with his business.

Aaida was a beautiful girl. So beautiful my heart stopped when I met her, hugging her to me like a long lost daughter, my soul threatening to collapse from the emotions that overwhelmed me. It felt like I was looking into my past, into the years that I had lost with my younger sister Aujene. For though there were 3 years dividing us, Aujene and I had been stuck at the hip prior to me being taken. And then nothing was ever the same after that as life caught up with us and we were destined to go our separate ways on opposite sides of the globe.

"It's uncanny," Hassan says to me, as we drive back towards our home in Dhar Khamra after we spend the day visiting at my mother's house. "Aaida looks more like you than she does her own mother."

"Yet Aujene and I look very much alike."

"You do, but there are differences. She looks exactly like you did when I first met you. You were similar in age, as well."

My mind floats back to the time in question. I laugh as I remember the first time Hassan and I met. I was in a jail cell and he was on the other side of the bars but didn't have the keys. He did, however, have a solution to my problem.

"She's very beautiful," I comment.

"How do you think Khaled will be towards her?" Hassan asks

me, and he turns his gaze away from the road momentarily to look at me curiously.

"What do you mean?" I frown.

"How do you think he'll react to her? To her similarity to you."

I shrug, contemplating his question, but not seeing the value in dwelling on the subject. "Does it matter? She's his cousin, of course she's going to look like us."

"You don't feel a special connection to her?"

"I do," I agree. "It's like she's been here this whole time. She's very close to the heart, and she adapted to us very quickly."

"Maybe they won't even meet," Hassan mutters, so softly I almost miss it.

"What do you mean?"

"Well, she's been here almost a week and the whole family has met her. Khaled's been so preoccupied with work and study, he hasn't been to see his aunt yet. Maybe he won't get a chance to come and they won't even meet."

I clucked my tongue and told Hassan there was no way I'd allow that to happen. My sister and niece didn't come all this way for him not to make the time to meet and welcome them home.

"I'll talk to him tonight," Hassan says. "It's 3ayb of him not to have come already to meet them."

"I haven't seen mother so excited in such a long time."

"Haram, she deserves to have some happiness after all these years."

KHALED

My first memory of Aaida.

It's 1991 and she's visiting Lebanon with her mother, my aunt Aujene, who I've never met before. It's a Friday, and the call to Prayer is blaring from the loudspeaker of the local mosque. I'm coming down the stairs from my great Aunt Samiya's house at the same time she's walking in from the *dhar* towards my grandmother Tala's house.

Our paths are going to cross. There's no way to avoid that-for either of us to get to our destination, we'll have to cross paths. She looks up at the same time that my mother and aunt Aujene emerge from the *dhar* in her shadow. We haven't been introduced, but immediately I know it's her. She sticks out like a sore thumb, with her white shirt, figure hugging jeans, and did I mention the ridiculous heels? She is, however, absolutely stunning-what I would've imagined my mother to look like at her age.

I introduce myself, but the girl just stands there mute, her eyes boring through me, and I wonder if my parents have foolishly omitted the fact that she is a deaf mute. Not to say that would have detracted from her beauty, but I would've liked to have a conversation with my foreign cousin.

When her mother jabs her in the side and reminds her of her manners, she sticks her hand in my extended one and greets me coolly, awkward and aloof. She reacts to me the same way every other girl does, although she tries her hardest to hide her misstep from me. While I am used to this sort of behaviour from others, it somehow holds a different meaning coming from her and I am almost flattered.

My father, who appears out of the periphery to come and stand by my mother's side, says something funny about all the girls falling over themselves at my feet, which I quickly dismiss as I beckon Aaida to follow me so I can introduce her to all the other cousins.

"I think I've met pretty much everyone," she mumbles, struggling to keep up with me as we walk through the breezeway.

I stop walking and turn to face her. "Wow, so I'm the last. How long have you been here?"

"A week," she says, frowning at my strange question.

I frown right back at her and tell her I'd lost track of time and that's why I hadn't managed to see her until now. She shrugs as though she doesn't care and merely stares at me, her molten brown almond shaped eyes boring deep through me. I notice that I am at least a head taller than her and look down at her face.

"You'll need to lose the heels," I tell her.

She shakes her head. "Why?" she demands, her brows forming a frown.

"Well, if you hadn't noticed, there are potholes everywhere here. So unless you're looking forward to spending your time in Lebanon in a cast, it would be best if you stuck to flat shoes. Heels may work in the fancy streets of Australia, but out here, they're just a hindrance."

"And if I don't?" she asks in defiance.

I shrug nonchalantly. "Suit yourself," I tell her. "You've been warned."

AAIDA

Khaled was not what I expected.

I had met all my other cousins, and everyone kept mentioning Khaled, but I had yet to meet him. So when I do, I'm not exaggerating when I say the earth stopped revolving for a few seconds while I gathered my thoughts.

From the moment I met him, when I stumbled over myself and lost all sense of being as I looked at him, I knew even then that Khaled would be my undoing.

He was everything I was not.

He was cool, calm and patient where I was anxious, rebellious and stubborn. I fought him and debated him at every turn, and he seemed to thrive on that. Rather than getting mad at me like any normal human being would, he would smile and take a strand of my hair in his hand and wrap it around his finger, his wistful gaze lingering on me as he told me I still had so much to learn about life.

"You can talk," I snickered, looking back at him through my hair. "You think I'm an immature girl trying to find my way in the world, but you're only 20! What makes you wiser than I?"

"Merely the fact that I am open to criticism," he explained "whereas, you are not."

He was so matter of fact, I blubbered in response rather than coming up with an adequate comeback.

"You know," he started, "things would go so much smoother for you if you just admitted you were wrong most of the time. But your arrogance clouds your judgement. You're so stubborn, you can't see 10 feet in front of you when you're worked up."

"Thank you, Einstein. Thank you for your explanation on why

I am the way I am. From *your* point of view," I said, stabbing a finger at his chest. And with a flourish, I turned and walked away, leaving Khaled standing there laughing at my foolishness and shouting after me that he'd pick me up early the next day so we could go horse riding.

"You're dreaming if you think I'm going anywhere with you!" I shouted, my back to him.

"You will," he exclaimed, as I continued to walk away quickly. And as I did, my pace picking up as I tried to get away, my heel got stuck in a hole I hadn't noticed, falling away from my shoe seamlessly until my shoes were rendered useless. I looked down at my feet in horror, my mind racing and my lip trembling anxiously as Khaled let out an enormous burst of laughter at my misfortune.

The thing is, he had warned me. But I had been too stubborn and too arrogant to listen. And now I was one pair of heels down. Truth is, my heels were my comfort; they afforded me height, and the subconscious ability to stand above things, especially in my darkest hours. I looked back at him with what may have seemed to him to be tortured eyes, then quickly fumed at the way his eyes continued to dance with mirth. I slipped my feet out of the remaining good shoe, picked up the broken pieces of the other, and proceeded to throw them in his direction in defiance, before turning to walk away barefoot.

"Tomorrow!" he called after me in a loud voice, no doubt to remind me that he would be there regardless of how I felt about him in this moment.

◆ ◆ ◆

Out of all my cousins, Khaled, though not the eldest amongst them, was the one who seamlessly commanded everyone's attention whenever he walked into a room. People regarded him with the highest respect. In fact, it seemed almost like people, both old and young alike, revered him.

I watch as a group of older men practically bow before him as we walk into a local store. One goes so far as to grab the back of Khaled's hand to his lips in an attempt to kiss it, a familial sign of great respect amongst the clansmen when dealing with their leader.

"*Astagfirullah!*" Khaled says, pulling his hand away quickly.

The old man makes another unsuccessful attempt to grab his hand, telling Khaled it is his *"wajib"*, his honour to celebrate the meeting respectfully.

"*La'a ya Abu Firas. Walaw,* we're all brothers here. Your Salaam is more than enough."

"May God protect you, my son," Abu Firas says, lowering his head in respect. "May God bless you with his bounty and keep you safe."

"I don't understand," I say to Khaled, as we weave between aisles. "How old are you again?"

Khaled laughs and chucks his head in embarrassment. For all his power and standing and place in society, he was extremely shy and not immediately accepting of praise.

"Does it matter how old I am, Aaida?" he asks. "Respect knows no age and it can't be sought, it needs to be earned. I have proven myself beyond measure in these parts."

"I can see that," I amend. "It's just so odd seeing men so old deferring to you as their leader. What's stranger still is that in this day and age, tribal structures still exist."

"That's the one thing I think the bedouins will never let go of. In order for there to be order amongst them, there must be a hierarchy that everyone abides by. It's the only way to maintain peace here."

"Can you wait for me in the car?" I ask him, as we near the items I'm looking for. Khaled shrugs and shakes his head, silently asking me why he would do that.

"I need some personal items," I explain.

"So go on," he says, unmoving.

I roll my eyes and bend my head to the right as I watch him

carefully. Not only is he smart, but he's also dumb as I try to drop hints to him about certain things.

"I know what you're thinking," he says, raising his eyebrows and smirking. "You're thinking how daft I am for not getting the point and giving you your space."

I roll my eyes again and shake my head in exasperation. "Come on Khaled, I'll only be a few minutes, don't make this any more awkward than it needs to be."

"I'll wait for you by the counter," he negotiates, and I know by the past few outings that there was no point countering his offer, as there is no way he will cave.

He never ever left my side, once explaining the fact that my broken Arabic was enough to put ideas in the wrong person's head. "We've just come out of a bloody war," he had explained. "Nothing is off limits. Kidnapping, murder, rape, disappearances without an explanation. With the constant chaos surrounding us, there is next to no police presence to deal with non-war related crime. Most go unpunished. Unfortunately, as long as Syria has a stronghold on the ground in Lebanon, we can continue to see more or less of the same crime until a strong police presence is created."

"What does this have to do with me?" I had asked him.

"Everything," he had replied, his thumb swiping against my lip as he stared at me. "Your broken Arabic is a dead giveaway that you're a foreigner. Foreigner equals ransom."

"That's it? That's what you're worried about?" I asked, wide eyed.

"What else would there be?"

"There has to be more to it, Khaled. Because I assure you, anyone who kidnaps me and has to deal with me running my mouth would definitely pay you to take me back."

At that, he had chuckled and put his hand in the small of my back as he ushered me out of one store and into another.

AAIDA

I am a listener.

I am a keen observer and an even sharper listener.

When people talk, I'm extremely delicate with my ears. I lend them, and I listen. I saturate what everyone around me is saying. And what they are not saying.

I'm an observer. I watch and I listen and I confine things to that lock box called memory.

The characteristics of my long held memories are retained within my senses.

When I unpack my memories, I can describe the exact sequence of events, down to the feel and smell of the moment. I can tell you the way this memory made me feel, or how it affected my mind. I can tell you what was cooking the day of a particular memory because all memories have a particular smell. And every time I get a whiff of a particular smell, a different memory from a bygone time flits across my mind.

And I can give you a litany of memories floating like colourful ribbons through the air to fall at your feet. Every memory will take you to a certain place and a specific time. And each and every single memory will evoke within you tightly held secrets you had long relegated to your own tightly sealed lock box.

1991 is a year of firsts.

It's the first time I leave Australia after our arrival in 1977.

It's my first trip to Lebanon.

It's the first time I meet my extended Lebanese family.

It's the first year after the war in Lebanon has ended.

It's the first time I hear Fairouz and fall in love with her music.

Fairouz is an icon in Middle Eastern circles. She is considered the "soul of Lebanon", and no wonder; her music dives into your heart and pulls at the chords, severing your nerves and rendering you helpless. Her voice is like smooth syrup dictating to your soul and offering hope in a world otherwise paralysed by fear and war and heartache.

When we drive through the olive groves and Khaled puts on the radio, Fairouz's sweet melodious voice floats through the car as she sings *"Kifak Inta"*. I listen on in silence, my physical being melting at the gliding sound that smoothes over the wrinkles of my heart. My Arabic is minimal, basic, but I understand almost every word of the beautiful tune, and turn to look at Khaled's profile as he sings along as though humming a lullaby.

Fairouz sings her prose with a soul jarring nuance that wrenches at the deepest internal crevices where our emotions dwell. It is a beautiful song. And it becomes our song. Our anthem. Our battlecry as we drive on through the grove until we come to a densely wooded area that offers some shade. Years later, in reconciling my relationship with Khaled, the song is even more powerful and resonant than ever as I realise our love story played out exactly the way the song depicted.

Khaled brings the car to a stop and emerges to the throng of excited voices as my mother and aunt join us from the car already parked under the trees. Tayta Tala is already sitting on a stool under an olive tree, clapping her hands in happiness to a silent song in her head. Our great aunt Samiya is sitting on a *haseeri* mixing the *tabouli* as her children run after their children through the *karam.*

I cherish these picnics, where we all get together and frequent the groves where our mothers spent most of their childhoods, picking olives and figs and oranges. More than anything, I love hearing their funny stories of the way things were, and commit their beautiful recounts to the back of my memory, devouring every last morsel of history I can extract from the family.

When my great aunt Samiya says something about the olive grove we're sitting in and my mother and aunt Farida whip their heads towards her in murderous glares, I realise I have barely peeled back a fine layer of my family's history, and there is still so much more to elicit and learn.

"*Wlee, skiti!*" My aunt Farida hisses, baring her teeth angrily as she urges aunt Samiya to shut up.

"What happened?" I ask Khaled. "What did she say?"

Khaled just shakes his head and rises, pulling my arm up so we can go for a walk. I pull my arm back and look down at the women as they continue to stare each other down. Tayta is wringing her hands in what I have come to learn is her anxious tic. Not many things make my grandmother nervous, but obviously, something is going on. Khaled pulls at my arm again, urging me away from the confrontation.

"Come on Aaida, let the big girls sort out their drama."

I look at him, irritated that he would think I wasn't old enough to hear whatever it is that is going on.

"You go!" I snap. "I want to know what's going on, so I'm staying."

Khaled purses his lips in disagreement, and I can see he's irritated over my unwillingness to budge.

"Whatever is going on has nothing to do with you," he reminds me. I turn my nose up at him and turn away, brushing my shoulder away in dismissal as I cross my arms over my chest and watch the conversation unfold.

"Aaida!" my mother admonishes. "Go with Khaled for your walk."

I raise my chin in defiance but say nothing, and my mother looks at me and frowns at my stubborn insolence.

"She's not a child," Samiya speaks up, looking toward me. "Why are you so intent on keeping things from her?"

And that just fuels the fire as my mother and aunt, as well as some of Samiya's grown children all speak simultaneously and their voices are drowned out by one another. I can't make out anything that is being said as I swing my head this way and that trying to keep up with the conversation, but instead only manage to grab fragments of the conversation over the constant din of shouting and accusations.

"Khalas!" Khaled finally yells, just as my hands shoot up to cover my ears. Sometimes my stubbornness isn't my best trait; I now wish I had gone for that walk after all instead of living through the noisy chatter that complicates my mind. Everyone falls silent and looks up at Khaled as he looks back at everyone furiously. My aunt Farida swallows and gives her son what appears to be a look of shame. Aunt Samiya seems like she is in a spiteful mood and opens her mouth, possibly to defend herself, but Khaled holds up his hand to silence her. My mother looks at a corner of the *haseeri,* sucking her top lip under her teeth and looking guilty. I wonder what they're all hiding and realise my best bet is probably Samiya, but now question the wisdom of wanting to know if the conversation is only going to end this way, no matter what happens.

"Whatever you all want to talk about, whatever history you *think* is worth opening now, bury it and enjoy your day. We're here for a good time, not to relive bad memories."

Khaled admits, in a roundabout way, that there is a story to be told, but it isn't necessarily a good one. And that is all the validation I need. Some things are better left unsaid, tucked well away in that lockbox called history.

AAIDA

My family from my father's side don't like my family from my mother's side. We were obviously staying with my mother's family, but from the moment we had arrived in Lebanon, my father's extended family, his sisters and their husbands and their children, had ingratiated themselves in our lives. Father had come past once to visit, but his siblings and their spouses had literally set up camp in the *dhar*. They were nice enough, but I couldn't quite connect with them comfortably when my own father had silently renounced me.

"I don't understand why they're here practically every day," I mumble, throwing picked *molokhia* into a nearby tub. It was the season for Jew's mallow and it was tradition for the women of the house to sit around and pick the green leaves to prepare for drying and freezing and storing for the colder months.

At my complaint, my mother and my Aunt Farida exchange a knowing look then return to picking the mallow. My grandmother sits with us, her head oscillating between us according to who is speaking.

"They're your relatives, Aaida," my aunt Farida starts. "They're excited to finally meet you and spend time with you."

"But every day?" I ask, shaking my head in confusion. Again, the women exchange looks but say nothing. "What?" I ask.

"Well, Khaled is here a lot and I don't hear you complaining about him," my great aunt Samiya points out, setting her bucket of zucchini down and joining us on the *haseeri*. My great aunt Samiya is my deceased grandfather Amjad's sister and lives on the first floor above my grandparent's house with her husband and sons.

My mother and aunt stop what they are doing and look at aunt Samiya in shock. If I had come to learn anything about my aunt Samiya, it was that she had absolutely no filter, always saying exactly what was on her mind. Even my grandmother, usually always happy and smiling and following the conversation now looks down at the *haseeri* as though tracking an invisible bug, her smile falling from her face. She looks almost guilty.

"What?" aunt Samiya says, shrugging in nonchalance. "I'm merely stating the obvious. I don't see her complaining about Khaled being here all the time."

"That's different," I say, defending myself.

"Different, how?"

"Khaled is my aunt Farida's son. I have a connection with him because I have a strong connection with my mother, who is connected to *his* mother. I don't have a connection with my father, so why would I feel connected to his family?"

Aunt Samiya lifts her nose stubbornly and sniffs the air. She is so judgemental, but everyone puts up with her anyway. There would be long stretches of time when she would be exiled from the *dhar* for having offended someone with her tongue, but just as soon as she felt like it, she would resume her place amongst us and her tongue would weave its magic again. She was also known as the village snoop and gossip, most of which was obviously invented.

"I'm just saying, is all."

"Why did you specifically single out Khaled?" my aunt Farida asks, frowning. "All the other kids are here even more than Khaled, *laysh bas jibti seerto?*"

I can see that my aunt Farida is upset but I don't understand why. I try to decipher the dynamic shift between the women as I look from one to the other trying to read them. Aunt Farida and my mother have still not resumed picking the mallow as this latest conversation opens up, but aunt Samiya picks out a zucchini, cutting off the flower then proceeds to core it until it is so thin the sides touch when she presses the middle. She likes her *kousa* with a thin layer of skin, whereas I appreciate the taste of *kousa* in my meal.

"Khaled is the one who spends the most significant amount of time with Aaida, *hayk laysh*," aunt Samiya explains, somewhat matter of factly. "*Ba'daan*, I don't know why you don't just tell her."

"Tell me what?" I ask, looking around at the women, just in time to see my mother hit aunt Samiya with a stalk of mallow. Samiya yelps and moves out of the way, and I narrow my eyes as I turn to my mother for an explanation that does not seem forthcoming. "Mother?" I prod.

"Now see what you've done!" My mother, who is usually so calm and collected, clenches her teeth and snaps at my great aunt. "I didn't come all this way so you could put ideas in her head!"

"But Aujene!" my aunt Samiya exclaims, "why would you not allow your daughter to know people's intentions towards her?"

My mother and aunt Farida pipe up at the same exact moment, saying almost the exact same thing. That it was no-one's place to tell me what people's intentions were; I was to either deduce for myself or be told by my mother.

And that was when I learnt the true intentions of my relations from my father's side. Even before I had arrived in Lebanon, the race had been on to see who could win my hand first. There had been arguments and debates as to who would be the better suitor, with a few bowing out when the realisation hit that there were more worthy contenders amongst them and they didn't stand a chance. Like I was the prize at the end of a long drawn out competition.

Of course, as the male cousins from my father's side were older, the assumption would have been that I would wind up with one of them. Khaled, being as young as he was, and from my mother's side of the family (preference was always given to relatives from the father's side-it was tradition!), and still studying, hadn't even been looked upon as competition.

Until they all noticed how much time I'd been spending with

him and how close we were.

"I didn't come here to get married, nor even engaged," I say, turning to speak directly to my aunt Samiya. If anyone would put this news out there for all to hear, it would be my great aunt Samiya, or as we preferred to address her, the loudspeaker. It was a running joke that anything mentioned in front of aunt Samiya would be fodder for human consumption within the hour in our village. There was no such thing as a secret in her book of life.

"That may be true," aunt Samiya remarks, "but that hasn't stopped anyone from hoping. See, even Khaled is smitten with you!"

"*Hissee!*" my aunt Farida speaks up. "Don't you dare utter a word about Khaled or take his gracious hospitality and make a mockery of it! Khaled spends an equal amount of time with everyone. Aaida is no exception."

"You can see how this looks to others, Farida. And people have noticed the way they look at one another."

"Which way! Which way!" My aunt Farida is seething, near hysterical as she addresses Samiya. "All this rubbish you're talking is just that-things you have expanded in your head that you will run and share all over the village to set tongues wagging! I will not tolerate you causing problems for the children!"

"*Rouki binti,*" my grandmother speaks up, as a cloud of sadness cloaks her face.

"*Sharrira!*" Aunt Farida hisses. "Always causing trouble with your tongue!"

"*Khalas, ekhti,*" my mother says, trying to calm aunt Farida down, "don't waste your breath. What's important is that we know there is no credence to what she's saying."

"And what if there was?" My aunt Farida snaps, turning in aunt Samiya's direction. "What is wrong with my son Khaled, hmm?"

The argument has turned from the subject of suitors to why Samiya was attacking my cousin Khaled's good standing and spreading untruths to anyone who would listen.

"*Khalas,* Farida!" Aunt Samiya snaps back, like she is fed up with the conversation and everyone attacking her. As though she didn't bring this on herself. "I'm merely pointing out what everyone else is discussing, this shouldn't come as a surprise to you considering how much time they spend together."

"In the company of others!" My aunt Farida defends, and I can see from the look of frustration on her face that she has reached the end of her tether. "You are such a *sharrrira,* Samiya! You were born ruining people's lives, and you will *die* ruining people's lives! And I will be the first one dancing on your grave!"

And with that, my aunt Farida stands regally, lifting her chin in defiance, and stomps out of the *dhar.* But not before she lifts her leg and purposely aims it for the bucket, sending Samiya's precious *kousa* to the ground in a heap of unusable mulch.

KHALED

"You seem to be getting along well with your cousin Aaida," my father says, as we reign in the horses. I know he's only making small talk, but I get along with everyone, so I wonder if he's alluding to something.

"What's on your mind?" I ask him, turning his way.

My father's eyes twinkle when he smiles, the same way mine do. We could be twins, but for the age gap between us. My father is a rock. He has been my crutch and my most avid supporter my whole life, and we've never kept secrets from each other.

"She's a very beautiful girl," he tells me.

"I get that. But I still don't see your point."

"She reminds me so much of your mother at that age, the resemblance is uncanny. Aaida's had a sad life," he says, turning his body to face me. "She's grateful, I know she is, but that doesn't detract from the traumas she's lived through."

"Sounds like there's a warning in there somewhere," I tell him. "When there's no need; I'm only being hospitable. The same way I am with everyone else."

"I'm just asking that you tread lightly, son."

"Is there something you haven't told me, father?" I ask, looking at him curiously.

"Her paternal cousins are falling all over themselves vying for her attention. And she has given only you the time of day. You know the way things work in these parts, Khaled," he tells me. "The father's side of the family trumps the mother's side."

I tie my horse to a post by the fence and pause to take a deep breath before facing my father again. Culture and tradition have dictated our lives for so long, pitting families against one another as each in turn angles to have their way. I knew Aaida's other cousins well. Couldn't say I liked them much, but there had been, for many years, a healthy respect between us as we went about our lives.

"You're speaking as though there's something more going on between Aaida and I. When I can assure you, there is not."

"I know that son, but others may not. There has been some chatter; I just want you to be aware."

"You know," I start, "it's unfortunate that we still live the way our fathers and forefathers did many centuries ago. The fact that people can still hold firm in their belief that her paternal cousin is more entitled to her hand than her maternal cousin is absurd. That in itself is stupid enough. Never mind that *anyone* believes they are actually entitled to her."

"I've worked tirelessly for years to undo the damage these age old traditions have done. Our tribe has come a long way," my father tells me. "Other villages have remained firm in their beliefs, especially when there is something to be gained by doing so."

I nod my head in agreement and look out over the hill and down to our village, where I know mother is busy preparing an amazing lunch for us. Today Aaida and my aunt Aujene, along with my grandmother, are coming to visit and have lunch with us. My mother is over the moon that they are visiting and that she will have a chance to have her sister all to herself for several hours without restriction or intrusion from other family members.

"I should get going if I'm to collect the girls in time for lunch," I tell my father, as I mount the horse again.

"Take Turan with you," my father says, and I nod in understanding. This is the first trip the girls take away from their home without the company of her father's family, and my father expects there may be trouble. Truth be told, I know there's going to be trouble, but I'm more than capable of holding my own. However, to set my father's mind at ease, I pick up Turan on my way out of the village and we set out in the direction of my

AMAL IBRAHIM

grandmother Tala's house.

AAIDA

My cousin Aziz is an idiot, for lack of a better word. By now, the would be suitors have dwindled to a couple, and Aziz is one of them. The eldest son of my aunt Hasiba, my father's youngest sister, he is 26 years old and wears his hair parted to the side. It is ironic that I know my aunt Hasiba better than I know my own father, and even more ironic that I know all about his current life through my aunt.

Aziz is a would be solicitor, and everyone assumes he will be the winner in the quest for my hand, as he seems to be the most worthy with his degree hanging on the living room wall above the fireplace for everyone to see and admire. This I hear from my great aunt Samiya, who deems this fact noteworthy enough to share.

In all honesty, I find him boring as hell. But he comes past almost every morning without fail, sits and sips endless cups of *ahwi,* asks me ridiculous questions I have no intention of answering, and remains firmly planted on the couch for hours on end.

The day that we are invited to my aunt Farida's house for lunch, Aziz comes early and remains still seated in the same spot hours later when Khaled comes to collect us, refusing to allow us to travel via taxi service.

"You ready to go?" Khaled asks, ducking his head into the living room, where we all sit, ready and waiting, but with no sign of escape from Aziz. I look from Khaled to Aziz, not knowing what to say. I've been told it is impolite to usher a guest out of your home, but assume Aziz will understand and get up to leave.

"Are you going somewhere?" Aziz asks, smoothing his hands

down his thighs but making no move to rise.

"We're invited to lunch at my sister Farida's house," my mother speaks up quickly, sparing me. She, too, does not care much for Aziz.

"Oh, well..." he says, looking at Khaled, and I understand immediately that he is angling for an invitation. Khaled keeps his mouth securely shut, which is not customary for him. He is ordinarily a very hospitable person, but I can see that something is grating on his mind.

There is a long pause where no-one says anything, and I can see tayta sitting anxiously, wondering what will come next. Finally, Aziz stands, his back straightening to his full height as he stares Khaled down, obviously miffed at the sleight of not being invited to the lunch.

"Well, you don't want to be late," Aziz says. "I'll drive you." It was suddenly obvious he was more than a little miffed that no-one extended the lunch invitation to him and was intent on securing an invite any way he could. If he could just get us to Dhar Khamra, there's no way he'd be allowed to leave without at least joining us for lunch. The townsfolk would not hear of it!

The grating silence floats through the room as my mother purses her lips and a look of fury crosses Khaled's face. But if anything, Khaled is adept at setting people straight.

"There's no need, Aziz," Khaled speaks up. "That's why I'm here; Turan and I will drive them."

"That's okay, I'll drive them," Aziz insists, "It will give me and Aaida a chance to catch up. I've wanted to take her for a drive for a while now." He smiles down at me, and for once, I wish I'd worn my heels. He is trying to introduce the idea that there is something between he and I, where I could hardly bear to even be in the same room with him.

"*Ma'laysh ibni,*" my mother starts sweetly, turning to Aziz. "Khaled has troubled himself and come all this way, we'll be travelling with him."

"I have an idea," Aziz exclaims, feigning excitement. "Why don't you and tayta travel with Khaled, and Aaida and I will travel in my car behind you. Safety in numbers and all that."

The one thing everyone constantly accused me off was being overly stubborn. The fact that Aziz wouldn't take no for an answer was igniting a fire within me, the likes of which I'd never unleashed. Never mind that I had to deal with him for hours on end on a daily basis, and my mother's constant insistence that I not be rude to him, out of fear that my father would accuse her of turning me against his family.

"You know what," I pipe up, looking up at Aziz. Out of the corner of my eye, I see my mother's lips tighten as she silently urges me to stay quiet. "Thank you Aziz, for coming past again today. Aunt Farida has invited us to a quiet family lunch where we women will be catching up on some much needed girl time. So, sorry to be a drag, but this is a girl's only trip."

It is the polite way of telling him he isn't invited. I can see the wheels churning in his brain as his face turns red and he turns to Khaled again. He wants to ask why he can't still drive us regardless, but I nip that one in the bud by turning on my heels and grabbing my handbag before marching toward the door.

"I'll see you soon" I tell him, as my mother and grandmother follow in my steps and he reluctantly joins them, heading toward his car where he watches as we amble into Khaled's car where Turan sits waiting. I wave to Aziz as Khaled turns the car around and we drive in the opposite direction.

"You didn't have to be so rude to him," my mother admonishes as we make our way out of the village.

"I got rid of him, didn't I?" I ask. "He's been here since 8:30 in the morning. That's three whole hours of my life I won't ever get back."

"Still, once everyone finds out what happened..."

I cut my mother off swiftly. We never fought and we rarely argued, but ever since we'd come to Lebanon, I'd had to bow to societal norms that were wrong on so many levels. The sharp contrast between my life and freedoms in Australia and the pressure to conform to culture and tradition here had started to take their toll on me.

"I don't care what everyone will think when they find out, mother. I'm not in any way interested in Aziz, and he needs to know that, otherwise he'll just keep coming back day in and day out."

"*Binti*, you can't talk this way, and you can't be impolite when people visit you. That's not the way things are done here."

Khaled sits in the front seat driving, saying nothing. He looks at me in the rear view mirror and catches my eye, then quickly looks away. For all his quiet reserve, Khaled would never intrude on a conversation between my mother and I, even though he might have plenty to say.

My grandmother, usually so stoic and quiet, opting to speak only out of necessity or when asked to do so, now speaks up in my defence. "Leave her be, Aujene. She has a point."

"Are you condoning her behaviour?" My mother asks tayta incredulously.

"This is not about condoning her behaviour. This is about letting her voice be heard. We went our whole lives conforming to tradition and doing as we were told, even when it was the wrong thing to do. Do not suppress your daughter's voice. She has a voice, and an opinion, and a right to both."

FARIDA

"You really didn't have to go to all this trouble," Aujene tells me, as she looks at the spread before her. She was hoping to arrive early so she could help with the preparations, but I just tsked and shook my head.

"You should know better, *ekhti*," I say, taking her hand and leading her to the head of the table, where she'll sit by my side. "A guest is a guest is a guest," and we fall into each other laughing.

We sit side by side at the table, with my mother at one head, and Hassan at the other. Usually, it's Hassan and I sitting at the head of the table, but out of deference and respect for my mother, I now sit to her left, with Augene by my side, followed by Khaled and Turan. To my mother's right, and opposite me, are Aaida and the twins.

"I think you've made enough food to feed the whole village," Aaida says, spreading some baba ghannouj onto a piece of fried bread. Everything is home made, from the dips to the fried kibbe and the stuffed grape leaves.

"I made all your favourites, *ya Amar*," I smile at Aaida.

Khaled is quiet as he sits at the table, not participating in any of the conversations that arise and ignoring Aaida altogether. I notice he doesn't so much as look at her as he spoons lentil soup into his mouth. Khaled has always been a happy person, even in his darkest hours. He is always smiling and happy and thoughtful. But now he sits quietly brooding, almost agitated, looking as though he would rather be anywhere else but here.

Hassan notices me paying too much attention to Khaled's demeanour and shakes his head slightly. He knows I want to say something, but he sends me a silent warning to leave my questions for later.

Khaled stands abruptly as we're serving desert and announces he has work to do. I see the moment when Aaida's brow creases and she realises he's leaving. But she realises, also, that he hasn't said a word to her since they arrived, and she looks at him questioningly, trying to catch his attention, but he kisses the top of my head, then moves toward the door and disappears through the back of the house.

I look toward Hassan with worry all over my face. Even Aujene has noticed the dynamic in the room has shifted. This is so out of character for Khaled. And now Aaida will be left on her own or will spend her time with a bunch of old ladies instead of doing the fun things she's grown accustomed to in Khaled's company.

AAIDA

Some nights, I wake up gasping for breath.

Through the lens of my mind's eye, I see myself submerged in water, riding a tidal wave, then getting lashed across the face with a flood of water as though life were slapping me. My eyes open in horror, I hold my breath and try to avoid taking in water, flapping my feet as I fight against the tide and try to slice through the surface of the ocean . My hair floats about my head, almost luxuriously, as my hands flail and try to lift me, but I remain stationary, not moving an inch as the sea beckons me further down into its depths.

The thing about drowning is it can happen even out of water.

That's what I feel is happening when Khaled walks out the door after we'd barely finished lunch. I'd been looking forward to spending more time with him on the horses or in the fields, which is what we'd been doing a lot of recently, but with barely a glance my way and a scowl on his face, he'd simply picked himself up and left the room without so much as a goodbye.

I feel myself drowning as an overwhelming cloying sensation envelopes me. I find it hard to breathe. I can't understand what has happened between yesterday when he was making fun of me and this morning when he picked us up to bring us to lunch with his family.

"Aaida, *chai?*" my aunt Farida asks, and I shake my head, still in shock.

"I'll help with the dishes," I say, standing up.

"No need, *habibti*. The housemaid has that under control."

"Thank you, *khalty*. Everything was beautiful. The food was amazing."

Aunt Farida looks down at me sadly as I turn away, blinking

back tears. I will not cry, I will not cry, I will not cry, I keep telling myself. There is so much for me to be grateful for. First and foremost, just the fact that my mother is now happy, and reunited with her sisters and mother, is enough of a blessing for me to overlook anything else that is thrown my way.

"Aunt Farida," I say, standing to join the others in the living room. "When will you tell me the story of how you and uncle Hassan met?" I ask.

Aunt Farida looks at me and smiles, a knowing look on her face as she turns to my mother, who sits smiling conspiratorially at her sister. Even my grandmother is smiling, a far away look in her glistening eyes.

"If only you knew the depth of that story, *ya binti*," my grandmother says. "It's so unbelievable, it could only be true."

KHALED

I stay away for a week.

A whole week in which I brood and every breath I take is one of torture.

It's my mother who finally puts me in my place as only a mother could.

She tsks as she watches me walk into the house and set my keys down on the counter.

"I saw Aaida today," she tells me, and I remain silent, as though I didn't hear her speak.

"How long will you keep this up?" she asks, coming to stand before me, her face angry. My mother never gets angry. Ever. So she must be really mad. As she stands in front of me like a mountain, I can see all the emotions playing out on her face.

"The girl is miserable," she tells me.

"The *girl* is your niece, "I remind her. "I'm sure you can find something to entertain her."

"You shouldn't have spent so much time with her in the first place if you were just going to turn around and disregard her!" she yells.

When my mother yells, you know she is not only upset, she's fuming.

"That was not my intention," I mumble, looking down at my feet.

"Then what was your intention, Khaled?"

"Does it matter, mother?" I say, rising from my chair and grabbing my keys. My mother looks at me in horror and snatches the keys from my hand.

"Where are you going?" She asks. "You can't just walk away

from me!"

I sit back down and put my head in my hands. I don't want to fight with my mother, but there is no escaping this conversation.

"Just tell me what's wrong!" she screams. "What happened between you? Let me help you."

"There's nothing you can do, mother."

"The poor girl has attached herself to you and feels like she's lost her best friend in the whole world, Khaled. How is that fair on her? She's been bedridden since she left here and won't leave the house. Just tell me what happened!"

I lift my head and look at my mother, a deep sorrow burrowing in the depths of my soul.

"Nothing happened, mother. That's God's honest truth. Nothing happened."

"Then what?" She frowns, trying to understand why both Aaida and I were so miserable when we didn't even understand the reason ourselves.

"I don't even know," I tell her. "Many little things came together at once to remind me who we are and what shouldn't happen between us."

She shakes her head in exasperation.

"You said you weren't romantically interested in each other," she reminds me.

"This is an impossible situation, mother. If Aziz is to have any chance with her, I can't be the thorn in his side."

"Akkkhh!" She screams. "That reptile! You're worried about him having a fair chance with Aaida? Are you serious, Khaled? Aaida can't stand the sight of him."

"That's not my problem, mother. I can't be the reason she says no to him. I can't be the reason he thinks she's saying no to him. As it stands, the one thing she made clear to Aziz the day they came here was that she preferred this side of the family to her father's. That in itself is going to create problems for Aunt Aujene."

"And it has," my mother says, pointing a knowing finger in my direction. "But don't you worry about my sister Aujene. She can hold her own when the need arises. But right now, our main concern is Aaida and her well being. She's been absolutely beside herself since she left here. You need to fix this, Khaled."

AAIDA

I spend my days reading endless passages by Gibran.

I sit in the garden and while away the hours to pass the time.

I look out at the fields, then at the rich soil surrounding the vegetables, then the sky. Daily. Without anything ever changing.

At night I lay in bed, my eyes closed as I try to summon slumber, then open and staring at the wall, memorising every section of peeling paint and every scrape that lined the walls of the small room. My mind becomes my prison as I waver between lack of sleep and lack of nutrients. Anything I eat I throw up. And sleep evades me night and day as my life plays out like a news reel in my head.

Aziz comes to visit almost daily, and I turn him away every time, telling whoever answers the knock on the door to tell him I'm not well enough to receive visitors. I know at one point he raises his voice in defiance and demands to see me, accusing my family of hiding me away from him. That was the only time I ever heard my mother screaming at anyone, as she voiced her concern for my health and told him she had enough to worry about without having to deal with his narcissism. I had smiled slightly upon hearing that, imagining Aziz's face going beet red as he sputtered in response to my mother. She told him, in no uncertain terms, that he was not to attend unannounced again, then proceeded to call my father and tell him to deal with Aziz's situation. My father, in true fashion, did not see fit to concern himself with me, which I'll admit was a bit of a bitter pill to swallow, but the situation with Aziz must have been resolved as I didn't see hear from Aziz again for a while.

When my aunt Farida comes around to visit a week after the luncheon, she clicks her tongue and purses her lips as she looks down at me sitting in the shade of the fig tree in the garden.

"Aaida, *habibti!*" She is aghast. You're still sitting here day in and day out?"

"I'm going to sit here until he comes back," I tell her, and I'm sure I sound needy and pathetic, but I can't help it. The way that aunt Farida looks at me, with sorrowful eyes, I am sure she understands exactly how I'm feeling. And I know for a fact that she isn't taking sides or condoning her son's behaviour, no matter that he is her son.

"Turan is here," she tries, but I only shake my head. I don't want to see or speak with anyone other than the one who has splintered my heart in two.

"Aaida," my mother starts, coming up behind aunt Farida. "Aaida, come and eat with us. Look how thin you've become."

My mother's eyes are full of pained anguish. I can see that even she has lost some weight, probably from her concern over me.

"I'm not terribly hungry, mother."

"Then just come and sit with us. Your tayta has been crying over you all morning. Just come and sit with us and pretend you're okay, even if only for 5 minutes to calm her down."

KHALED

I find Aaida sitting on a chair in the sun in *tayta's dhar.* Her loose hair falls about her face and past her shoulders, almost to her waist, in a vision of loose black waves. The sun hits the top of her head, displaying rays of sunshine that make her appear as though she's wearing a halo of gold. Her back is to me and I can see a blanket sitting loosely at her knees. There's a book in her lap.

I stand at a distance and watch her for a while, take in the subtle rise and fall of her shoulders as she breathes in and out, the way she tips her head up to the sun and shakes her thick waves loose, then folds them to one side of her head so the other shoulder gets some sun.

My aunt Aujene is grateful that I've come. She practically fell at my feet out of gratefulness and I felt like scum, willing the ground to divide and swallow me whole for the pain I'd caused her. I'd been foolish and selfish, not taking into consideration what Aaida's condition would do to aunt Aujene. She had only the one child. Only Aaida. And she would move heaven and earth to ensure her safety and wellbeing, as well as her happiness. But Aaida was miserable and inconsolable for the better part of a week, ever since I'd shut her out of my life.

I walk slowly towards Aaida, and if I make any noise, she doesn't turn, but remains stoically seated looking up at the sun. When I am standing before her, blocking the sun from her view, she squints and looks at me, but it's as though she's looking through me. I lift the book from her lap and look at the cover. She has been reading *The Madman.* I turn the book over in my hand and notice it's been read many times over. There is a well worn page inside that has been creased and folded over. I notice the indent on the spine at that particular page; it's as though she's opened and closed to that particular section more than any other in the book.

"You're reading *The Great Longing*," I note aloud, and she merely looks at me. I close the book and pull up a chair, sitting across from her. The sun hits her hair again and I can't help but think how angelic she looks.

"What took you so long?" she finally asks, and I can't help but smile. Not too much, because I know she says this with sadness, and my heart is sad for her and the time I have wasted away from her. She is my cousin, but she is also my best friend. I have been miserable without her, and she has been miserable without me.

"Have you read it?" she asks, directing the conversation elsewhere. She has graciously given me an out so I don't have to explain to her where I've been and why I've stayed away. At the same time, in true Aaida fashion, she doesn't like to dwell too much on things-as she always says "the show must go on."

"I've read most of Gibran, if not all. I'm surprised you'd be reading it."

"Why? Too Arab for my tastes?" she jokes.

"I just always saw you as the type of girl who didn't go for fluffy romantics.

"Nothing fluffy about *The Madman*," she reminds me, looking serious, and I realise she is right. It may be romantic in places, but there was definitely nothing fluffy about it.

"*And I have found both freedom of loneliness and the safety from being understood, for those who understand us enslave something in us*"

She recites the verse by heart and so eloquently as her hand clenches the book against her chest, as though taking comfort in its written passages.

"Do you feel up for a walk?" I ask her. She looks frail and tired, and I notice the folds of skin under her eyes. My mother told me she hasn't been eating nor sleeping. Most days she's spent in the garden lamenting her poor broken self, and I want to hit myself for causing her this pain and torment. Even our *tayta* could not bring her out of her despair.

She tells me she doesn't feel like walking and just wants to sit in the sun, and when I ask her, she says she doesn't mind my company if I can tolerate the sun. I move my chair to sit beside her and take her right hand in my left, clasping it and sitting quietly. After a few minutes, I reach over and collect the book from her lap and open it, then start reading to her in a soft voice. Her eyes close as she tips her face to the sun, soaking the rays and taking in the warmth, her burdens lowered from her shoulders as Gibran's words weave and carry on the soft breeze to her waiting ears.

"My friend, thou art not my friend, but how shall I make thee understand? My path is not thy path, yet together we walk, hand in hand."

AAIDA

The second time I go to Lebanon, I'm there for a week before Khaled flies in from Canada, where he's been studying. I know the day he arrives because I've been waiting for him, but I don't see him until the day after his arrival, when a car screeches to a stop on the road outside, followed by a cacophony of doors closing and raucous greetings.

I find myself standing in the breezeway looking toward the front door, where Khaled is standing talking to aunt Samiya, his brother Turan standing in his shadow. Although I am about 15 metres away from him, I know the moment he's conscious of me being there, because he looks up to his right and sees me, and a huge smile spreads across his face. He closes the distance between us in what seems like only two huge strides, lifts me into the air and twirls me around, then sets me down and kisses the top of my head, asking me how I am.

Khaled mesmerises me. He always has. I try to label what it is between us, but I can't quite seem to do so. We're not romantic, although everyone else around us seems to think we're crazy in love. When we're in each other's presence, we're like two pieces of the same puzzle; when we're apart, we're both miserable. We talk easily and freely, sharing everything from our hopes and our dreams to our fears and burdens. Khaled understands me like no-one else can. And he always tells it to me like it is.

We're visiting aunt Farida a week later when Khaled suggests we go for a drive. However, he suggests that I drive, and I look at him awkwardly, then at the unsealed road littered with loose rocks and gravel, then back at him again, frowning.

"Go on, it's okay. You know how to drive, right?"

I scoff. "Of course I know how to drive. On roads, I do. This is anything but a road."

Khaled laughs and shakes his head. He thinks I'm being a princess as usual, and I can see he's looking forward to this little excursion and the laugh he'll get out of it.

"Come on, you've proved yourself at everything else. Hunting, you're a champion markswoman. Horse riding; even the horses love you. I'm sure you can manage a car."

He knows exactly how to phrase his words to challenge me, and he knows I've accepted the challenge when I shrug and get behind the steering wheel.

"Just one thing," he starts, putting on his most serious face as I turn the ignition "you sure you can handle driving left hand, since you drive on the wrong side of the road in Australia?"

We spend the afternoon laughing and joking as we drive around the general vicinity of Khaled's village before we slow down on the road leading towards his family home. At one point, I pull up to a side road with a clearing and go round and round in circles to convince a laughing Khaled that I can in fact drive in more than just a straight line. When we start to move again, I spy two girls walking up ahead, headed in the same direction as we are. They turn at the sound of the car and I see it's Khaled's cousins Soraya and Ghinwa, his uncle Waleed's daughters. The sisters could almost be twins with their identical frames and faces, the only discernible difference being that Soraya is a head taller than her sister.

"Stop a moment," Khaled asks, as we near the girls. I stop the car a few metres behind the girls, who have stopped off to the side of the road, and watch as Khaled exits the car. I watch as he approaches the girls, then get out of the car myself, following slowly. I watch carefully as he reaches the girls, dragging my steps to keep my distance but not wanting to be rude and stay in the car without saying hello.

"*Marhaba,* Khaled," Soraya is the first to speak. "Welcome back." And I realise she hasn't seen him yet since he's been back. They live in the same village, and she still hasn't seen him! Although this makes me feel somewhat special, I feel some unease as I look at Soraya and notice the deep crimson blush creeping up her neck to her face.

"*Kifik* Soraya?" Khaled asks, keeping his distance. I notice his awkwardness addressing the girls, and even more so, the fact that he didn't greet them the same way he greets me has not escaped my attention. "Ghinwa, how are you?"

"*Hala,* Aaida," Soraya calls, and Khaled turns back to look at me. It's when his gaze lingers on me a little longer than it should have that I notice the frown that settles on Soraya's face. And that is the first awareness I have that Soraya wishes herself to be more than Khaled's cousin.

The girls decline an offer to drive them the short distance to the village, telling us they are enjoying their walk. When I drive away, my foot heavy on the gas, the tyres turn up a great amount of gravel, squealing noisily as it leaves a blanket of dirt in our wake.

"Whoooaaaa," Khaled says, holding up his hand to calm me down, and I drive steadily in silence the remainder of the way home.

My mind is in an introspective mood as the drive comes to an end. Khaled doesn't say anything either, as though sensing it is time for silent reflection. He is so attuned to my feelings, he reads me like a book. When I park the car in front of his house, I turn the motor off but remain in the car. I notice my hands are clenched tight against the steering wheel in what I understand is anxiety, and loosen my fingers off the wheel one by one before I let my hands fall in my lap. I turn in my seat to face Khaled, who sits in his seat without saying a word, looking at me expectantly.

"Just say it," he says.

"Say what?" I ask.

"Whatever's on your mind. I know when you're thinking about something because you go all quiet on me. Usually, I can't shut you up." Khaled speaks in a light tone, meaning to inject some humour into the conversation, but I turn away and look through the windshield at the fields in the distance.

I don't know why I'm so irritated by Soraya's feelings for Khaled. It was written all over her face. And I know I shouldn't, but I guess I feel a smidgen of jealousy and possessiveness where he's concerned, even knowing that he's different with me than he is toward her.

"Spit it out," Khaled says. "Otherwise it's going to hang over us like a dark cloud."

"She's in love with you," I whisper.

For the longest time, he doesn't say anything. He looks out the window of the car and I watch as his chest rises and falls with every laboured breath he takes. I long to touch my hand to his chest and feel each breath as he exhales. I shake my head at myself, shrugging off the emotion that courses through me like electricity.

"Does it matter?" he asks, and I notice that he doesn't deny it. A thin rod of jealous fire pierces through my heart with this knowledge.

I shake my head and look away, feeling like I'm in an impossible situation. There's something brewing between Khaled and I, there is no doubting that, but I have to remind myself that he's my cousin and that is just a no go zone. I just don't understand why I feel so resentful and jealous of Soraya.

"Then why are you upset?" he asks.

I shrug in response. How could I explain something I didn't understand myself?

"I think it's time I go home," I tell him softly.

He sits quietly for the longest time, then gets out of the car and comes to the driver's side. He opens the door and waits for me to get out of my seat.

"Lunch first," he says, ignoring the conversation that has just taken place. Like this never even happened. "It's bad manners for a guest to leave without breaking bread," he reminds me.

TALA

When Aaida comes home, she is visibly upset. I can hear it in the tremble of her voice as she leans down to kiss me and asks *"Kifik, tayta."* There is a wetness against my cheek and I realise she's been crying. Aujene is in her room resting, a migraine having crept up on her unexpectedly. I pat the stool next to me for Aaida to sit down.

When she does, she is so close, I can smell the beautifully subtle scent of gardenias invading my senses. Aaida has a unique smell that I would know anywhere. She wears her perfume like no-one else.

I feel a heavy weight in my lap and realise she has rested her head there, and reach down to smooth her hair back. My beautiful, troubled Aaida, there is something on her mind. I continue to play with her hair as we sit in the *dhar*, her quiet sniffles breaking my heart.

Aaida is the strong one in the family. The women...my daughters and grand-daughters-none of them hold a candle to Aaida's strength. She is strong and outspoken and well-versed in the way of the world. She will not fall victim to the customs and traditions that have plagued our women for generations before her. I know that she will be the one that makes the changes required to pave the way for further generations. She is the first girl in our family to get a proper education and go to university. She will make her own destiny. She will choose her own spouse. And she will not be told what to do. Of this, I'm certain. Aaida is the conductor of her own symphony, and she will not be silenced because she challenges the status quo.

I know many in the village view her with suspicion, as though she has come into the village to wreak havoc and cause mayhem. In all actuality, the men are simply afraid because she challenges their way of thinking and they fear losing control over their wives and daughters.

In many ways, Aaida is not unlike the first Farida, the bedouin girl who arrived in Tul Ghosn a hundred or more years ago and proceeded to educate the women and children of the village. The men, feeling threatened by her, hung her and threw her into the sea. However, there'd be no silencing a woman's powerful voice this time. My son in law Hassan's standing in the North ensured Aaida's protection; no-one would *dare* touch a hair off her head.

I can't help but draw comparisons between the two girls as Aaida sits weeping, her head in my lap. The men in our village are weary of the power Aaida wields in providing the women with a voice. She stands up for what she believes in, what is right, and is a staunch defender of the oppressed. The women and children of the village absolutely adore her, and this is no more apparent than in the way they refer to her as *"al Amira"* - the princess. In their eyes, Aaida is a saviour who has come from a far away country to bring about change and teach them how to live better, more meaningful lives.

"What's wrong, Aaida?" I ask, as I continue to brush my fingers through her hair.

She doesn't say anything for a long time. Instinctively, I know it could only be one thing.

"Khaled?" I prompt.

I feel her head nodding in my lap, but she doesn't move to verbalise her pain. What seems like an eternity passes and still she continues to weep quietly.

"As a child, my mother used to tell us a story to try to get us to sleep, especially when we were unsettled," I start. "Truth be told, we deliberately acted out because mother was a brilliant storyteller. We loved to hear her relate stories; the way she narrated made you feel like you were living the story, not hearing it. One particular story stood out, and we always asked specifically for this one. And each time my mother would recount the story of the first Farida, it would be as though she were telling it for the first time."

When I start to recount the story of the first Farida, knowing it would inevitably lead to more questions, for one brief second I question the wisdom of telling Aaida the truth. She is a foreigner to our way of life-what good would come of inviting her into a history of our past tragedies? But I push on, remembering that Aaida is old enough and wise enough to know-and deal with-the truth of what happened here so many years ago.

And so we sit there in the *dhar*, grandmother and granddaughter, and I recount the story to her as best I can considering my memory, until her sniffles grow few and far between and I feel a calming breath leaving her.

"Once upon a time, a very long time ago, a beautiful bedouin girl by the name of Farida came to Tul Ghosn and set up a tent on a vacant plot of land in our small village. She was a Syrian bedouin who broke with her tribe and exiled herself in Lebanon after her one true love chose to marry her sister over her.

Farida was welcomed into the village by the children, who she taught to read and write, and the women, whom she helped on many an occasion when the need arose. As time passed, it was soon apparent that Farida had an amazing talent and she began to be viewed with suspicion by the councilmen of the village, who accused her or sorcery.

Her talent, you see, revolved around predicting events before they occurred. Farida was able to predict the weather. She was able to tell you who would marry whom. She was even able to predict the gender of unborn babies.

One dark night, in the absence of any women in the village, the councilmen took Farida to a deserted plot of land and hung her up by the neck to die. Before her poor soul departed the earth, Farida took one last breath and cursed the councilmen and their families for generations to come. The men lowered her body to the ground then threw Farida into the sea with her belongings, erasing any indication that she had ever even existed.

Nothing was ever the same again in Tul Ghosn after Farida was martyred. A heavy storm blew into the village and destroyed all the people's crops. Many of the livestock perished, as did a boy who was swept away to his death in torrential rain.

Some of the councilmen, consumed with guilt, now sought to cleanse their souls of their misdeed and started to share the truth of what had happened to Farida with their wives. Soon, the whole village was awash with the news, and a certain terror enveloped the women as fear of the curse planted itself firmly in their minds and took hold.

The women of the village understood Farida's special gift-she had been a true nomadic bedouin, travelling from place to place all her life, so of course she was able to predict the weather! How else would she know when and where to pitch her tent? She was a keen observer of people-why would she not be able to deduce who was going to marry whom by the way the children looked at one another? And as for predicting genders-didn't all women do that?!?

The women were incensed by what the men had done, killing an innocent young girl due to their ignorance and lack of insight. In a bid to make amends, the women built a water-well in Farida's memory. They planted a tree for her in the place where she had pitched her tent. And they started to name their daughters Farida in memory of the bedouin girl who had sought refuge in their village but found her resting place at the bottom of the sea."

Aaida shifts as the story comes to an end and I notice that her sniffles have subsided.

"Aaida?" I ask.

"Tayta? Tell me another story," she says, settling her head back into my lap.

AAIDA

Every year, I go back to visit family in Lebanon. Like clockwork. I don't skip a year. I fly in from Australia and Khaled, my best friend in the whole world, flies in from Canada where he is studying. We always manage to catch up and spend time together. However, there is one year when our trips overlap; I am flying out of Beirut the day he is arriving. It's the year I turn 19 and he turns 22.

Khaled calls me as he makes his way home from the airport and I make my way towards it.

"Lets meet in Junee," he suggests.

I tell him I don't want to miss my plane. I had been devastated that he had not been able to come any sooner-the first visit I'd ever spent in Lebanon without him, and it had not been the same as other visits, but I still needed to get home in time for my exams.

I can't refuse Khaled anything. I ask the driver to take a quick detour through Junee and the car skids to a stop when I pat the taxi driver on the shoulder excitedly and tell him to pull over next to a parked Mercedes. Khaled is leaning against the car waiting, his long legs crossed in front of him and his hands in his pockets. His face erupts into a broad smile as he sees me. I fly out of the car even before it stops, leaving the door open as I rush toward him.

Khaled holds his arms open and I rush into his embrace as he lifts me off the ground and twirls me around. When he finally sets me down, he kisses the top of my head and chucks my chin, then looks off to the side as my mother approaches.

He hugs my mother to him and tells her how happy he is to

see her and he wishes we'd be spending more time together but it was unfortunate that we had to leave.

I pull my top down self-consciously and watch him as he interacts with my mother. Khaled is sincere in each and every word he says, as he is in all his dealings. He is sincere and polite and fair, and there is no man more giving or compassionate than he is. Finally my mother hugs him again, telling him she'll miss him, then turns to me and tells me she's waiting in the car.

"When will you be back?" he asks, and I shrug, telling him I'll let him know closer to the date so we can co-ordinate our trips.

"I've missed you, *ya zgheeri*," he tells me, taking a lock of my hair in his hand and wrapping it around his finger, then watching it snap back into a curl after he lets it go.

"Same," I tell him, and I lean up and kiss his forehead before explaining we're out of time and I have to leave, otherwise we'll miss our plane.

"So, miss your plane," he tells me, a mischievous look in his eyes.

"Exams," I explain, and he nods his head in understanding.

"Let's not wait too long, Aaida."

There is a wistful sadness in his eyes, even though he is smiling. The hardest part of leaving Lebanon is always saying goodbye to Khaled. Every time I leave, I feel like I'm leaving a little part of me behind, and I have the acute sensation that eventually, I will stand with nothing left to give. He holds my face between his hands, his forehead to my forehead, saying nothing as he breathes me in then quickly pulls away like it is physically painful for him to be so close to me.

"Til next time, Aaida."

I turn and start to walk away, turning back once, then move toward the car where my mother waits, looking at us. She waves toward Khaled then turns to me as we drive away.

"You're too close to that boy," she tells me, as the car meanders down the hill and moves back in the direction of the airport.

"That *boy* is your nephew," I remind her, a touch of resentment in my voice. She purses her lips and turns away.

"I didn't mean it in a negative way, Aaida."

"Then what did you mean, mother?" I ask, turning back to face her. "What did you mean?"

My mother exhales and looks up at the interior roof of the car, as though seeking guidance from some unseen power.

"You're in love with each other," she says, and I scoff at the mere idea.

"He's my cousin," I remind her again.

"That doesn't mean you love each other any less," my mother starts. "Every one from North to South can see it as clear as day-you two are in love with one another."

I shake my head in response, dismissing her words. My mother and I never fight. We never argue and we hardly ever disagree about anything. This was probably the most intense conversation we had ever had, one that we were now most likely about to disagree on.

"And what would it matter if we were, mother? Not saying that we are, but what's the big deal? I thought you like Khaled."

"I love Khaled. I don't like what's going to happen to either of you though when this goes south."

"And why would it go south, mother?"

"Because there is no way on this earth that Khaled would ever leave his parents, and you would never leave Australia to come and live here. His life is here, yours is there. In a nutshell."

I feel a constriction in my throat as I listen to my mother tell me the reasons why Khaled and I would eventually cease to be. Even though we aren't romantically involved, or maybe I'm just fooling myself into thinking that, she is right. There is no way either one of us would thrive full time in the other's native environment. And this was the crux of the problem...no matter how we felt about each other, we were doomed even before we started.

AUJENE

For many years, I tried my hardest to shelter Aaida from the ugliness of my past and my family history. So many times, I thought she should know, but the thing was, I couldn't tell her one thing without going into the next, as our whole sordid dirty laundry connected like a lifeline from one window to another. Out of context, each significant event may have been tolerable, but when combined, our past lives before she was born read like something out of a Greek tragedy. Travelling back and forth between Lebanon and Australia, recollections were bound to converge at some point as we flitted between past and present.

My aunt Samiya is hell-bent on unlocking our tightly sealed Pandora's box. She doesn't think I notice, but I'm aware of the moment she calls Aaida and surreptitiously steals her away from me and up the stairs to her home, where she can gossip to her heart's content. I'm not sure what her angle is, but she is determined that Aaida should know all about our checkered past, even knowing that it will undoubtedly paint all the players in a different light.

I eye her suspiciously as I climb the stairs and make my presence be known. Her head is lowered to Aaida's and she is whispering something to my daughter. Whatever she's telling her, Aaida is a captive audience, her eyes wide in disbelief.

"Aaida!" She is startled and looks up at me with something like fear in her eyes. She knows she's not supposed to be here and she's not supposed to be entertaining Samiya's tendencies toward gossip. I beckon her to me, and she rises quickly, as if caught in the middle of an act, and her stool falls backward and lands on the ground with a heavy thump. I meet Samiya's eyes and give her a stern look, my lips pursed in disappointment; she is aware that she has crossed a line, and I can, surprisingly, see regret starting to formulate in her expression. She can't help but gossip, but this is not *her* story to tell.

"*Emshee*." I grab Aaida's arm somewhat roughly and force her down the stairs before me. She is a grown woman, but I am so disappointed that she felt the need to go behind my back and I feel like I should be punishing her for going against my wishes.

I keep a close eye on Aaida because I know she'll want to try to finish the story with Samiya- Aaida has always been a little too curious for her own good. Farida arrives two days later, her arms laden with breakfast pastries and I pull her quickly into my room before Aaida has a chance to join us and outline my plan to her.

"Do we *have* to tell her?" Farida whines, and I feel like I could slap her.

"Farida, she's going to find out. Would you rather we tell her, or she finds out from someone like Samiya, who has a reputation for embellishing what doesn't necessarily require embellishing?"

Farida looks at me with uncertain eyes then relents. She is afraid. Aaida has voiced her opposition to arranged marriages many times. She is horrified as it is that I was forced into marriage to her father, so there's no telling how she'll react when we lay everything out for her.

"I think mother should tell her," Farida says, her eyes crinkling with concern.

"Stop being such a coward!" I pinch her like we used to do when we were young girls and she yelps. "What's past is past, she can't hold us accountable for past horrors which were forced upon us. But she has to know."

FARIDA

When I think about my past, it is as though I am recalling a friend from a long time ago. I try to limit the amount of time I linger on that period of my life, but no matter how I try, it always seems to catch up to me.

My life as it was 25 years ago winks at me, and the fragments of my collective memory shift before my eyes like a mosaic of still life frames. Blink and I might miss it. I don't often discuss the events of that time with anyone other than Hassan, when we are in a nostalgic mood and our hearts linger on the thing that brought us into each other's sight. My mother, God bless her, aches with the memory of her endless search for me, then the ensuing burial of a daughter she thought she had lost, so I spare her the pain and never gloss over that part of my life so she doesn't have to relive it. That's when she lost her eyesight. After she lost me, and after she held the hose they used to wash what they presumed to be my dead body before putting me in the ground. I want to spare her the ache of remembering, so I walk with Aaida through the village until we get to the Boden olive grove where once we were young girls and we roamed free and all we had was our innocence and our youth.

Aujene and I have agreed. I want to tell Aaida the story on my terms. It is my story, and it needs to be told. In my voice. She follows us at a short distance, to offer the support her daughter may need once she knows the truth.

The young girl looks at me quizzically as she recognises the contemplative look on my face. I stop walking in the exact spot where it happened all those years ago, and I start to narrate my story.

"This is where it started..."

AAIDA

The women in my life worry about me. I know this because they treat me like a fragile flower that needs constant watering. I was scared, then mad, then scared again when my mother stomped into my great aunt Samiya's house and pulled me out by my arm just as Samiya was about to reveal more of the story of what happened to my aunt Farida. I know my aunt was kidnapped; I know this because that's how Samiya's version started out, by telling me that aunt Farida was kidnapped before she was married and she wasn't the only one.

I can see that aunt Farida is struggling to reveal her secrets, and as she starts to talk, all I can think to myself is "*does Khaled know*?" Mother walks behind us at a distance, and it would seem like this was the agreement between them - that Farida would reveal, and mother would pick up the pieces. I know something very bad happened here, and I'm about to find out what that something is as Farida musters up the courage to dig into her lockbox and bring out the memories that she would probably prefer to keep dead and buried.

FARIDA

"There were 4 of them. Big, burly men with their faces covered, who hauled me into the back of a truck and took me away. One of them followed your mother on foot, but Aujene, always the nimblest one among us, outran him.

I was taken to an underground cell where I was held for two months. The only person I spoke to during this time was one of the guards that took me, who pitied me and checked up on me sporadically. Eventually, I understood that I'd been mistakenly kidnapped in place of another girl named Farida. Having no use for me, the clan members decided to kill me, but the guard who had befriended me worked tirelessly to find a solution for my predicament. He approached another tribe, where the leader offered to marry me in order for me to escape a death sentence.

It was an offer I chose to accept.

I married the clan leader, Hassan, who was a compassionate man both feared and respected throughout the region. Over time, and owing to his enormous generosity toward me- he respected me and treated me extremely well- I fell in love with him.

After the birth of our first child, my husband took me to my old village to see my family. It was the first time I would see any of them since I was taken more than 2 years ago. There, I learn that my parents had believed I was dead, and had even buried a girl found dead at the water well believing she was me.

Mother had gone blind after I was taken, and father was still a tyrant. My husband had to hold him back from attacking me, so consumed was he with what everyone would think of him now that his daughter was back from the dead. To many, it may have looked as though I had willingly left my home and gone off with a man, *especially when I turned up again with said man. And father, like many others, considered honour one of the highest levels of society's moral fabric. If not for your honour, what did you have?*

AAIDA

In 1994, I'm attending my cousin Zanjabeel's wedding. She's my aunt Moraya's daughter. They live in a village in the hills high above the other villages, looking down at the vast network of interloping orchards. Whenever I stand on the clearing in front of their house, aunt Moraya is quick to come and stand beside me and point out all the land that once belonged to my paternal grandfather before it was squandered away. She points out two thirds as far as the eye can see and I look on in wonder as she gives me the history lesson again. But no matter how many times she tells me, I always look forward to hearing the story as though it's the first time.

"That way, and that way, and over there," aunt Moraya says, spreading her arms wide in a sweeping movement in front of her. She is not exaggerating. Several people have mentioned the fact that my grandfather was a land baron who met his untimely death on the road to Syria.

His siblings, my father's uncles, had started selling off chunks of the land even before my grandfather's body could settle beneath the earth, and by the time the courts got wind of the situation, it was too late to recover what was already gone, but the remaining assets were tied up in litigation until all those involved could stop arguing long enough to agree on how to divide the estate.

"Such a tragedy," she murmurs, looking out to the distance sadly. "At one point, your father's family was one of the most illustrious in the North." She shakes her head and I'm sure we're thinking the same thing; how can a family go from having literally everything to almost nothing?

"People still talk about him," I say, but I can hear the question in my voice.

"To this day," she says. "For all his faults, he was a very generous and kind man, Aaida. If it's any consolation. Your father turned out nothing like your grandfather; you would've liked him. And all the good he did for the people is still paying off. People remember him and his kind ways and always say a prayer for him." I found it hard to reconcile the sharp contrast between my father and my grandfather.

When the guests start to arrive, we walk back toward the garden and start to greet those we've overlooked during our history lesson. We check on Zanjabeel and find my beautiful cousin all done up and breathtaking in her wedding dress, a bouquet of wild flowers held loosely in her hands. I can't help but notice how confident and happy she looks-I have butterflies on her behalf, so I don't understand how she's so calm.

My aunt Farida comes bounding into the room and hugs us all close, as usual a huge smile plastered on her beautiful face. Aunt Farida, even at this age, with grown children, is probably one of the most beautiful women I've ever seen. Even her sisters were enchanted by her any time she walked into a room. I stood mesmerised, watching her as she spoke a mile a minute to my aunt Moraya.

Once we leave Zanjabeel with my aunt Moraya to share a few final moments before Zanjabeel is to become a married woman, we make our way back outside to the garden and mingle with more guests as they arrive. Across the perfectly manicured lawn, I see Khaled, and to my surprise, his cousin Soraya standing nearby, shyly tucking a lock of stray hair behind her ear as she watches him. Without consent from my brain, I feel my lips open slightly in surprise, an overwhelming wash of heat rising from my feet to the very tips of my throbbing head as I watch them in silence. They are not standing together, but close enough to one another that I can see she wants to remain in his proximity.

"Zanjabeel's father does a lot of business with Waleed," my

aunt Farida tries to explain Soraya's presence at the wedding. Did it really matter that my cousin's father and Khaled's cousin's father were associates? We moved in the same circles either way, so I don't know why her presence has surprised me so much.

I turn to my aunt and shrug as though I don't care. She shakes her head slightly and gives me a sympathetic look, and I feel like such a fool. I won't admit I have feelings for him, yet I'm furiously jealous of a single look that passes between Khaled and Soraya, and I don't understand it. Even when he doesn't return her glance, just the mere fact that Soraya lays her eyes on him, her expression telling a thousand stories, makes my hackles rise.

"Don't look now," aunt Farida whispers, and I resist the urge to turn and face the direction she's looking in. "Aziz is here." Of course. He lives in the same village as my aunt Moraya; by default, all village dwellers are invited to such events.

I frown and look in the direction furthest away from him in an attempt to avoid him, but when I instead find him by my side, kissing my cheek, an embarrassed flush colours my face as I realise what he's trying to do. He's trying to stake his claim on me by displaying his affection, which would in effect send the single males scattering with the interpretation that I'm spoken for. I shrug his hand off my arm and don't smile as I thank him for coming to share this joyous occasion with us.

"I've missed you," he tells me, smiling down at me arrogantly. Even in my heels, high as they are, he is taller than me and doesn't fail to make me feel small. "I should have thought to pick you up and drive you here," he states, his gaze firmly planted on my face as though searching for something he can't quite find. His eyes dart left and right across my face, as though trying to read something. This little act in itself, of him looking into my eyes with such intensity, tells passersby that we are intimate enough for him to be doing that. I feel my skin crawl as I understand what Aziz is trying to do, and I don't understand why it's so hard for him to understand that I'm in no way interested in him.

"There was no need."

"I'll drive you home once the day is over," he decides, taking the choice out of my hands.

"Still no need," I tell him.

"Don't mention it, I'll drive you home." He's being forceful with his language, making decisions for me and insisting things happen his way. He lifts his head and looks over my shoulder, a smile firm on his face as he continues to direct his words at me while looking elsewhere.

When I look over my shoulder, I realise he is looking directly at Khaled, who's looking back at him as though at any minute he will take flight across the room and pin Aziz by his collar to a wall. Khaled is standing with his father, who is also looking our way, while Soraya stands off to the side, brooding as she watches the events unfold before her eyes. I suddenly understand Aziz's demeanour and his attempts to make our conversation look intimate.

Before I can walk away, Aziz's hand touches my arm, an obvious sign of affection. He's walking a very thin line. I don't want him to touch me, I don't want people to get the wrong impression about us, and I definitely don't want to be the cause of a problem at my cousin's wedding.

"I need to check on my cousin," I tell Aziz, moving away from him, but not before I hear him call after me "Save the first dance for me." And as I walk away, I realise with a heavy heart that he was loud enough for everyone at the gathering to hear him.

KHALED

My father is talking but I don't really hear a thing he's saying as I continue to watch Aaida's interaction with Aziz. I saw him the moment he walked into the garden and zeroed his efforts directly on Aaida. I don't understand why he doesn't just get the point and leave her alone. She obviously isn't interested in him.

And now he's touching her. My father puts his hand to my shoulder before I can walk in their direction and tells me silently to stay calm. No-one wants to be the one who ruins a girl's wedding, and I hold myself in check, promising not to do anything stupid to ruin the evening. There'd be plenty of time later to deal with Aziz.

"Why don't you dance with your cousin Soraya," my father suggests as the music starts. I look at him like he's grown two heads and want to say something sarcastic enough to ruin anyone's celebratory mood.

"We've had this conversation before," I remind him.

"And we've also had *that* conversation before," he counters, nodding in Aaida's direction.

"Now is not the time nor place."

"Then be on your best behaviour," he warns me, before tucking his hands into his pockets and walking away.

I try to avoid Aaida for the rest of the night and stand, for most of the evening, in a corner of the garden conducting conversations with my brothers or other cousins while surreptitiously glancing at Aaida from time to time.

I'm not the only one. Half the men, both single and not, are enamoured with my beautiful cousin as she flits about the garden in her gorgeous blue dress and heels. She has curled her hair into loose strands that hang delicately down the front of one shoulder, diamond studs sitting prominently in her ears, her long neck on display for all to see. She makes the rounds and greets family, drawing people's attention away from any little mishaps like the coffee taking too long to be served. I can't help but stare at her, and when the music plays and females are offered the floor to do their *dabke* without the men, I watch as she fumbles through the steps like a beginner, yet somehow still manages to make the dance look exotic.

After the *dabke*, there is a lull, then more dancing as couples merge on to the dance floor. I watch as even the youngest boys try to catch Aaida's attention and ask her for a dance. But it is only when I see the look on her face after Aziz leans down and whispers something in her ear that I make a move. I excuse myself from my current company and stride in her direction quickly, doing a pirouette before lifting her hand in mine and wordlessly guiding her onto the dance floor. I can feel Aziz's anger as we walk away, but choose to ignore him as I hold onto Aaida and take in her scent.

There is an invisible curtain between us. Something that identifies a deep yearning within ourselves, but won't allow us to act on our feelings. Our hands are entwined as we move to the beat of the music, then I do something so forward, so daring, I know I'll pay the price for it later. I let go of her hands and move her closer, putting my left hand on her arm as my right hand sits in the crook of her lower back. I almost hear the gasps from the crowd, but I don't care, and Aaida doesn't seem to either as we continue to dance in our own little world.

Even men who have come with their wives are not brazen enough to dance so close to their spouses. I can see Aziz standing in a corner watching us, his hand held up to his mouth in consternation. Soraya, too, is standing off to the side, holding one arm with her other hand, a wounded look on her face. I haven't danced with her as my father suggested, and although I feel a twinge of remorse, I don't want her to get the impression that there is something between us. I feel nothing but a brotherly concern for Soraya. Aaida is different. Although I can't put a name to what I feel for her, there is a churning in the pit of my stomach whenever she crosses my mind, and I know she feels more or less the same way I do.

When the song comes to an end, Aaida pulls away from me, even as I hold onto her hand. It's like she was in a trance for the duration of our dance and now she's come back down to earth. With a thud. Aziz tries to steal her away for a dance, but she just shrugs him off and tells him she needs space as she scrambles away and into the relative safety of the house.

Miraculously, Zanjabeel is off the *barzi* and following her cousin into the house to check on her, on her own wedding day. I make to follow her, but my mother pulls me back, her lips pursed in disappointment. She has warned me off playing with Aaida's emotions, but what she doesn't realise is that I was not the one to play with Aaida's emotions. The girl stole my heart from the moment I set eyes on her.

AUJENE

The whole night plays out like a Shakespearean drama.

Zanjabeel is marrying the love of her life.

Aaida and Khaled share an intimate dance (well, it's not so intimate, but in a small town village in North Lebanon in the 90's, their dance is enough to set tongues wagging).

Several mothers and aunts approach me about suitors for Aaida, and I spend most of the night fending them off.

Soraya sits brooding in a corner of the garden, and I have serious concerns for Aaida's safety, worried that Soraya will give my daughter the evil eye for all the spite she carries in her heart.

Aziz, when he isn't shadowing Aaida, has taken it upon himself to follow me around like a wounded puppy in an effort to prove himself worthy of Aaida, reminding me so much of my ex husband Samer.

My sisters all remark what a beautiful couple Aaida and Khaled make, and their chemistry all but overshadows the bride and groom.

Zanjabeel's new husband practically throws my niece off the *barzi* to attend to Aaida when she goes running into the house in tears, and I love him all the more for his compassion towards Zanjie's family.

Oh, and did I mention that the groom is crazy in love with Zanjabeel?

When I find the two girls in an alcove inside the house, they look up as I enter the room. Aaida has been crying. Zanjabeel's mascara is streaking because she's concerned for her cousin. Beautiful Zanjabeel, with her gorgeous soul and beautiful heart, is distressed at Aaida's sadness. Even on her own wedding day, which should be the happiest day of her life, she is selfless as she gives her time and patience to Aaida, offering her words of reassurance. Zanjabeel is probably the best person to deal with Aaida at the moment; they're the same age and they have so much in common. She is like the sister that Aaida never had.

"*Khalas* Aaida," Zanjabeel finally says, wiping at Aaida's tears. "You're so much stronger than this."

"I can't," Aaida gasps, more tears streaming down her face. The plea in her tone tells me she is in so much turmoil, and it breaks my heart to see her this way. I've never had to worry about my daughter, my only child, and the issue of boys and emotions and heartache. I thank my lucky stars for this small blessing. But now I watch her falling apart in her cousin's arms, and I wonder if it was ever the wisest thing to bring Aaida to Lebanon in the first place. Each year she comes and grows more and more attached to her family, and then struggles to fill the time between visits with precious memories that play with her emotions like a tug of war. I fear I've lost my daughter to the common problem of being lost between two alternating universes, two very differing cultures, and not knowing where she belongs.

Zanjabeel looks at me helplessly as she holds Aaida to her chest, and just as quickly as Aaida has broken down, she is stretching out, straightening her back, and pulling herself together in a remarkable show of strength I'd not expected of the girl who'd been falling to pieces just moments ago. I immediately recognise the change in her composure and the reason for it-if ever a saying was true, it was the one that Aaida had always adopted in her darkest hours; "the show must go on."

Soon, she is the one wiping at Zanjabeel's streaked mascara, plastering a smile on her face, and slinging her arm around her cousin's shoulder as she walks her back out to the waiting crowds. The change in her is so rapid, it is almost unbelievable, and I watch on, mesmerised at my daughter's ability to so easily switch her feelings off, a trait that I realise, with some sadness, she has probably inherited from her father.

TALA

Aaida is exactly like her cousin Khaled. They are a mirror image of one another. And no matter how I describe it, one could not understand until you sat in their presence and saw for yourself how one complemented the other.

They like the same things, and they speak the same language. When the two of them are together, all I feel is fire. She speaks her mind and he lets her. I see them without seeing. And I see what no one else sees because without my sight, I have to rely on all my other senses to assess their companionship. They are but a moving blur before my eyes, and I follow their movements in my mind's eye, or maybe it's just me imaging that Khaled tucks a strand of Aaida's hair behind her ear and she blushes. Maybe I just imagine him popping a grape in her mouth as they discuss their favourite foods from those set out in front of them. It could be just my imagination, but I could swear that they are holding hands as they stand under the huge avocado tree at the border of our land, which droops slightly and falls into a small *wadi* with a creek running through it. I could be imagining all these things, and I could not. But I know what I feel, and that is light and love and hope.

When they sit huddled in a corner talking and laughing, the only thing radiating from that corner is fire and it warms my heart. It fills me with joy to see them so happy, because I can't remember a time in our family when two were so happy and so in love. In our family history, you see, a man and woman didn't marry because they loved each other. They married because the union would be one of convenience, a trade-off, if you will; something for something in return.

They are in tune with one another to such an extent that they finish off each other's sentences. They are immune when there is a shift in environment around them, so entwined are they in their own company. When one asks what they feel like eating, they will speak simultaneously and say the same thing. And one will not eat without the other. Our immediate family has grown used to seeing Aaida and Khaled joined at the hip, and I hear that everyone is entranced and mesmerised when in their company, as though watching a real life soap opera and waiting for the hero and heroine to finally decide they cannot live without each other. The village, too, is abuzz with the couple, and everyone looks upon them as though they are a star couple. I believe everyone knows it's just a matter of time before the two are engaged then married, and from the whispers I hear here and there, I think everyone is looking forward to this royal wedding.

Year after year as Aaida visits and becomes closer to Khaled, so too her cousin Aziz continues to insert himself unsolicited into Aaida's life. No-one really likes him, and I don't know how many ways Aaida can show him that she's not interested in him, but he just won't back off. The man has no pride. He's the cousin from her father's side, and when he sits and I hear him speak, I am transported back many years to a time when his uncle Samer was courting Aaida's mother. Well, not so much courting, as she really didn't want to have anything to do with Samer, but Amjad, God rest his soul, had thrust him forcefully upon our daughter. Aziz sounds the same way Samer did then. They have the same views, the same big dreams and ideals, both their egos full of self-important fluff.

I had to suffer interminable hours in his company when he came to visit. Aaida always insisted that someone sit in with her so she wouldn't be alone in Aziz's company. For a while, he disappeared because Aujene had spoken sharply with Samer about telling the boy to back off because Aaida wasn't interested in him, but he had resurfaced during this year's trip and made himself an almost permanent fixture in our home.

Sometimes I nodded off as he spoke, so bored was I. I could

only imagine what poor Aaida was going through as she nodded her head, or replied in one word answers. An "mmm" here and sometimes a discordant *"Na'am"* to show him she was listening, when really, she was not. For her mother's sake, and to keep the peace between the families, she put up with his visits, although they were making her terribly miserable.

I don't really know what Aziz was thinking, spending endless hours visiting a girl that had no interest in him. None whatsoever. Maybe he liked the sound of his own voice and Aaida was a great listener. That had to be it, I surmised.

Then one day, a miracle happened. It was like a lightbulb moment, and I wondered why Aaida had not done it sooner, but so many things became clear and were settled after the day that Aida asked Aziz "the question." He had been talking non-stop, and barely paused to take a breath, when Aaida jumped in and threw a verbal assault at him.

"So let me ask you something," she started, and I could hear the crunch of a potato chip as she bit into it. If Aaida was good at anything, it was not giving a shit. I perked up, lifting my head from it's semi sleep, like a cat unfurling it's tail and lifting its neck exotically, waiting to see what Aaida would say. Everyone wanted to listen when Aaida had something to say.

"Why aren't you married yet? You know, you're getting up there in the years."

Aziz seemed to pause and stutter before he answered, maybe not entirely sure how to respond.

"Well yes, of course I look forward to getting married, but these things take time. The right girl…"

"Don't tell me you haven't found a girl yet, Aziz. There are plenty of girls around. And I'm sure you have cousins aplenty in your village."

"Well, yes, but…"

She cut him off deftly, delivering her final act.

"I'm *never* getting married," she told him, sounding a little sad. But I could discern she wasn't really sad, but merely putting on a voice as realistic as he needed to hear it.

"Never?" he asked. "Well, why ever not?!?" And his voice rose in such a way that the shrill of his tone reminded me of a shrew.

"Well, what for?" she replied, and my mind saw her shrugging. "I've no desire to marry and be tied down to anyone. And I definitely don't want children-I mean, I still need someone to look after me!" And she roared with laughter. "So I definitely won't be getting married."

There was a long pause before he answered. "Never?" he asked.

"Never." She said it so matter of factly that even I began to think she was being serious.

Aziz followed with a few mumbled words, something about remembering he had to be somewhere for a meeting before he excused himself and left the house hurriedly.

"Do you think that did the trick?" she asked me, coming back into the room after walking him to the front door.

"You almost fooled me," I told her, chuckling heartily. "If that doesn't scare him off, I don't know that anything will."

AAIDA

My mother and aunt Farida decide we need to have some quality girl time together, and play a guessing game of what activities would be fun to do together. I think they're just creating a diversion to give me something to do when Khaled is not around, and it seems to be working. I'm laughing til I almost pee my pants as they bicker back and forth about what to do, and the only person laughing harder than me is tayta Tala, sitting on a stool in the corner of the kitchen rolling the beads of a *masebha* between her fingers. She loves her rosary beads.

"How about I choose an activity," I tell them, and they stop what they're doing and look at me in surprise.

"What would you like to do?" my aunt Farida asks tentatively, and she seems almost afraid of my answer.

"I'd love to learn to cook Lebanese food," and no sooner are the words out of my mouth than a burst of noise spills forward as all three women start talking above each other marathon-style about what they deem worthy dishes for me to learn. And before I know it, aunt Farida is throwing a frypan on the stove, mother has brought out the knife and chopping board, and my tayta is shuffling toward the door, presumably to fetch some local produce.

Tabouli
Generous bunch of parsley
1 bunch mint
1 bunch shallots
4 tomatoes
2 Lemons

20 ml olive oil, preferably Boden
Sprinkle of fine burghul, washed
Sprinkle of salt
Secret ingredient

"We're missing an ingredient," I tell the women, as we sprinkle the salt and put the final touches to the *tabouli.*

"We have all the ingredients we need," my aunt Farida says.

"Where's the secret ingredient?" I ask, looking around the kitchen counter to see what we'd missed.

"Right here," my aunt says, washing her hands. "Aaida, every Lebanese dish has a secret ingredient, which varies from dish to dish."

I frown at her to let her know I don't understand what she's saying, but she just smiles and plunges both hands into the bowl of tabouli and proceeds to mix the ingredients with her hands.

"The secret ingredient to tabouli," she starts "is to mix the tabouli with your hands. Always wash, then mix. Mix well."

"Why not just use a spoon?" I ask.

"It doesn't mix well with a spoon. It doesn't taste the same."

She continues to mix and I watch in fascination as her hands weave expertly through the parsley and tomato and oil. I could probably spend the whole day watching her perform this mesmerising dance which captivates my soul.

"Here, taste," she says, bunching the fingers of her right hand together and spooning the mixture into her hand before holding it up to my mouth to taste. Immediately, there is an explosion of zesty parsley and lemon as they invade my tongue, and I close my eyes in satisfaction as I swallow the tabouli and lick at the corner of my lips. My mother laughs and my grandmother claps her hands together when she hears my joy and praise over the food.

"Farida makes the best tabouli," my mother exclaims, dipping a spoon into the mixture to try it.

"Mother taught us to make tabouli," Farida explains. "My mother in law, whenever she makes tabouli, captivates me with the way her long fingers work the parsley. I always insist on her scraping the parsley off her fingers and feeding it to me because that is always the best part of the dish. She puts her heart and soul into mixing it, and I can taste it in the residue on her fingers."

I smile in awe and I'm so surprised that something so simple yet unique could grant someone so much pleasure.

"I want you one day to make tabouli," my aunt continues. "Split the mixture into two bowls, mix one with a spoon and the other with your fingers and taste the difference."

"What's next on the menu?" I ask, eager to learn more.

"Well, now we eat," my mother says, weaving her hand around her sister's waist and hugging her close.

After a lunch of tabouli with friend eggplant and potatoes, we sit in the *dhar* and sip *ahwi*, as my aunt promises to come in a few days so the women can teach me how to make *kibbe a'raas*. "This dish is very intensive," my aunt tells me, "but what sort of a teacher would I be if I didn't teach you this one national dish?"

FARIDA

I am an apparition, floating through the halls of my memories, back in time to a place a long time ago. I am locked in my past, and lost to my present, whilst the future seems unclear.

When Hassan collects me from my mother's house, after I've shared an afternoon with the girls, cooking and eating and laughing, he finds me in the garden, lost in my own world as I stare at Aaida intensely. When I look at my niece, it is as though I am travelling back in time. I wonder, if I feel this way, how must Hassan feel? How must everyone else around me feel?

My mind is playing tricks on me. It is 1970 again. I am cloaked, bound and tied, and thrown into the back of a truck and taken to an underground bunker, where I am imprisoned for the better half of two months. I spend my days laying on a tattered old mattress that's seen numerous occupants, all unknown to myself. I don't know where I am, but I do know it's dark and dank and definitely not the sort of place someone would stumble upon accidentally and release me.

I've learnt that I was not the girl they were supposed to take. Therefore, I am worthless to the clan that has me shackled to this underground nightmare. I am a casualty of someone's mistake, and within days, I will inevitably be executed and my body thrown into a ditch to rot. Callously. To hide someone's stupid mistake. They came for another girl, but they took me.

Jihad is my only friend in the whole world. He is what is keeping me sane as the days edge closer to my death. I am doomed, and even Jihad cannot help me. But at least we have made a pact, and he has agreed to let my parents know what has become of me should the worst come to pass. I can at least take refuge in that fact alone.

One day, Jihad brings a visitor. I have never seen him before. But he is tall and well built and commands authority. He is someone important, this I can see.

The man tells me what I already know. That I've found myself in a bit of a situation. Although, he understands this has been through no fault of my own. He lets me know, in no uncertain terms, that there is no physical way for him to release me from my prison. He does make me an offer, though.

The irony is that there is no other option but to take the offer, otherwise I will find that I have become an inhabitant of the earth no more. When I consider his words, and weigh up my options, there are only two ways. Either accept his offer of marriage or die a certain death at the hands of those that have imprisoned me.

I chose life. Even not knowing what the outcome of a marriage to a man I didn't know would be, I chose life. There was still so much I wanted to do. And my mother...why would I ever choose to leave my beautiful mother and my sisters?

So I married the man, who turned out to be a local clan leader, one that was ultimately more powerful that the one who took me.

Hassan has treated me well. It took mere weeks for me to fall in love with him. For even though we had married, and I was his wife, he never took advantage of the power he wielded over me, allowing me instead to surrender to him on my own terms. He was soft and gentle and smart and compassionate. A lesser man would have handled the whole situation a whole lot differently, but the man had morals and a heart, and he tethered me to his soul without so much as lifting a finger.

"Does Aaida take you back there, Hassan?" I ask my husband, as we make our way towards our home.

"Looking at her is like looking at you when you were that age. It's uncanny how much she resembles you," he tells me.

"I don't know why whenever I look at her too intensely, I am transported back there. Back to that bunker. Back to meeting you."

"Any regrets?" he asks, casting his eyes in my direction.

"None," I whisper. "That bunker gave me you. It gave me my

here and now. And it gave me all my tomorrows."

AAIDA

Khaled comes into the living room holding a stack of papers neatly rolled tube style with an elastic band holding them in place. I'm not expecting him today. I'm expecting my aunt Farida, though, to teach me how to roll mince and rice stuffed vine leaves. I look forward to the weekly cooking sessions that are reserved for just us girls and I'm slightly irritated that Khaled is here.

"Where's aunt Farida?" I ask him.

"Talking to aunt Samiya. I just came to drop her off."

My relief is audible in the sigh I let out, and Khaled frowns at me, for once not understanding my mood. I love spending time with him, I do, but I need structure. I don't like surprises. Tuesdays are for aunt Farida, my mother and my grandmother to cook and talk and laugh, and for me to spend this time with them learning not only how to cook, but also about our customs and traditions. I need to know who I am and where I came from. The only way to do that is to learn the history of my country and its people.

"What's that?" I ask, pointing at the papers in his hand. He beams, his smile threatening to splinter as he unrolls the papers on a nearby table and beckons me over at the same time that my mother enters the living room.

"*Salam Khaled habibi*, where's Farida?"

"With aunt Samiya," he says, looking up. "She'll come down soon."

He looks back at the papers, and I follow his gaze to where he smooths his hand over the drawings. There are plans for a home, one of grand proportions, with soaring ceilings and marble pillars.

"These are the preliminary drawings for my home," Khaled tells me, and I continue to look at the drawings, then up at him, saying nothing. My mind has gone completely numb, devoid of any thought, and I don't know how I'm supposed to respond to him.

"Ok," I say, waiting for him to say more.

"I wanted you to see them," he says.

"Why?"

He looks at me quizzically, then shrugs nonchalantly, trying to shake off the hurt. I'm not trying to hurt him, but I am trying to understand why he believes I should see the drawings.

"I just thought you might like to see them and give me your opinion."

"Why would *my* opinion matter?"

And now I have really hurt him. Khaled is adept at hiding his feelings though, and he bounces back quickly from situations like this. I notice that every time it's that time of the month, I am especially testy with him. Not purposely, but my hormones really bring out the beast in me.

I can feel my mother loitering in the background witnessing the interaction until she is uncomfortable enough in our presence to announce that she is going to search for her sister.

"What's wrong with you, Aaida?" Khaled snaps, and it's the harshest he's ever been with me. "We do everything together. You're my best friend and your opinion matters to me; that's why I'm asking."

"Don't you think decisions about your home should be made with the one you marry, Khaled? It will be her home, so she should have a say."

Khaled exhales then mutters a curse under his breath, loud enough for me to hear him. He gives me an exasperated look, and I could swear if he had the courage to kill me, he would.

"Yes, but my future wife, wherever she may be, is not here now. And I need a woman's opinion. That's why I'm asking you."

Khaled is freaking me out. My hands get clammy and I can feel a thin streak of sweat as it tingles down my back. He's asking for my input on something I have no business being involved in. We're best friends and we tell each other practically everything, but this seems a little too intimate for us and I'm freaking out as I stand there clenching my hands shut tightly, agitation riding through me.

'There you are!" my aunt Farida laughs, coming into the room and hugging me to her. I know she can feel the tension in the room. Mother probably warned her she'd be walking into a war zone. "*Wallahi* I missed you, *ya zgheeri*," she says, chucking me under the chin before she turns to Khaled and says in a stern voice I've not heard her use with him before "Pick me up at *Asr* time." I wince and close my eyes as I realise how bad this is. It is so much worse than I imagined it to be when aunt Farida takes that tone of voice with Khaled.

She turns to me after he walks out of the room and takes my hands in hers. Slowly, she starts to unclench my fists. I watch as though I am removed from my body as she struggles to lift back my fingers, one by one. They are wrapped tightly, like stone, and I can see the anxiety in her eyes as she looks up at me with some concern. She is talking to me, but I cannot hear what she's saying. I'm in a trance-like state, immune to any and all movement outside of my orbit until she grips me firmly by the shoulders and shakes me.

"*Wallah* I think she went into shock," I hear my aunt gasp as my head jerks in a slight shake and I come out of the spell.

"He may as well have proposed to her," I hear my mother say as she comes into view.

"Tsk, it's not that bad. You know Khaled is very fond of Aaida and appreciates her opinion," aunt Farida explains.

"And you know Aaida is still very young. She's bound to misinterpret intentions. And she doesn't understand some things that may present themselves but mean different things to different people."

"*Ekhti!*" Aunt Farida raises her voice. "I know all this! Khaled just got a little excited, that's all."

"Well, it didn't help that Aaida is on her period," my mother explains, and I see my aunt roll her eyes at her. "You know how she gets at that time of the month."

"Of all the times he could've chosen to ask her about the house..." my aunt reflects.

"*Yallah, ma belashtou???*" My great aunt Samiya says, coming into the room. She looks around and doesn't find anything prepared for our cooking event and clicks her tongue. "*3an jaad?*" She asks, like a petulant child. "You haven't prepared anything yet? Were you waiting for me to do it, *ya3ni?*"

AAIDA

When I visit when I am 20 years old, Spring in Lebanon is especially beautiful. Tul Ghosn in particular, is a picture of perfect radiance as we drive through the streets bordering the groves. The almond trees are in full bloom, their beautiful white flowers blanketing the countryside like a sheet of snow. In the distance, the snow capped mountains blend with the natural environment as the flakes continue to melt slowly down the sides of the mountains, creating a mosaic of grey and white tiles.

Spring in Lebanon is beautiful.

When we arrive home, we are getting out of the car when another car pulls up behind us. I turn to the new arrivals, my hair a mess from the wind blowing through it as we sped through the countryside, a huge smile plastered across my face. There is nothing like driving through the countryside and feeling the wind floating through your soul and caressing your mind.

My mother stands discussing our next trip with the driver. He's a trusted neighbour from the village who's available exclusively for our use the whole time we're in Lebanon, any time we come home. Mother pays him a monthly salary, plus enough for petrol to drive us from the north to the South of Lebanon 10 times over, and he's more than happy to oblige.

My aunt Farida and uncle Hassan emerge from the car, followed by a man I have not seen before, who stands watching my mother curiously as she talks with chauffeur Hani. I see the precise moment she turns around and sees my sister and her husband, but it's when she lays eyes on the stranger that a certain look cloaks her face, rendering her speechless as her mouth falls open. My aunt and uncle turn to the stranger then look back at my mother, a silent understanding passing between the four of them, which makes my heart quiver as a sparking jolt surges through me. There are secrets. Secrets I don't know but would like to know. Secrets that need unearthing.

My aunt Farida comes to stand beside me before I even realise she's moved, so mesmerised am I by the silent exchange happening between my mother and the stranger. She hugs me to her side and plants a kiss atop my head, saying *"Kifik ya helwi"* in her affectionate tone. If I know anything, I know that my aunt Farida loves me as she would her own daughter.

"Who's that?" I whisper to my aunt, as my mother walks toward the stranger and stands but a metre away from him. My uncle Hassan stands next to the stranger with his hands in his pockets, looking on quietly.

"One of Hassan's friends. He met your mother once a long time ago."

"And?" I ask for an explanation.

"It's complicated," she tells me, leading me into the house. I struggle a little, wanting to stay with my mother and watch this chapter unfold. I have never seen my mother so entranced in my life, and I realise, with a deep ache in my heart, all the things my mother has had to sacrifice and missed out on because of my father. With my father, even the little things in life had been a burden.

I look at the stranger, trying to gauge what my mother sees. Tall. He is tall. With dirty blonde hair and bottomless dark blue eyes that crinkle at the edges when he smiles. He is a handsome man, perhaps in his mid 40's, with a smattering of light hair sprinkled on his cheeks and chin like he hasn't shaved in a few days.

"I see you made it out alive," he laughs, addressing my mother in a thick Arab accent.

My mother extends her hand in mid-air then drops it back down helplessly. It's like she thinks she's seeing an apparition.

"Lets go inside," Hassan says, leading the way, kissing tayta

Tala on her cheeks as he passes her in the breezeway. He takes her hand and leads her to the *dhar*, where we sit under the shade of the fig tree and look out over the neighbouring fields in the distance. Uncle Hassan loves my tayta to death, and this knowledge comforts me to no end, to know that she is in good hands when we are away from her. She is well looked after; he has organised good doctors for her, and although she can't regain her sight, the doctor's have helped her to manage her pain and prevent further issues from arising. For his undivided and unwavering attention to her, I am eternally grateful.

"*Kifak ya ebni,*" tayta says, and the stranger bends to kiss her hand. She is too blind to see what he is about to do and he is too quick for her, so his lips have landed on the back of her hand before she is able to pull her hand away. "*Astagfirullah, ebni!* How many times do I have to tell you not to do that!" and tayta laughs in her little girl laugh as she takes her seat and nods her head, agreeing with no-one in particular that this is going to be a good day.

"This is Jihad," my uncle Hassan introduces the stranger to me. My mother sits mutely on her stool, looking at the stranger but saying nothing. There is a story there. "He works with me."

"For you," Jihad clarifies, looking over at Hassan.

"With me," Jihad repeats, turning away from the man. "He's modest. He's also one of my oldest and most loyal friends."

"Well, I guess any friend of uncle Hassan's is a friend of ours," I mutter, looking at my mother again. She notices me looking her way and looks away quickly, a red flush marking her cheeks. "But it doesn't explain my mother's interest in you."

"Aaida!" my mother screeches, and everyone starts laughing at how forward I am and I don't think it's possible, but mother goes even redder.

"And what did you mean when you told her she made it out alive? Of what?"

"Oh, for the love of...," my mother starts with an exasperated sigh, but my aunt cuts her off.

"Aaida, there's a whole story behind how your mother knows

Jihad, but that is a story for another time. Let's just say she was once in danger and he saved her."

"Well, that doesn't tell me anything," I say, shrugging nonchalantly, "but whatever. Not sure why you all feel it's important to keep secrets in this family-you know I love history."

Everyone goes quiet as the topic is unceremoniously closed and I look down at my feet and then look up, rolling my eyes at the sun.

"So what would everyone like to talk about, then?" I ask. I'm actually a little irritated that even at 20 years, my family still thinks they need to protect me from the truth.

"Actually, let me just put it out there," Jihad says. "I can see you're old enough to understand and there's no need to beat around the bush here." A man after my own heart, I think, finally sure that I will get the answers I need. And then he continues with his bombshell.

"I've come today with the intention of seeing your mother and potentially, if she is agreeable, asking for her hand in marriage."

I look at Jihad for the longest time. Aunt Farida gasps and holds her breath, unsure of what is to come next. Uncle Hassan has a twinkle in his eyes and looks like he's about to erupt in laughter. And my grandmother clucks her tongue and starts wringing her hands, a nervous habit we don't see so much anymore. Are they all nervous because they're concerned about *my* reaction to the news?

"You see," I start, putting on my most serious face and directing my attention to Jihad "I knew there was a reason why I liked you."

AUJENE

Sometimes I'm surprised by the little ironies in life.

It's funny that Jihad should surface after all this time, and that we would, more than 20 years after first meeting in an olive grove in Tul Ghosn, be sitting in the same room exchanging stories about what got us here.

The first irony is that Jihad once ran after me through an olive grove and held a gun on me.

The day they took my sister Farida, I ran through the grove and Jihad was tasked with following me and returning me to the waiting convoy. But when he caught up with me, he jabbed his rifle into my side and ordered me to run. I thought he was going to shoot me in the back. I thought maybe he was a coward and wouldn't be able to shoot me if I were looking into his eyes. But it was the exact opposite-he told me to run and not look back, granting me a silent freedom. I took one last look at his mesmerising blue eyes and took flight as fast as I could, making it out of the olive grove before any one else could catch up with me.

The second irony is that when Samer was asking my father for my hand in marriage, Hassan and Farida stepped forward in a humble but vain effort to save me from a marriage to the narcissistic Samer. Hassan had recommended, but not named, Jihad as a possible suitor for me, an offer which my father refused.

I had gone on to marry Samer and live a miserable life with him. Jihad had gone on to marry a woman who later died due to illness.

Jihad and I had already met briefly in 1970, even though not under the best of circumstances, and we had the opportunity to meet again two years later, but that was not to be. Instead, we went on to live separate lives, before we ironically came full circle and made our way back to each other again.

That which happened and came to pass in the years before our union *had* to happen to bring us here today.

AAIDA

My mother is not an easy woman to convince.

She doesn't like change.

And she's damaged after so many years of trauma. But I can't believe it was all my father. No. My mother has suffered traumas so deep I wonder if there is any coming back from them.

My aunt Farida and I stand facing her squarely as she stands silently by the kitchen window.

She is afraid.

Afraid of the unknown.

Afraid of what people will think.

Afraid of having the same dumb luck again.

Jihad treats my mother like a delicate flower. He is everything my father never was. My tayta has already given her blessing. She's known Jihad for many years and she dotes on him the way I imagine she would have doted on her own son had she had one. I learn that over the years, Jihad has made a point of visiting tayta and checking up on her. He takes good care of her.

Jihad has been married before. He was married to the same woman for 15 years, until her passing, and wasn't lucky enough to be blessed with children. For him, marrying my mother is his second chance at love. For my mother, it would be her first love story. I know she never loved my father. What was there to love about a narcissistic man who only thought of his own selfish needs and inflicted emotional and psychological warfare on those he was supposed to protect? For that's what it came down to when all was said and done. Sometimes, a father that is there but not present does more damage to a child than a father that is not there at all.

I always asked myself why my father didn't feel there was a need for him to be a father to me; constantly blaming myself when I couldn't find any other explanation. The fact that he went on, remarried, and had children that he adored further confused and destroyed my already frail psyche.

Yet still, my mother remained adamant that she would not marry again, her lips trembling as she delivered the news. There is a real and distinct fear there, and I don't know what she is more afraid of-being tied to someone again, or having the same dumb luck twice.

"Jihad is outside," I tell her, crossing my arms over my chest dramatically. "If you won't marry him, you can tell him yourself."

Her eyes widen and she shakes her head, disbelief registering on her face. She doesn't believe we would actually put her in the position of breaking the news to him.

"Just go out and talk to him," aunt Farida tells her. "Give him 5 minutes of your time."

AUJENE

My mother tells me I owe Jihad the courtesy of a few minutes of my time.

"*Ya binti,*" she starts "what is wrong with Jihad? He's respectful and charming and he's choosing to be with you. No-one is forcing him. And no-one will force you either. This will be your choice. But choose wisely, my dear."

She points out all of Jihad's beautiful traits. She doesn't mention any imperfections, and I know that is probably because there are no apparent issues with him. Hassan has vouched for Jihad. Farida absolutely adores him and treats him like the brother she never had. And I know that over the years, Jihad has been checking in on my mother and ensuring she had everything she could possibly need or want, without the need for recompense.

When I walk outside into the sun and see him sitting on the swing between the two fig trees, his back turned to me, I pause then gingerly make my way down to him, sliding into the spot on the other end of the swing. Jihad turns to face me but says nothing, merely watches me for the longest time as he waits for me to take the first step. And that single selfless act alone tells me a lot about him. This is not about his needs, this is about my needs. He's willing to listen and he's willing to meet my needs. And for the first time in my life, I feel like I am being put at the forefront of someone else's priorities. I am at the top of his list. And I do matter.

The way he looks at me is not the same way Samer looked at me, and I hate that I make the comparison. There is *no* comparing the two men; they are as different as night and day.

But when Jihad looks at me, with a wistful glint in his eyes, it feels like he is consumed wth just the thought of me. I fulfil that need for him, and the depth of his eyes as they bore into me tells me I have his undivided attention.

"I'm scared," I tell him, my voice a vulnerable whisper.

"I know."

And in that simple short interaction is my acquiescence and his confirmation that he knows how I'm feeling and is willing to make things easy for me.

We reach a compromise, Jihad and I. The thought of moving to Australia irks him, but he's willing to make the move for Aaida and I on the proviso that we spend at least 3 months out of every year in Lebanon. And when Aaida is married, the option to spend longer stretches there, if circumstances permit. It's an easy trade-off; this way I get to spend time with my aging mother to make up for the 15 years I spent away from her. And I can visit with my siblings and forge the relationships I was never able to because of my exile.

◆ ◆ ◆

Everything that came before didn't matter.

For once in my life, I felt complete...whole.

Jihad made me forget I was ever married to a man named Samer, and I walked about and readied myself for my impending marriage as though it were the first.

Aaida was over the moon and took to him like a bee took to honey. He filled within her a void I never realised existed. Although she was now 20, I had always been so consumed in my own misery that I had never understood what Aaida had needed in her life. A father figure.

The fact that Jihad had never had children of his own ensured he became all that much attached to Aaida, treating her like his own daughter; spending time with her and never taking a step towards our future without including her in the discussion.

Some days, I woke and looked up at the ceiling and caught myself, wondering if I dreamt Jihad into my life. What he means to me and what he has done to my life seems beyond a reality, beyond anything I could have ever dreamed up. By the time we had completed a month in Lebanon, it was official and I had formally agreed to marry Jihad.

The whole village was abuzz with the news of my engagement. Mother, to say the least, was overjoyed and welcomed Jihad into the family with open arms. Everyone else in my family was also obviously happy for me, although not many of the neighbours with their whispering tongues could understand why I would even be considered for marriage at my age, with a grown daughter in tow.

However, there was one person that was not at all happy to hear the news of my impending marriage.

Samer came charging into the house one morning as I sat around with my sisters discussing my *jhaaz*. My aunt Samiya tried to stop him, but he just pushed past her, banging the great iron door into the wall as he shoved his way into the house, making a ruckus as he barged unannounced into a room full of only women.

"You!" he fumed, pointing a sharp finger in my direction. "How could you do this?"

"Father..." Aaida started, but I held up my hand asking for silence. This was one battle that I would be fighting on my own.

"Do what, Samer?" I asked, standing to my full height. Even then, I was still shorter than he was, but the strength I felt, the empowerment I felt, ensured I stood on his level and didn't feel as small and inconsequential as he'd always made me feel.

"I offered to take you back!" He screamed, and I could see the veins in his neck popping as his anger rose. "Why are you getting married to someone else?"

"You offered to take me back," I mused. "Because I'm a possession that you can just treat badly, discard, then take back whenever the urge arises?"

"You. Left. ME." He reminded me.

"Noble of you to admit that, Samer. Where were you when I was beating the gossips back because everyone thought *you left me* because I wasn't a good wife?"

Out of the corner of my eye, I saw Jihad and Hassan come to stand in the doorway. Samer is so angry that he doesn't even notice them standing there. He wouldn't have known that they were upstairs having tea with the men and must have heard the intrusion.

Both men must've heard enough of the conversation to understand what was going on. When Jihad makes a move to come forward and intervene, Hassan holds him back, understanding that this has to happen. Samer is my demon to deal with.

"You can't marry him," Samer screams, almost pleading.

"Why not, Samer? Why can't I marry him? You've remarried and moved on. You have children."

"But I had you first," he replied.

I shook my head in disbelief and looked at the ground before taking a deep breath, mustering the courage required to defend myself to him yet again. Aaida stood and put a quiet hand on my arm, as though telling me he wasn't worth my energy. Even now, he had not looked at his daughter once, had not acknowledged her presence or even directed his attention her way. I moved closer to him until we were standing barely a couple of metres apart. He had never wanted me as a husband should want his wife, but neither did he want anyone else to have me.

"You may have had me first. You may have had me once, but I am no longer yours. You have no more entitlements over me."

"Do it for our daughter," he said, using the one card he had no right to use.

I scoffed then let out a low chuckle, which seemed to anger him ever more.

"*Our daughter* is the one who convinced me I should marry Jihad," I revealed. "And she was right to do so."

Samer's gaze turned in Aaida's direction and lingered there

briefly, before turning back to me again. Just as quickly as his gaze had flicked her way, his shutters came down as resentment festered in his eyes at the thought of defeat.

"You need to leave, Samer," I told him. One of my sisters rose and came to stand behind me in a show of solidarity I hadn't realised I needed. Without him in my life, I was that much stronger.

"Not until I've said what I came to say," he said.

"What more is there to say?" I asked him.

"You can't marry another man, I won't allow it!" He bellowed, and just as soon as he'd lunged toward me, Hassan threw his hand down and Jihad sprinted through the doorway, grabbing Samer by the back of his collar and flinging him across the room.

Hassan roared for the women to leave the room, and they all scurried away as the sound of a rifle cocking echoed in the almost empty room. Hassan turned at the sound of the gun to face his son Turan, who aimed the weapon in Samer's direction, ready for whatever was required of him. I remained, watching on indifferently as Jihad lunged once again at Samer and brought him to his feet.

"They'll settle this like men," Hassan said, directing Turan to lower his rifle.

"Now, before I decide whether or not I'm going to beat you to a pulp," Jihad started, "let me give you a little directive."

He points towards me, his gaze raking over me and settling in my depths comfortably before starting to talk again. He didn't take his eyes off me as he directed his words at Samer, looking at me with an intensity I had not seen since that day in the olive grove when his gun grinded into my side. Samer followed his gaze with some contempt, the collar of his shirt tight against his throat.

"This woman right here, this QUEEN, who you so stupidly gave up…is going to be my wife. You have no rights over her. No right to come in here, into a room full of women, and cause so much trouble. I could kill you for this alone. I could kill you for many reasons. But I won't. Today, your sons saved you. They are the only reason you're still alive."

Jihad let go of Samer's collar and Samer went thudding to the ground with a loud thump.

"Make no mistake, Samer. Next time you come near my wife, I *will* kill you."

Samer had the audacity to remind Jihad that I wasn't his wife yet, insinuating that there was still time for me to change my mind. This comment earned Samer a kick to the ribs and Hassan grabbed Jihad before he could do any further damage.

"Take his advice, leave and don't come back," Hassan warned.

"My daughter lives here," Samer yelled.

"Your daughter lives in Australia. If you really want to see her, make an effort and buy a ticket," Jihad replied.

"You have no right to stand between us," Samer said, speaking to Jihad while chucking his chin in my direction. I wondered what was in his head. We'd gone 5 years with very minimal contact, so why was he all of a sudden so concerned with me getting remarried? Was it the mere fact that I would now be with someone else? Was it the threat that I would finally be happy? Maybe the thought of me in constant misery was what he thrived on? And now that I was finding my happiness, it didn't sit well with him.

I moved forward until I loomed above Samer, staring at him with the same contempt he held within his own eyes. "The thing is Samer, we may have once been married. But you never really had me. Not really. Not at my best. And I'm okay with that. I forgive you for everything you put me through, but know this. I don't want to ever see you again. And if you do ever come near me again, know that there'll be nothing left of you for Jihad; I'll kill you myself."

Jihad and I were married that same night, with protestations from Aaida, who argued that my *Jhaaz* was not yet ready. Jihad gave her the car and enlisted the help of my aunt Samiya and gave them a two hour deadline, telling them we'd be married regardless of whether or not they were back with the remainder of my *jhaaz*. I didn't argue with him. I wanted to put this to bed as quickly as possible without the possibility of anyone else interfering again.

Last time I got married, everything I wore was dictated by someone else, from the dress to the makeup. The man I married was not of my choosing. The life I lived was written for me the moment I was born, however it was not a path I would have willingly chosen to walk on.

This time, I wore a simple blush coloured dress and gloss, keeping it simple as my immediate family gathered around me to celebrate and wish us well. Aunt Samiya threw out *zalghouta* after *zalghouta,* and I could swear that the *tabal* was obscenely loud on purpose, if only to reach the ears of everyone else in the village.

With this marriage, I felt vindicated. For so long now, I had been referred to as *el mtalka,* the divorced one. People had thrown around the expression in a derogatory manner, and whispers and stares had followed me everywhere I went, be it in Australia or Lebanon. There were even a few instances where men-married men-had approached me; for some reason, they viewed the divorced woman as being immoral and loose. It was the same outcome no matter where I went; divorce was still frowned upon.

What was even more unusual was the fact that I would be worthy of remarriage. Most viewed a divorced woman as one who would live out her days broken and alone, and the majority sought to compound this scenario by defaming the divorcee any chance they got.

So it came as a huge surprise to anyone and everyone who was not in my immediate circle when my marriage was announced. Who would want to marry a divorced woman with a child when they could have their pick of fresh young virgins? It didn't make sense to the narrow minded and weak. But surprisingly enough, the one person who initially had reservations but now had my back was my aunt Samiya, who is the loudest and most boisterous at my wedding, and who has shut down each and every criticism as it surfaced.

And with my marriage came the whisper of something more. Hope. Belief. That fairytales did happen, and everyone deserved a second chance at a happy ending.

AAIDA

Pomegranate Molasses
30 large fresh pomegranates
50ml freshly squeezed lemon juice
1/2 cup Sugar
A whole lot of patience

My aunt Farida suggests we make pomegranate molasses. Every year, she makes a huge quantity using pomegranates from their own land. Crate upon crate of this vibrant fruit is tapped to remove the seeds and then distilled and mixed to make a thick juicy syrup.

She doesn't want to overwhelm us, and she's using this time to teach me this technique, so she suggests about half a crate, which is equivalent to about 30 large heads.

We sit outside on a *haseeri* spread out under the shade of the fig trees of my aunt's home, and aunt Farida demonstrates the method of tapping out the seeds by cutting the pomegranate in half then holding the half upside down and tapping hard on the skin with a pestle until the seeds rain out and scatter into a waiting bowl.

"Just like this," she says, showing me precisely how to do it. My mother sits with the other half of the head in her head and watches us, a look of confusion on her face. I can see it's probably been so long since she's done this, she's forgotten how to do it. My mother breaks my heart sometimes; she's been away so long, it's obvious she's lost her connection with her cultural identity.

We continue to tap tap tap, and all too soon, I have mastered the craft of deseeding a pomegranate and my mother has found her footing again. Tayta Tala comes out to join us, shuffling through the dirt slowly, guided by my cousin Yousef, who deposits her on a nearby stool that digs into my shoulder. After a while, we are joined by Farah, Khaled's other grandmother.

Khaled's grandmother and tayta Tala are alike, but they're not. They are like two peas in a pod, and they get along so well, they are more like sisters. They joke and heckle and laugh, and are often seen walking through their respective villages arm in arm as Farah guides Tayta through the streets she once roamed through freely, when she had her sight. Where Tayta is reserved yet happy, Farah is boisterous and a straight shooter. She will always give it to you like it is, no holds barred, and I think that's the foundation of why the two elderly women get along so well; they rely on each other's unfiltered advice.

I have been lucky enough to get along with everyone, and Farah is no exception. She's that little old lady who pinches my cheeks and looks longingly into my face, telling me how cute I am. When she does this, I am transported back in time and feel like I am 8 again. I wonder at the hand of fate which deprived me of the comfort of having a grandmother around, for I feel lucky enough to now be surrounded by so many loving souls. For even though she may not be my biological grandmother, the way she treats me is a damn sight better than the way I've been treated by my father's own mother.

When we are joined by Soraya, Khaled's uncle Waleed's daughter, there is an awkward silence as she sits on one of the nearby stools and watches us. Aside from the initial *Salam* she whispered as she took her seat, she doesn't offer up any other conversation, and a blanket of caution automatically cloaks us as she sits amongst us.

Soraya scares me. She stares at me with such an outward intensity, it's hard to know what she's thinking at any given time. The fact that everyone is on their guard in her presence tells me I'm not the only one who feels the air shift with tension whenever she is around.

Instinctively, I turn to my right and look at tayta Tala, who is always smiling and nodding and enjoying life in her blind version of utopia, but who now sits frowning uneasily, her fingers stitching together in a sort of mini dance of the hand wringing she is so well known for. Beside her, Farah has also pursed her lips, but looks down and says nothing, opting to refill everyone's cup of coffee instead.

There is minor chit chat, and the two elderly ladies lean into each other and laugh about something quietly. I smile at their friendship, and notice that Soraya scowls when she looks at them but remains silently absent from any of the discussions that arise. I wonder what it was that brought her out here only to sit without contribution, silently criticising the gathering.

The only reaction I see from her is when Khaled and Jude approach, and Khaled smiles broadly and greets us with "*Salamaat*". He pulls up a stool next to tayta Tala and winds his arm around her shoulder, asking her how she's doing, and Yousef does a tap tap tap on his thighs to mimic the thumping of the pestle on the skin, humming a tune as he does so.

"*Yallah*, Aaida," Khaled says, grabbing my hand and lifting me to rise to him, and there in the open grounds of the villa, underneath the shade of the fig trees, he raises his arms and spreads them out like the wings of a bird and turns slowly this way and then that in a slow happy dance, taking me with him. I move with him slightly, both our arms outstretched but not touching, my fingers dripping the deep red liquid of the pomegranates as I laugh and turn with him, amused by his actions in the middle of our cooking session.

"*Ya ibni*," aunt Farida clucks her tongue. "You're holding us up."

And with that, Khaled and Yousef take their leave, and I smile as I sit down to continue the pitting, but not before I spy Soraya sitting on the edge of her seat, a look of utter defeat on her face. And I know, I know, just by that look on her face, and the look of contempt she throws me, that she was hoping that she too would get her chance to dance with Khaled. I look away quickly, choosing to ignore her expression and the unease she brings to the gathering.

When we are done emptying the seeds from their shells, Farah offers to pulse the pomegranates so we are left with the juice and the pulp is discarded.

"*Ma'alaysh, tayta*," I say, rising with the pot in my hands. "I'll do it." I will do anything to move away from Soraya's evil eye, if only for a few minutes.

"You can't pulse them too much," she calls out after me "or they'll turn to mush and the syrup will be bitter."

I nod and make my way inside to find the blender. When I emerge from the house a few minutes later, I hold up the glass bowl for all to see and I'm met with positive remarks and a guarantee that I have pulsed the seeds "just right."

"*Ya ayni ala hal bint*," Farah says, smiling my way. "I don't know why that foolish grandson of mine hasn't married you yet!"

There is a collective silence as Farah's words register, and everyone stops what they're doing and stares ahead. They look everywhere but at Soraya, who is emitting such negative energy, it feels like she is about to suffer a spontaneous combustion. Tayta Tala starts wringing her hands, a full blown hand folding over hand wringing that mirrors the stress on her face.

Soraya stands, looks at us one by one, then turns and walks away without a word.

Aunt Farida shakes her head and lets out a breath she didn't know she'd been holding.

My mother lets out a sound of relief then starts to recite supplications to ward off the evil eye and envy.

Tayta Tala recites "*Masha'allah, la quwata illah billah.*

And Farah. God bless Farah, you had to love her, bellows out about her own grand-daughter "Soraya *boomeh*", causing us all to erupt in a fit of laughter.

KHALED

I watch Aaida as she sits outside with the women, stringing beans. Well, they work on the beans, and Aaida just watches. I sit on my perch by the window on the top floor where no-one else can see me, watching her in private. I see her wince as she leans over in her stool to pick up a beanstalk, then thinks better of it and drops it back on the tray.

My mother whispers something to her, the concern evident on her face as she frowns. She calls over her back, and momentarily, Lita comes outside carrying a tray with a small cup, which my mother lifts and raises to Aaida's mouth.

My mother is like a mother hen around Aaida, treating her like the daughter she never had. And I'm glad-Aaida has given my mother something she never knew she needed, while my mother has given Aaida what I suspect is a montage of our family history, a subject I know Aaida holds near to her heart.

Aaida finishes drinking and nods when my mother asks her something, then proceeds to squeeze her hips, as though willing the pain to remain subdued. She's been off all morning, feeling sick from the moment I pick her up, when she insists on staying home instead of hunting with me. I don't want to miss spending what precious little time we have left away from her. So I compromise.

"Ok, no hunting for you," I agree. "But let me take you to our house so I can at least see you after we're back. *Yallah,* get ready, mother is waiting for you," I prompt her.

She is reluctant to go, but stands up and pulls her oversized shirt down, as if to hide something from me. For all her bravado, Aaida is very self-conscious about her body, even though she looks amazing. When it comes to body image, her self-esteem is in the gutter.

We all scramble into the car and I drive us to Dhar Khamra. My aunt Aujene sits up front with me, while tayta Tala sits with Aaida in the back. As I drive, I sneak surreptitious glances in her direction in the rearview mirror, noticing how she is withdrawn and pale.

I watch her now and realise not much has changed. She is still not well enough to go hunting with us, even though I know how much she loves to do so. So she'll sit out this session, staying back with the women as the men take several cars out to the field to hunt. Afterwards, we'll come back and enjoy a hearty meal as a family, and I can spend more time with her. She's leaving in two weeks, and I know the next 14 days will fly past in the blink of an eye, so I have to make the most of our time together.

Something squeezes at my heart when I think of Aaida leaving. Just the thought of being apart from her for another year does things to me I can't explain.

"You ready?" I hear from the doorway, and I can't bring myself to turn away from her. I'm rooted to my spot by the window, mesmerised by every movement she makes. My father comes to stand beside me and looks out the window to see what I'm looking at.

"You know, you could so easily marry her," he says, turning to face me.

I cluck my tongue like that is the most ridiculous thing he's ever said. "She's my cousin," I remind him.

"You don't need to remind me," my father says. "In these parts, marrying a cousin is a normal enough concept."

"Not where Aaida is from," I say, turning to face him. "She's made it quite clear she thinks the practise is archaic."

My father regards me quietly for the longest time, then shrugs indifferently and says the one thing I've been hearing constantly over and over again. "She may hate the practise, but that doesn't mean she's not in love with you."

Everyone thinks we're in love. I don't know; maybe we are.

We haven't put a label on what we mean to one another. We haven't so much as uttered promises to each other or voiced our feelings. I do know that without her, there's a void in my life. And everything I do revolves around the next time I see her. But that doesn't mean I'm in love with her, or her with me. We're simply two people connected in a way that most people aren't.

My father shakes his head and looks at me in a way that tells me he thinks I don't have a clue, and it feels as though he's read my mind. It feels like he's reached in to the deepest recesses of my mind and pulled out something so fragile and given it to me, yet I don't believe what I see. I know what he's thinking. But maybe it's easy for my father to feel that way; after all, he's lived his love story, so maybe he sees things differently to the way I do. Not everything can be a bed of roses all the time, and sometimes where one sees colour, as I believe he does, another may see black and white.

"You coming?" he asks again, turning toward the door.

"I'll be down in a minute," I say, grabbing my rifle. I take one last look out the window at Aaida as she leans her head into my mother's shoulder, resting there, looking more like her daughter than her niece, and make my way out to the car to join the men. Perhaps an outing away from Aaida is just what I need to clear my head, I think, as I take my place in the back seat next to my father. Two of our men sit in the front, and my brothers follow in one of two other cars travelling with us.

We hunt birds for almost three hours, revelling in the clear weather as we toss our bullets into the air and birds come screeching out of the sky to land in the fields. Two younger boys run through the grass to retrieve the birds and put them in baskets. Truth be told, I'm not very fond of the taste of the game we hunt, but it is a sport I've loved since I was very young. On the other end of the spectrum, my brothers, the twins Yusuf and

Jude don't care much for the sport, but like to pick the bones of the birds clean.

I marvel at our catch as we fire off round after round, filling up two large baskets as the morning wears on. Aaida bosses my mind, as she oftentimes does when I'm doing something she enjoys. She loves hunting. A big part of that, I believe, is due to her natural ability as a marksman. Hunting is in her blood, and it would seem that she inherited this talent from her father, who she still refuses to acknowledge as an integral part of her life.

Not that he even tries. I would never say it outright to Aaida, but the man is the scum of the earth, abandoning her, his eldest child, to start a new life with a whole new family, thus erasing her from his history as though she'd never even existed. He didn't deserve her compassion. Nor did she owe him anything.

I aim my rifle and take another shot. Aaida should be here beside me, I think to myself, doing what she loves doing.

We've piled back into the cars and are on our way back to the village when we're stopped on the side of the road by a man waving us down. We recognise him as one of the locals from a nearby village, and my father orders the convoy to a halt and emerges from the car to talk with him.

Abu Rabie tells us he was on his way to our village when he happened to have a flat tyre and no spare. By chance, and to his relief, we happened across him.

"*Kheir,* Abu Rabie," my father starts, as the men use their own spare tyre to fix Abu Rabie's car to get him back onto the road as quickly as possible. "What was it you wanted to discuss?"

"Abu Shaker sent me. He's distressed over some infighting that has happened between he and his neighbours over water. The situation has reached a point where it seems outsider intervention would be necessary to diffuse the situation."

"How can we help?" my father asks, and Abu Rabie reveals tensions are so heightened, the only intervention that anyone would benefit from would be that of the highest ranking Shaikh in the region, meaning my father.

My father never turns down a man who holds his hand out for help. No matter the circumstance, he would never. He also happens to be adept at de-escalating situations and reaching the best outcomes for all parties involved.

And that is why my father agrees to follow Abu Rabie to Abu Shaker's house, where we will meet with Abu Shaker, discuss the situation, and figure out the best angle to tackle this complication. We re-arrange our men so that two cars follow Abu Rabie, and the third car, carrying the twins and a few others, goes ahead with the baskets to the village so the birds can be prepared for lunch upon our return.

I settle beside my father and look at him as he looks out his side window, a look of deep contemplation upon his face.

"Sometimes I wonder at the ridiculous reasons that people find themselves in conflict," I tell my father. "Why can't people just get along?"

"It's human nature," he says, turning to me. "Mankind will always need something to fight for, even when it is something as ridiculous as water."

"You don't ever get tired of it?" I ask him.

He shrugs and looks at me thoughtfully. "I'd be lying if I didn't say I have my moments. Man can be so stupid. But if we all gave up without trying to settle our differences, there'd be no-one left."

We follow Abu Rabie until he stops in front of a huge imposing home with marble pillars and a wide wrap around balcony. I count about 30 men in total, some with rifles slung against their shoulders, and the whole setting looks more like an army barrack than a family home. This will be no ordinary mediation. The fact that there are so many men present means the situation is dire enough to have the house locked down like a fortress with guards in place.

Abu Shaker is the head of the household. After we have removed our muddy shoes, he welcomes us into his home and offers us *ahwi.* He knows exactly who we are and what we represent. And he understands, very well, that the situation at hand can only be diffused with our help, and it is obvious that he has sought us out specifically. By this time, we are the strongest and most powerful clan in the North, and our standing and fortune attest to that.

The old man explains the situation to us in detail. His neighbours have bought land adjacent to his and put up tents instead of homes with proper plumbing. They have installed a makeshift pipe leading out of the tents, where their dirty dish and bath water runs out onto the land and across the unsealed road into Abu Shaker's land. Abu Shaker's access on the unsealed road has been restricted because his car keeps getting bogged down, and part of his land has also become water logged. In one instance, one of his cows fell into the muddy patch and broke her leg. Abu Shaker is fuming, but willing to work toward a resolution if it means there will be no bloodshed between neighbours.

We promise to look into the matter and guarantee Abu Shaker that God Willing, the matter would be resolved by the next day, and we would return with good news.

Abu Shaker insists we stay for lunch with the men, but we take our leave and promise him there will be other times to dine together, but right now, there was much work to be done.

We collect our boots from the front stoop and file down the front stairs as we leave the house and make our way to the car.

No-one sees it coming. A spray of bullets piercing the air at the same time that all time stands still.

The first bullet hits the doorframe behind us, ricochets and hits something metallic. Before we can duck, another round of bullets is sprayed toward the front of the house and there is the sound of heavy slumping as bodies fall to the ground like dominoes.

I feel something sharp and warm hit my right shoulder and I stumble back, just in time to see men emerging from the house with guns raised, aiming for the intruders who have assaulted us.

I push the person in front of me to the ground and fall on top of him just as another bullet rips through my torso. I turn to reach for those behind me. My brain cannot connect with what is happening, and my unflinching eyes open in horror as I see the bodies laying on the ground, drenched in flowing blood. There is a river of blood.

We were talking about the flow of water, but now it's rivers of blood that are flowing, drenching the ground, the metallic smell assaulting my nostrils in defiance. We're not armed. Our hunting rifles, hopeless against such aggression, were left in the car out of respect for Abu Shaker.

I look around to gather my bearings, and there behind me and slightly to my left is a lifeless body. I know this body well, and I cannot accept what my eyes are showing me. His eyes are open in one last blink as his soul marks the earth one last time, his face and chest coated with blood.

My mouth is open in a silent scream, my voice drowned out by the yells of men as they start to drag bodies away from the line of fire. And just as soon as it started, the spurt of gunfire retreats and I hear the slamming of car doors in the distance and more indistinct yells and shrill wailing.

We never saw it coming.

That day, we lost a few great men.

And we lost my brother Turan.

AAIDA

We first realise there's something wrong when a man on horseback rides into Dhar Khamra as though he's racing a marathon. He's off the horse even before it screeches to a halt, tumbling onto his back then rising again and heading to Waleed's house. People are emerging from their homes to see what all the commotion is about as a series of yells pierces the quiet silence of this small familial village.

I emerge from the house in time to see Waleed raising his palms to the sky and muttering a prayer, before springing into action and gathering the men of the village around him. My aunt Farida, as though sensing something in the air, wears a worried look as she comes up behind me, just in time to catch Waleed's gaze as he glances in her direction. Instinctively, she knows. And I wonder what it is she knows as Waleed looks at her with eyes full of sorrow. She almost tumbles down the stairs in her haste to get to him, clutching at her chest as though knowing whatever it is, it threatens to eviscerate her heart.

"*Mart akhi*," he says, sternly, addressing her as sister in law. I've never heard him take that tone with her.

"Who?" Farida asks. "Who is it?"

She knows. Her heart knows. Something. But not the specifics.

The minute Waleed opens his mouth and says "Turan - i*nna lillahi wa inna ilayhi iraji'oon*", my aunt Farida faints and flutters to the ground like a feather. Instantly, she is surrounded by women who clutch at all sides of her, lifting her and carrying her into the house. I stand mesmerised, unable to fathom what has happened, but then understanding dawns on me as I translate Waleed's words in my head. "Verily we belong to Allah and verily to him do we return." Words of condolence. Turan. Something bad has happened. To Turan.

I look up and watch Waleed as he starts throwing around commands, ordering the community to be locked down. By now, the village in its entirety has come to stand before him, and I notice that some men are carrying rifles. He addresses those before him, telling them Hassan's convoy was attacked earlier and we're waiting on more details.

"No-one leaves. No-one enters. Everyone is to stay indoors until we know more. There will be men on the rooftops protecting the village, but for your own safety, stay inside and lock your doors. Load your guns. Protect yourselves if anyone gets through. We don't know what we're looking at."

"Are our men okay?" a woman yells out.

"We've lost a few good men. My nephew Turan is amongst them."

Murmurs rise from within the crowd as the villagers utter prayers and condolences. Whatever has happened must be serious to have ended in the death of one of the clan members of the Damour tribe, they realise.

"I urge you all to practise extreme caution until we know what we're dealing with. My brother's convoy has been attacked. Our village could be next."

Waleed goes on to tell them he's making a quick trip to the hospital to check on casualties, and assigns one of his best local men to stand guard at the gate and act as keeper of the village. Shortly, he comes over to me and tells me to get ready so he can drop me off in Tul Ghosn on his way to the hospital.

"I'm not going anywhere," I tell him, folding my arms over my chest petulantly.

"It's not safe for you to stay here, Aaida," he explains. "Hassan would kill me if anything happens to you."

"I'm not leaving, Waleed." I grab the gun in his arms and cock it, then look him squarely in the eyes. "I can outshoot any man here," I remind him. "I'm staying."

Waleed squints and looks at me as though I have lost my

mind. And maybe I have. In his world, the woman's place was in her home and the man's place was to protect. But here was this little girl who'd come from half way around the world to challenge his beliefs and traditions. She spoke her mind and did what she did, and God help anyone who dared stand in her way.

"This is not the place for you to be right now, Aaida. I can't be worrying about you while I try to protect the whole damn world against this threat."

"Then don't worry about me," I tell him. "Let me be your crutch and help until the men are back and we know more."

He shakes his head in desperation but realises he can't waste any more time arguing with me to leave. "Keep the gun near you. Take care of your aunt," he says, as he starts to walk away to a waiting car.

HASSAN

The country is slowly rebuilding itself after 15 bloody years of civil war, and the government is cracking down on lingering clan warfare in an effort to stamp out crime and corruption. A shooting like this, with several dead and multiple injuries, is bound to reach the attention of the newly formed army, which is now dealing with all major crimes, especially those involving bloodshed.

The good we put out in the community affords us some luxury. Like visits to the hospital. We've driven the dead and injured to this local hospital where we have worked with good doctors previously and donated generously, and we know they'll be instrumental in getting the injured treated quickly and with as little fuss as possible, without raising any alarm bells with the local police or the army.

I'm too numb to feel anything but a blanket fury at what has happened. I will have to bury my second son. My first born has been shot several times in the thigh and the chest, that bullet narrowly missing his heart. I thank God that the twins were sent back to the village ahead of us, avoiding the massacre altogether.

My main concern now, aside from seeing my son Khaled stitched up and well again, is Farida's welfare. I can't contemplate what will happen to her when she finds out what has happened and I'm not there to support her. She will be devastated.

My second concern is the aftermath of what has happened. By now, the shooters, so obviously part of the problem Abu Shaker was explaining to us, would know that they had shot and killed people not involved with the ongoing feud between the neighbours. By now, they would have realised the damage they've done, and who they've attacked. An attack on the Damours would not go unpunished. Everyone knows this. I wonder if they will try to finish the job and try to extinguish the remainder of my family to save themselves. It has happened before to other clans; when self preservation kicks in, there is no telling what people might do to extricate themselves from a situation.

I don't have long to wonder as my brother Waleed comes rushing into the hospital, a few men on his heels.

Our little village is a fortress unto itself. It's a village within a village, so sparsely populated and so fortified, it would literally take an army to cross the drawbridge and scale the towering stone walls that envelope it. When we lock down, we really lock down, and I don't think there would be a place on earth safer than Dhar Khamra when we've shut the world out. Other families from neighbouring villages who fall under our umbrella and therefore our protection, find their way to our village to offer their unwavering support in our time of need. Waleed advises me the village is locked down tight, with hundreds of loyal men dotting the boundary to the outside world.

"They're safe," Waleed assures me.

"Farida?"

"She's fine, *akhi*."

"She knows?"

Waleed gives me a solemn nod and lowers his gaze to the floor. "She knew before I opened my mouth to speak. She just didn't know who."

I run a hand through my hair and flatten it against my neck; never have I felt so helpless and ill prepared to deal with a situation. I realise this is unlike me and I have to pull myself together for the sake of my family and my community.

"What do you want me to do?" Waleed asks.

He is older than me. But he has always been the weaker one between us. He never wanted the mantle of clan leader, and that's why the responsibility fell to me upon my father's death. Yet he has always been there right by my side, happy to walk in my shadow as I took the Damour name to new heights. I worked hard to establish a healthy respect between the other clans which meant no in-fighting and an unprecedented term of peace between the neighbouring tribes. Waleed has been my rock, for although he was not equipped to rule, he has been a necessary weapon in my arsenal when it came to establishing law and order amongst us.

"Nothing for now," I mutter, putting my hand on his shoulder. "Just ensure the safety of the townspeople and make sure there are guards at the hospital gates. As soon as Khaled is well enough, we'll move him."

"Is that wise?" Waleed asks me.

"We can't stay here indefinitely. It won't be long before news reaches the police and they come through those doors. The safest place for us is Dhar Khamra. But not until it's safe to move him."

AAIDA

Some would say there's a fine line between life and death.

You hear stories of people crossing over to the other side, swearing they saw a light at the end of a dark tunnel and turned back.

There are those, who like me, would otherwise be pronounced clinically dead, were it not for a young boy pulling me out of the water while I was on my last breath.

And yet others, having suffered man-made atrocities, damaged beyond all repair, who become permanent inhabitants of the earth when their life is extinguished by the snipe of a rifle.

Turan was that person for me.

He was the first dead person I had ever seen who related to me.

That afternoon, when the men trudge home to a village surrounded by men and guns and protection, Turan is carried quietly out of the car and laid to rest on a makeshift gurney in the basement, where he is washed and wrapped in the customary white shroud in preparation for his burial.

My aunt Farida sits on a chair by the door softly weeping, as the men file in to pay their last respects. Finally, my uncle Hassan orders the men to leave the room to make way for the women. The women in the immediate family want to pay their respects and say their final goodbyes. He escorts aunt Farida in first, with Turan's aunts and cousins following. Farida is exceptionally stoic, resigned to the fact that her son is gone, kissing his cheeks and his forehead as she bids him farewell, tears staining her cheeks.

I feel my own warm tears flow against my cheeks as her pain consumes me. She is so heroic about it, and I wonder at the depth of spirituality she possesses which allows her to accept such an end to her son's life and allows her to continue on with a life without him in it. She is truly blessed to understand and accept that this is the way of the world, it is God's will, and no amount of hope could undo what has been done.

I look down at Turan's glowing face. For glow, it does. His eyes are closed, and there is a calm tranquility about his peaceful face, as though he is finally at peace. His lips are turned up at the edges, as though attempting to smile, and a perfect light emanates from his face. Nour. Light. That is the only way to explain what I am seeing as I look down at my cousin's face for the last time. I had heard stories of believers who had died in such a state. Their connection to the Almighty coupled with their good deeds in the time they roamed the earth ensured them a swift transition into the afterlife.

Turan holds a special place in my heart. He was my aunt Farida's second born son, the quietly reserved polite son who was always playing pranks. Although I am closer to Khaled, Turan nevertheless still meant the world to me. To now be saying goodbye to him and knowing that I would never see him again was breaking my heart. I envied my aunt Farida's quiet determination to stay strong and hold the family together in their darkest hour as I swallowed my pain and brushed my hand against Turan's glowing cheek.

"Bkhaatrak, ya ibn khalti el aziz," I whisper my farewell into his ear, referring to him as my darling cousin.

I wipe at my tears and turn away, moving through the crowd to allow others to pay their respects. I reach the door just as Waleed is pushing a wheel chair carrying Khaled into the room. My cousin looks up at me as he enters the room, a pained look on his face. More tears come as I remember how easily we could've been burying two brothers today, rather than one.

"Khaled," I whisper, putting a hand briefly to his shoulder as I walk past.

"We mustn't delay the burial any longer," Waleed says, and I know that he is right. It is Turan's right to have a speedy burial.

I watch as Khaled is wheeled past me to farewell his brother, and leave the room to stand outside on the front porch, where I see no less than a thousand or more men milling about the front of the house. I feel like I am in a dream, and at any moment, I will wake up. Things move too quickly, and before I know it, there is movement and noise behind me as I hear someone yell "Coming through! We're bringing the deceased out!"

I move out of the way and watch as there is a break in the crowd in front of the house. Turan is held like a prize above the heads of four men who lift him as though he weighs the measure of a feather. And just as soon as he appears, he disappears into the crowd as he is passed through the throng of men and they surge on foot towards the cemetery, where they will bury him and recite Quranic verses at his gravesite.

It is said, in Islam, that those that are of the most pious, of the highest standing in their religiosity, enjoy a speedy funeral and burial. Everything sort of falls into place and the road to the next life is smooth and transactional. I would be lying if I said the whole affair, from start to end, took more than 30 minutes. It took just 28 minutes to say our farewells and bury my cousin. I look on in astonishment as the men converge on the village after their return-on foot-from the local cemetery, which on any given day, would have been a 20 minute walk either way.

"Did something happen?" I ask a lady standing near me. "They came back so quickly."

"No, *ya binti*, Turan is one of the lucky ones. His good deeds ensured he had a swift burial."

KHALED

Massacre: the deliberate and brutal killing of many people

I hate myself.

I am unlucky enough to survive five bullets piercing my skin and bones.

I say I'm unlucky because I'm one of the few that survived the massacre that claimed eight lives and left twelve others seriously injured. We lost two of our own men, one being my younger brother Turan. So I hate myself. Hate that I got to live while he died. I know, I know, it may be a sign of the fraying of my spiritual soul when I think such things, when we consider that we all have plans, but God is the greatest of planners.

Yet I still hate myself nonetheless. I hate myself enough to refuse visitors. And I hate myself enough to send Aaida away. I am in so much physical pain, but that is nothing compared to the mental anguish bruising my heart. I contemplate seeing her and telling her myself, but I'm a coward when it comes to facing her with the awful truth. And I know this will break her heart, but it has to be done, so I meet with my father and Jihad and I briefly outline what I want them to do on my behalf.

Both men, equally fond of Aaida, look at me as though I've lost my mind and argue back and forth for a few minutes, before they realise I'm fading and quickly.

Despite what the doctor says, I know I still may not make it. There's something wrong with me, and if it doesn't get fixed soon, I know I'll reside under the earth beside my brother. The possibility gives me pause for thought-would it be such a bad thing if I just took a bow and faded into the background? For what sort of a life could I expect, when most likely, I'll be confined to a wheelchair for the rest of my life?

I feel my chest throbbing at the bullet wound there, and it's as though a red hot fire is seeping outward from the place where the bullet entered me, and I know it must be the spread of an infection. I feel warm all over, and I know my temperature is spiking yet again. It would just be so easy to let go and give in, and fall into a deep slumber from which there is no waking.

But then I remember my mother. My poor, beautiful mother, who would not be able to deal with any more loss. Her heart would not be able to handle any more grief. I feel my head drooping heavily to the side as Jihad and my father talk over each other trying to make me understand that what I'm doing is wrong. And their protests as I fade in and out of semi-consciousness, their voices becoming soft and distant as I strain to listen.

"...will break her heart," my father is saying.

"There's no coming back from something like this," Jihad sighs, urging me to reconsider what I'm doing.

"Son, you're on so much medication, you don't know what you're saying."

"She's been here the whole time waiting to see you. She's beside herself with grief and fear."

And my parting words to them before I feel myself finally shut down. I hear my own voice as though in the distance, yet I can't be certain I actually said them...

"She has to go."

AAIDA

My mother is beside herself with grief over Turan's death and falls into Farida's open arms as they cry together, sharing their unfettered grief as more mourners flow into the house to pay their condolences. It was almost as though everyone had forgotten that evil thing that had happened that took the life of a beautiful young man, and Hassan sought to remind everyone it was no time to let their guard down.

"I'm staying with Khaled," I say, later that afternoon when my mother announces our departure. Hassan, Jihad and my mother stand around in a semi-circle and seem to look from one another without responding to me. When I urge them to speak, it is Hassan who says it would be best if I left to ensure my safety.

"I'm not leaving him. I'm not leaving aunt Farida," I add.

"Khaled's going back to the hospital shortly," uncle Hassan tells me.

I shake my head in confusion, not understanding why Khaled would be going back if he's come home. No one has been allowed to see him except his father and a doctor that they have brought in to monitor his condition. Even I haven't been able to see him; uncle Hassan explains to me that he hasn't been the same after he bid his brother Turan farewell.

"He's had a fever all night and through the morning," Hassan explains. "The doctor was hopeful that it would break, but it hasn't. It looks like an infection."

My hand flies to my mouth in distress, my mind not reconciling that things could go from bad to worse.

"What will happen to him?"

"We shouldn't have brought him home. It was his insistence

to farewell his brother, and that alone, that made us bow to his request."

"I should be with him," I whisper, more to myself than anyone else.

"Aaida," Jihad finally speaks up, somewhat reluctantly, and I realise this is the thing that no-one else wants to say. "Khaled's not in a good place right now. Understandably. He needs some space and time to heal."

"Space from me? Me?" I ask, stabbing a finger into my chest, the hurt enveloping me like a typhoon.

"Aaida, come Aaida," my mother says, her hand on my arm, ushering me away from the men so we can talk in a quiet little corner. I shrug her hand off my arm and stare her down defiantly as she tells me he just needs time alone to mourn.

"When am I going to be there for him if not on the worst day of his life?" I cry, looking at her then back at Hassan and Jihad watching me uncomfortably. I know I am being irrational, but I can't help knowing that he is in pain and I'm not sharing that pain with him. What if something happened to him and I was not there to say goodbye? What if I never had the chance to tell him all the things I always wanted to say?

"Aaida," Hassan begins. "Khaled has asked me to send you home." Hassan's words are sharp and distinct, slicing through my heart and severing the arteries.

Plain and simple. Nice and easy. A heartbreaking finality. This is what Khaled wants. He's hurt and he wants to send me away. To discard me. Abandon me. Reject me. Just like my father did. This was no different. Sending me away, no matter what the reason, was a rejection. Of the greatest kind. I rear my head, tossing it from side to side in disbelief. Then my whole body shakes in disbelief, as though I've been dipped in a barrel of icy cold water. There are tears streaking down my cheeks and a sharp throbbing in my chest, where my heart is, and I clutch at that place, sure that I'm about to expire. It hurts. It hurts so much.

"I want to see him," I gasp.

Hassan looks down at his feet, then back up at me, his hands firmly planted on his hips in the stance of a leader. Hassan was born a leader.

"He's already gone, Aaida," he tells me, and it feels as though he's taken a stake and driven it straight through my heart. Another rejection. Another failure.

I'm about to tear myself to shreds resigning myself to being rejected by literally every man I've ever known, and wondering what I've done to deserve this.

I'm overwhelmed with so many feelings, and the only thing I can hear above the throbbing in my head is the word "gone, gone, gone" playing over and over in my head as though it's set on auto repeat. He's already gone. He didn't even say goodbye. He just left. Just like that. Without a word.

I wipe my sleeve against my eyes and stifle a further sob. If aunt Farida were here, I know we'd be having a very different conversation, but the doctor had to sedate her when the realisation hit her that Turan wasn't coming back and she was consumed by agonising wails.

"I can't do this," I say, to no-one in particular, a choking sob lodged in my throat.

"Let's go home," my mother says, moving to put her arm around my shoulder to comfort me.

When he sends me away, something inside me snaps. A cold, aching wall blankets my soul and extinguishes my heart. I am devastated. I am torn. And I know that I will never be the same again.

Some people spend their whole life searching for "the one."

I was born with the one already written for me.

I was lucky enough to stumble into him quite by accident. On a trip to Lebanon. When I was 17.

Khaled was it for me. Meeting him was like meeting my other

half, the missing part of my soul that I didn't know existed until I met him.

I was lucky like that. Most people spend their whole life searching for that one person that will make them whole.

Every day, I sit quietly in the garden and wait for his car to come screeching to a halt in front of tayta's house, where he flings the door open carelessly and bounds from the car to run into the *dhar* and pick me up, throwing me in the air as though I weigh nothing. I would squeal and laugh with delight, punching at his shoulder to put me down because my fear of heights would weigh in, causing my breath to catch abnormally. Every day I would wait, but that day never came. For two solid weeks, I waited, but he never came.

Aunt Farida visits once, a day day before we are due to get on a plane and leave for home, and looks at me with sad, grief stricken eyes. She has not only lost Turan, but she has also lost everything that Khaled *had* been, and everything that Khaled and I could have been. She is mourning her son, but she is also mourning the death of a possible future for me and her other son. She holds me for endless minutes, wailing into my shoulder as I cling to her for dear life, then just as quickly releases me and goes to wait in the car as Hassan says his last goodbyes.

"I'm sorry, Aaida. You know under any other circumstances, he would have come. But he just hasn't been himself since..."

I nod my understanding, telling him there's no need to go on as I step into his embrace with tears rolling down my face. Something about the way he held me felt like a certain finality that told me this was the end of the road for me with the Damour family. The mere thought of that being the case ignited a raging inferno within me as grief overwhelmed my senses. I knew then, with the same clarity I had when I first met Khaled, that my life would never be the same again.

KHALED

The last time I saw Aaida.

The last time I saw Aaida was in 1996, when I was 25 and she was 22. That was the year of the massacre. That was the year that everything changed. If I had known that would be the last time I would ever see her again, I never would've let her go.

But then, I was the one to push her away.

The massacre changed everything. My brother's death changed everything. After that day, I spiralled out of control, my anger and depression overwhelming me, until I lost all control and started taking my anger out on everything and everyone. Aaida had been grief stricken by the events that transpired that day. She had been shocked and horrified, and I know she probably needs therapy to this day after what she saw. Yet still, stoic and loyal Aaida had stood by my side, clutching my heart and soul in her strength as I fell apart with no concern for her own well-being. It was only after I had started to heal that I realised what her strength had cost her.

The day before she left, Aaida enlisted the help of Jihad, who drove her to Dhar Khamra, and above the protestations of my brothers, she burst into my room and tried to lay claim to my soul one last time. In that moment, I couldn't see straight in front of me, so full of sell-loathing was I. I was sick with worry about her being so close to something so horrible. She screamed and called me a coward for acting the exact same way toward her that the men in her family over the generations had acted, dictating and assuming we knew what was right for the women in our lives. It hurt that she compared me to those men, all of whom had let her or her ancestors down. Her father, her grandfather, her great grandfather...had all sought to stifle their wives and daughters by dictating their lives for them.

"Lower your voice, Aaida." I had been agitated ever since the massacre, short-tempered and, truth be told, maybe even a little self-centred. "You're leaving tomorrow, why do you want to end things on this note?"

"Look, there you go again," and she whisked her hand in the air helplessly, trying to demonstrate a point. "You push me away then you pull me back, and then away again. You're being so selfish and you're taking the coward's way out!"

Which was the wrong thing to say, and she knew this as soon as the words came out of her mouth, because she sucked in a sharp breath and her hand flew to her mouth in regret. That was so not the right thing to say. I had just lost my brother and I was bound to be selfish and angry without her throwing that unnecessarily in my face.

"You should go, Aaida."

"I want to stay here with you," she pleaded. "You're not in the right frame of mind at the moment. You don't know what you're saying; you need time to think with a clear head," she told me, grasping at straws.

"I need time away from you," I told her, and with one fell swoop, it was as though I had cut her off at the legs. She swayed and looked at me in disbelief, a wounded look in her eyes. I needed her to understand that this was not where she should be. "I need time away from you."

"What about what you started here?" she gasped.

"I started *nothing*," I spat at her, somewhat spitefully. I was hurt and wounded and needed to lash out. "There's *nothing*. Neither of us made any promises to the other."

I spoke the unspoken without actually saying anything, slicing her heart in two as I looked at her. Aaida's pain and anguish were so deep, I thought I could easily go insane with what I was doing to her. Years had gone past and we had grown closer with every visit she made to Lebanon. But why had I never told her that I loved her? Why had I never articulated my feelings for her so that there *was* some sort of a promise to hold on to? Saying it now would only reek of desperation and it would be said for all the wrong reasons. Maybe distance was exactly what we needed.

"This is true," she whispered, hurt beyond all measure.

I *would* tell her I loved her. I *would* tell her I wanted to spend the rest of my life with her and only her. I *would* cherish and worship her in the way she deserved to be. But I just needed some time. Time to sort through the jumble of my emotions and show her what she meant to me.

"Khaled, I don't want our last goodbye to be this way," she said, looking at me helplessly. "If I leave now, I'm never coming back."

I shrugged as though I didn't care, hitting the last nail in the coffin until it sealed our fates, shutting our feelings for one another within its walls.

"This isn't fair. You know my time here is limited, and yet this is how you choose to spend our final moments?"

"But the circumstances are different," I reminded her. "Things have changed."

She nodded. "I understand that. But I'm not sure that my leaving will make any difference. You can't move on, you're so fixated on what happened."

I wanted to remind her that it was *my* brother who died, but that would have been callous and would have diminished the pain that she felt. What she had seen, she could not unsee. That in itself was enough to make her go crazy.

"I won't be going to the airport," I told her, playing the only card I had left. She realised this was the last goodbye, yet she just shrugged in defeat and turned away from me, looking out the window. Almost every other trip, with the exception of when I'd been in Canada, I'd been with her up until the end. I'd spent every last minute with Aaida, even driving her to the airport. It hurt now that she didn't seem to care, and I felt the crease in my forehead as my brows knitted together.

Usually I was the strong, level headed one, but in this

instance, I realised I was the one that was falling to pieces and had to distance myself to save my sanity. She was right, I *was* a coward.

"Aaida." I waited but there was no response from her. "Aaida," I called again, but still there was no answer and she didn't turn around to face me.

"I think we've both said all there is to say, Khaled. Don't make this any harder than it is."

Her dismissal of me was all the incentive I needed. I realised this was probably her armour going up, her safety mechanism to distance herself from my rejection.

Despite the overwhelming urge I had to touch her one last time, I merely looked at her back as her chest rose and fell in a quivery shake. I realised she was crying and closed my eyes to stem the pain radiating through me. I did this to her. I caused her pain. I caused her devastation.

"Goodbye Aaida," was all I said as I turned and wheeled myself away. And that was the last time I saw Aaida.

AAIDA

The last time I saw Khaled.

The last time I saw Khaled was the night before I was due to fly out of Lebanon.

Even after he banished me from his life, and the knife twisted in my heart every time he refused to see me, I went against his wishes and went to see him. I burst through his bedroom unannounced to have my say. I would not leave without giving this one last chance. I had already extended my trip by weeks, most of which were spent living with his rejection, and now I begged him to reconsider his position.

Khaled was vulnerable after Turan's passing; he had seen the dregs of hell after the massacre which claimed the life of his brother and the others. I realised and understood this. I, too, had seen and heard and been a part of things that no person should ever have to go through. So I was not entirely immune to his pain. But although he had not previously made any claims or promises or plans for us, he was now pushing me away for all the wrong reasons.

I tried everything I could to sway him, going so far as to beg him to let me stay with him, but it was impossible to change his mind. I wanted one word, one inkling, one small indication that what had once bound us to each other was still there. Otherwise, I was leaving the next day, and would never be back. But my threat fell on deaf ears and there was nothing further to talk about as he bade me one final farewell. I was glad my back was to him and he couldn't see my tears as they fell silently down my cheeks, the pain so overwhelming, I swore I could feel my heart collapse.

And as he bid me a curt farewell and turned away, my tears streamed unabated down my face and I thought of all the things I wanted to say but was too much a coward to say, having already been ordered to leave.

When what I really wanted to say was that I loved him and had done so from the moment I had met him. That invisible hand that had reached out, causing me to stumble and fall, weaving its magic as it brought us together, had ensured he was the one, the only one. The better half of me. Without him, I was only a shell of a woman, wandering aimlessly through life and asking *"what if?"*

But instead, I held my tongue and shed my tears. I cried endlessly into the night, in the car on the way to the airport, and then finally on the plane, I cried myself to sleep, sandwiched between my mother and Jihad, who each took one of my hands in their own and held me as I fell apart into a million little fragments.

Khaled was the heartbreak I would never survive. He was the one, but he was also my destruction. Not willingly. But by all the things that were never said. All the feelings we should have raised but were too afraid to do so. All the fears we should have been straight about, but decided it wasn't important enough for discussion. And then when all was said and done, I went my way and Khaled went his, the frail subject of our last fractured conversation never having been resolved, a sad last goodbye that tortured our souls and left our hearts tattered and bleeding.

AAIDA

Some days I wake up, drenched in sweat, my heart racing, my head beating like a drum. I clutch at my temples, squeezing, pushing back the pain. At times, the pain has been so bad, I have wished for death, the migraine thumping away loudly in the confines of my head and draining the energy out of me.

Some days I wake up in confusion, my eyes fluttering as I look up at the ceiling, my mind unsure exactly where I am. The dreams are so vivid, the memory of my motherland embracing lme ike a tomb, I almost believe I am back there in Tul Ghosn.

No one can understand the depths of what I left behind. No one even tries to understand. Friends tell me I should be grateful that I live in a country where my freedoms and safety are guaranteed. They don't understand the clenching desire I have to return to my mother country. Somewhere, deep within me, is an invisible thread that binds me from one side of the globe to the other. I love my adopted country, and wouldn't dream of leaving it, but I've left something of myself back in Lebanon, and it feels like I have unfinished business there. Something intangible binds me to that tiny plot of land on the map, sandwiched between other nations constantly at war with one another.

Other times, I wake up screaming, my face pale and my voice hoarse as my mother comes running into the room. Not Jihad. He never comes immediately; he is always courteous enough to allow the worst of it to pass before he enters the room to soothe me. Which is exactly what I need. He understands that I can't bare for him to see me at my worst.

One particular night, I wake up screaming and scratching at

my chest. My mother shakes me into consciousness and has to slap me in order for me to calm down. She knows these nightmares can be brutally harmful, as displayed by my last one, where I thrashed about so hard, I ended up with bruises on my arms and legs.

This time, I wake up with horror in my eyes and fear in my heart, gasping for breath as my heart beats erratically out of my chest. My mother looks at me, worried at my dishevelled, wild eyed state. I tuck my hands into my hair and pull, lurching forward into a rocking motion as I scream; one loud, unforgivable roar before I fall into my mother's open arms and sob uncontrollably.

Jihad is worried enough to come running into the room, rapping on the doorframe before coming to sit on the bed on my other side. He grabs me and shushes me, stroking his fingers through my hair as I clutch at his shirt, soaking it in my tears. He knows exactly what mother and I need, at the exact time when we need it. And he somehow knew this was bad enough that it warranted him saving my mother from having to deal with this alone.

"Just a nightmare," he whispers. "Just a nightmare, I've got you. It's over. You're ok."

And he rocks me back and forth for endless minutes as my sobs subside and the silence envelopes us well into the night.

Mother makes me my favourite, *"sahlab"*, the Middle East's answer to hot chocolate. It's a rich milk pudding topped with crushed pistachios and cinnamon sugar, and it never fails to calm my nerves. She pushes the mug into my hands and watches as I blow against the steam rising from the milky concoction, eager to take a sip. The first sip burns my tongue, but I can't help myself. The thick liquid slides down my throat and I close my eyes momentarily to savour the rich aromatic taste.

"Your nightmares have been getting worse," my mother says, when I set the mug down on the table.

Jihad stands against the doorframe, his hands crossed against his chest and his legs folded over one another as he watches us carefully. I have spent more time in his presence since he married my mother than I spent with my father in 15 years of him being my "father." Where I wondered what cruel hand of fate could have given me Samer for a father, I now marvelled at what miracle was bestowed upon us that we now had Jihad, a sturdy rock-like foundation that propped us up at every breakdown. I know it irritates Jihad no end how my father treated and discarded us, but by the same token, Samer's loss became his greatest asset, and for that I know he's grateful.

"It was a bad one this time," I explain, without mentioning that it involved Khaled. Even without me saying it, the way my mother sucked her lips into her mouth in concern told me she already suspected.

In my dream, instead of it being Turan, the congregation is carrying Khaled to his burial site. I stand above the congregants, watching the events unfold, as though suspended in the sky like a fragile bird looking down. I open my mouth in a silent scream, tearing my hair out until it falls in clumps on the ground. Khaled is gone, which means my world will cease to exist without him in it.

I heave a deep breath and exhale. Most times I wake up from my nightmares and I don't remember what I've seen. I have no recollection or memory, just that it was something awful. But not tonight. My nightmare tonight was clear as could be, and tears start to well in my eyes again as I recall the horrifying images I was subjected to in my sleep. An overwhelming sadness floats over me, severing my heart-strings and shattering my self-control. My lip starts to quiver, my head falling into my hands as I lower my eyes from my parents to compose myself.

"How bad was it?" Jihad asks, concern lingering in his eyes.

"I can't," I stress, shaking my head. I can't even recount what I dreamt about tonight, for fear of speaking the unthinkable and having it replay in my mind. I squeeze my eyes shut and try to lock out the images that are still dancing across my mind.

I look around in desperation, a tight cloying sensation gripping my throat. If I talked about what happened. If I opened that lockbox. There would be no shutting it. There would be no going back. And I would have to face the horrible truth of what happened, accept it, then move on, relegating my memories to that compartment in the back of my mind where hopes and dreams went to die.

KHALED

Revenge: to inflict hurt or harm upon someone as an act of retribution for a wrong suffered at their hands

We do things differently in these parts.

A sleight upon us is a sleight which must be returned, and my need for revenge overrides all common sense.

Everything that ever was, everything I had built, from my good standing to my international education, to my strong business connections, was set to the wayside as I plotted and planned to avenge my brother's death. This one single act consumed me, and the amount of time I had on my hands during my rehabilitation meant I was able to refine and finesse and fine-tune my plan until it became fail-safe. I would not rest until my thirst for blood had been quenched and my dead brother had been avenged.

So when we identify the men who carried out the ambush that took my brother's life and those of countless others, it is incumbent upon us to ensure that our rights have been exacted.

I'm not going to lie.

At the moment, I'm bound by a wheelchair, so I'm pretty much useless. But what I can't do physically, I more than make up for mentally.

Time. It's all I have. I am confined to a wheelchair and my bedroom and my mind, so all I can do is plot and plan and refine my plan until it's ready to be executed. Right down to the finest of details.

By the mercy of the Almighty, I will walk again. And when I do, there will be much bloodshed. Aaida can't be here to witness that. She will hate me if she does. Nor can she be here to suffer through my pain and rehabilitation. It will take some time to accomplish the task at hand, but once it's done and dusted, I will send for Aaida to come back. It will be safe to do so then. Never mind that she warned me she wouldn't be coming back; I know she didn't mean that. Once everything is taken care of and the dust has settled, she'll come back. I know she will.

Aaida and I are finally together.

I've built her a house on the hill above the olive grove that she loves so much.

It's only a small house, but it's comfortable, made of sandstone and built to withstand the test of time.

She loves the house.

She loves the green beyond the house, where an array of dandelions and wildflowers bloom.

Sometimes I find her collecting daisies, which she keeps at their original length and arranges in a tall vase, their delicate white petals one of only a few colours that litter the greenery that brightens her day.

Today, as I approach the house from the north side, my rifle slung over my right shoulder, she looks up and sees me, raises her hand in greeting, then drops her basket and runs towards me.

I drop my rifle to the ground and stride forward to meet her, taking her by the hips and twirling her around and around as she looks down at me with happiness, then up at the sky and laughs.

She is the happiest I've ever seen her.

I am the happiest I've ever been.

And all I want, all I've ever wanted, is for this moment to never end and for time to stand still as we are entwined in each other's arms and souls this way completely.

I wake from the same recurring dream bathed in sweat and my heart beats rapidly as I stumble to collect my bearings. Aaida is gone, this much I know. She had tried and tried, suffering in the process, but I had held my ground and insisted she leave.

Even when she so courageously and fiercely pummelled through my door and begged me to let her stay, I had loved her all the more for her obvious commitment to me, yet still I had sent her away, believing this was the only way I'd be able to spare her a life with a cripple. I was full of self loathing, hating yet feeling sorry for myself at every turn. And maybe I was selfish in letting her go, but I loved her enough to give her a second lease on life away from me.

The day I walk is the beginning of the end for me. It is the day I sell my soul to the devil. The day I make a secret pact with myself not to rest until my carefully thought out plan has been executed.

After my revenge has been orchestrated and played out, I send for Aaida. The danger of retribution is non-existent; with the help of Abu Shaker, I wiped out every last member of that family to put this war to bed and move on with my life. Did my revenge have the taste of victory and satisfaction I believed it would? No. The only thing it really did was cement me as the beast of Dhar Khamra, a mantle I never really wanted, but one I was crowned with nonetheless.

I contacted Aaida to ask her to come back.

She wouldn't speak with me.

I begged and pleaded with my aunt to get her to talk to me, but Aaida, it seemed, was lost to me. Perhaps all my cleverly laid out plans had been for nought after all, when the one single plan that mattered the most was the one I hadn't accounted for completely.

Aaida never got over me sending her away. For her, it was just another rejection in a long line of disappointments, and I realised she probably would have forgiven me anything, but not my pushing her away.

The distance from her burned a hole in my heart and left a void in my soul. When I suggested following her to Australia to bring her back, my mother shot me down and told me I'd done enough damage without inflicting more harm on poor Aaida. And so I settled into a safe routine of life and work and new projects which opened up because of the fierce reputation I'd built for myself.

Every night I dreamt of Aaida. Every day I thought of Aaida. And every moment away from her, as time went by, chipped at my heart as the weeks grew into months and they in turn became years.

FARIDA

Under any other circumstances, Hassan and I never would have met.

I can curse the day I was taken all I want, but what it came down to was this...

If I hadn't been in that olive grove that day, I never would have been taken. And if I hadn't been taken, I never would have found myself in an underground bunker, praying for a miracle that would guarantee my survival. If I had not been where I was at the precise time that I was there, Hassan and I would never have crossed paths. My destiny would have been much different, the hand of fate gifting me to another, while Hassan may have gone on to marry a girl from his own village.

I could not begrudge the good fortune that had been bestowed upon me. For when I thought of the road I had been travelling, engaged to be married to Farouk, who I had no feelings for and who was basically thrust upon me by my father, versus the life I went on to live, I would do it all over again if the end result was always Hassan. He has been my rock since the moment I met him, his protection comforting me like a warm blanket, willing me to fall in love with him.

Hassan has always moved with a spirited grace, the true essence of a man whose presence shook the earth wherever he went. I watch him now as he sits in the rocking chair on the balcony, looking out over the fields, a faraway look on his face. He has always been the strong, silent, dependable type. Ever since Turan's death though, he has folded into himself.

That day, we lost two sons. One we put in the ground. The other we put on a mantle as we waited for the ghost of him to re-emerge and join the living. Hassan had to bury one son and watch another go slowly insane with grief as he mourned his brother and learnt to walk again.

To make matters worse, we also lost Aaida. My beautiful, Australian niece with her free spirit and unwavering love for us. She loved us still, I knew. But Khaled had pushed and pushed and pushed until he shoved her right out of our lives, onto a plane, and out of the country. She had left us, bruised and broken hearted over Khaled's rejection. Aaida would have been able to live with and accept anything-except rejection. It only served to remind her of what her father had done, and that in her eyes was the biggest disservice a person could inflict upon another.

So when she refuses to accept Khaled's calls, I am not surprised. She has told me, in no uncertain terms, that she will not come back to Lebanon. She wishes Khaled all the best, but for her own mental stability, she believes it's best if she quietly exits the stage and doesn't return.

Although I am heartbroken, I can't say that I am surprised. The lengths the girl went to trying to talk sense into Khaled were extraordinary. She had done everything she could, very nearly pulling her hair out at the frustration she felt when he had not budged. Even Hassan and I had tried to talk him around, with no success. He was firm in his belief that Aaida had to leave in order for him to right himself before he could move on with his life.

And there lay the whisper of Khaled and Aaida united as one, the daughter we never had betrothed to our first born son, as each went their separate ways and time moved on.

Khaled is consumed with guilt. He survived when his younger brother didn't. He will go on to live, and love, and have children, a life well lived. Turan will not. It's hard to think of such a young life so easily removed, and harder still to think of all the things you will be deprived of from the loss of this one life. Khaled and Turan were close, best friends, and Khaled watching his brother die only served to make his trauma that much more pronounced.

I have been spending most of my time the past few days with

my sister Aujene, who is preparing to fly back to Australia this week. She has come alone with Jihad this trip; this is the second consecutive year that Aaida has not made the trip back. When I arrive home that afternoon and Hassan drives us down the long pine covered path toward our villa, it's not lost on me that several members of the community lower their gazes as we pass them, or turn to whisper to each other conspiratorially. The one thing we have had from the members of our community over the years is unwavering support, so their behaviour is a little odd to say the least.

"What's happening?" I ask Hassan, as I watch Em Diya look towards our house sadly. Hassan shakes his head and tells me we'll soon find out as the car comes to a standstill in the circular driveway. The front door is flung open even before we emerge from the car and Jude is standing by my side, holding out his hand to help me out of the passenger seat. His face has taken on an ashy hue, and his features, usually so soft and fragile, have turned to stone. His stern expression catches me off guard as I hold my breath and ask him what's wrong.

"Come inside, mother," he says, scaring me.

"Jude?" Hassan calls. "*Kheir, shu fi?*"

Jude shakes his head and heads toward the house, asking us to follow him.

Inside, he breaks the news to us.

Khaled got married.

In secret.

To his cousin Soraya.

And the whole village knew because he drove into the village with Soraya by his side in a white wedding dress, then held her hand as he helped her into his home-the home he had built with Aaida's help.

AAIDA

Six years.

For six years, I went back and forth from Lebanon to Australia, visiting my country of birth every year and taking comfort in the arms of my extended family. In the sixth year, on my annual pilgrimage, the unimaginable happened. That one year changed everything and put my life in a tailspin, and I wondered if I would ever recover from the after effects of that one trip. Mother and Jihad continued to go to Lebanon twice annually, and it was not lost on them that I would ask about every family member and omit the one that had caused my heart to break.

After mother and Jihad exhausted all the information they could give me, brilliantly sidestepping any mention of Khaled, I would purse my lips and suck them into my mouth, fighting the overwhelming urge to ask about him. They would look at me expectantly, perhaps hoping that I would ask, thus proving that I was well and truly recovered from that traumatic part of my life, but I would merely shake my head and turn away before the tears could gather in my eyes.

I knew that Khaled was walking again. He had done what he needed to do and stood on his feet again, taking his first full steps 8 or 9 months after I had returned from Lebanon. He then proceeded to pick up the phone and call our home, asking to speak with me. But just as he had turned his back on me, I turned my back on him and refused to talk to him. I would not go through that rejection again.

I miss my home country with an aching thirst. I miss aunt Farida and tayta Tala and even my great aunt Samiya. I miss them all. But most of all, I miss my cousin Khaled. By now, I've missed a few of his calls and not made an effort to reach out to him. The scene of my last trip, the tragedy that still flickers through my mind on auto-repeat is still freshly imprinted on my psyche, and I can't let go of the feeling that things would be better off the way they are. That doesn't, however, diminish any of the pain in my heart.

When my mother returns from her trip in 1998, she is a changed woman. Changed in the way that she is carrying a heavy burden that she just won't let go of. I greet her at the airport and immediately realise that something is wrong. Jihad holds her by the arm, and I see that she is in a fragile state, and she falls into my arms and heaves heavy gulps of air before she starts to sob and tell me that she's sorry. A few passersby turn and regard us curiously, and I look toward Jihad for some answers to my questioning gaze, but he merely shakes his head and mimes "later".

Jihad helps my other into the car and I drive them the short distance home, where mother is laid on the couch after I give her some painkillers for her migraine and leave her to rest. Jihad won't tell me anything, indicating he thinks it's better if my mother told me, but assures me no-one has died. That, if nothing else, is all the consolation that I need. It can't be *that* serious if no-one is dead. How much worse that that can something get?

When mother wakes and sits up on the couch, I am on the chair beside her, and I take her hand in mine and ask her how she's feeling. She assures me she's fine, though tears glisten in her eyes as she looks toward Jihad standing by the window regarding her thoughtfully.

"Are you going to tell me what's gotten you into such a state?" I ask her, smiling softly. Mother reaches up her hand to my left cheek, holding it in her hand for a few moments and looking at me longingly before she folds her hands in her lap, one over the over. This is her serious pose. She's doing something she really doesn't want to do, but something that has to be done nonetheless.

"It's Khaled," she says finally, and those two words stop my heart short as I hold my breath. No one has dared to utter his name in front of me in years. I don't think I would survive anything happening to Khaled.

"What about Khaled?" I ask.

My mother bites her upper lip then looks at the ground. At the ceiling. At Jihad. Anywhere but at me. This must be bad, I think. Why else would she find it so hard to look at me?

"What about him, mother? Just tell me."

It was many more moments of her looking everywhere but at me before she finally faced me and dropped her bombshell.

"Khaled got married. To Soraya."

Her words come out in a rushed jumble. If I was expecting anything, that was not it. I probably would've been able to handle anything and everything, but not Khaled getting married. Without so much as a word. Not that he owed me anything, but I thought at the very least, he would let me know that he was getting married. And to his cousin Soraya, no less.

"Married," I whispered, stunned. "Khaled got married."

JIHAD

Aaida sat stunned, as though not comprehending what her mother said. Then she whispered his name, ever so quietly, but I heard her. I heard her voice, the anguish so apparent in her disbelief. She was heartbroken. Devastated. And suddenly I understood why Aujene had been so fearful to tell Aaida. Suddenly I understood what even Aaida herself had not-that she had been in love with her cousin Khaled all these years but was too afraid to label her feelings. The same way he had been.

Unconsciously, they had been waiting for the hand of fate to do something to push them together without either of them being in the awkward position of admitting their feelings and possibly getting rejected. Aaida, I knew, had a long standing issue with commitment, and a genuine, and not altogether unfounded, fear of rejection.

The moment she stood up, I was across the room and ready as she swayed then tipped to one side, fainting into my arms. Aujene screamed in despair and came to my side as I lay Aaida down and shook her gently. It was mere seconds before she came to, but when she did, her memory took a beat, then registered the events of the afternoon before realisation dawned on her and her lip began to quiver.

She cried. And cried. And cried. Until finally she screamed. She sobbed and rocked back and forth, her knees tucked gently under her chin, until Aujene agreed to give her a sleeping pill to lull her into peace and quiet.

Her pain knew no bounds. Even though she hadn't seen him in 2 years, and she had sworn off Lebanon after what had happened the last time she was there, the news had devastated her and left a shell where the girl should have been. She didn't sleep nor eat for days, dragging herself to the pits of hell and back as her mind locked her in a prison of her own making.

AUJENE

I had been heartbroken when, two days before we left Lebanon, word reached us that Khaled had married. Not that we weren't invited to the wedding; there was no wedding. Khaled had merely picked himself up and gone to the Shaikh with his cousin Soraya, where they had signed the marriage decree then gone home to the house that Khaled had built, which Aaida had helped to design during her time in Lebanon. I wonder what Khaled would be thinking now, any time he looked at a feature in his home which had been suggested by Aaida. I wonder what would run through his mind, what he would remember, or even if he would remember at all.

To say I was shocked would have been an understatement. My poor sister Farida had been devastated, and Hassan had roared in anger, raging at his son for having broken with tradition and done things on his own. To further compound his anger, Hassan seeing his wife so distraught over Khaled's secret wedding only made Hassan all that much angrier.

Although I had been shocked at his actions, in a way I understood what had led Khaled to do what he had done. Aaida had turned her back on Lebanon and not looked back. Khaled had tried his hardest to reach out to her, but she had shut him, and the whole entire world, out. After 2 years of not visiting Lebanon, and with no reprieve in sight, Khaled had decided he had a life to live and had moved on. He could have waited another year, or 5, or 10, but there was no telling whether or not Aaida would come around eventually. Khaled wanted to get married. He wanted to have children and live a complete life, not half a life waiting for something that might never happen.

For although nothing was written in stone, nothing was ever discussed or agreed upon, the silent declaration between all that knew Aaida and Khaled was that they would eventually end up together. For no matter what, what everyone who came across them could see that they themselves couldn't, was that they were insanely in love with each other. Though they never admitted it. No.

They couldn't even admit this to themselves, instead hiding behind the veil of their feelings with protestations against anyone who so much as suggested the mere hint of a love affair between them.

So Khaled chose his cousin Soraya and he got married, with the blessing of Soraya's father, Hassan's brother Waleed. I didn't even want to think of all the strain that would now arise due to Waleed's participation in the secret marriage.

I cried for two whole days along with my sister, my mother was beside herself with grief. Jihad suggested we extend our trip to stay close to family in their time of conflict, but in all honesty, all I wanted to do was leave and pretend that what had happened had not. For although I wanted to see Farida through her darkest hour, I knew for the sake of my own sanity that I should leave. I also wanted to be the one to break the news to Aaida; this news would break her heart and I needed to be there when she found out to pick up the pieces of what remained.

AAIDA

Fear: an unpleasant emotion caused by the threat of danger, pain or harm.

My mother never learnt to drive.

I never learnt to swim.

I never learnt to trust.

I couldn't trust the water and I never learnt to trust people.

My father's rejection made it hard for me to trust people for fear of further rejection. My school years were riddled with holes and gaps as I tried to seal my leaky boat with a fractured mosaic of friends who all had issues similar to mine and I seemed to attract only those that were broken like me.

Khaled was the only person in the world I had befriended who seemed to be well adjusted and lived a normal, healthy life that should have been the right of everyone to do so. When I looked at him and his interaction with his family, his neighbours, the wider community, all I saw was a solid, dependable and compassionate man.

Many years later, when he crossed my mind in that fond way that first loves do, I would think about him in a way that fractured my heart, almost causing it to stop. Fear. There was that fear again. There had always been fear. In everything I did. It dictated my past and my present, but I was determined not to let it carry me into the future.

PART 2 : 1999 - 2009

AAIDA

I continue to live with my mother and Jihad well into adulthood, and I can't help but respect the hell out of Jihad for making my mother so happy. The years we spent with my father have all but melted away, becoming a distant memory that no-one sought to dwell on. I have long since lost contact with my father, which is just as well, as he doesn't have a place in my life. Jihad has more than filled that void, and I can't help but wonder in amazement at the way he looks at my mother and the way he treats her, as though everything that came before her was non-existent.

My university years are dotted with study, work and friends. While I finish up my master's degree, I continue to work part time at a couple of women's shelters around the city, filling what little free time I have with community work. I have made a few select friends that I socialise with on the very rare occasion, but mainly, my life is too full to have any time for anything else.

Mother is fortunate to have retained most of her friends from her early migration days to Australia, and while many have since moved to other states, a handful are still by her side as the years pass. Although they don't pass the time as they used to, with long winding girl's nights, they do meet up on occasion, and Jihad is considerate enough to make his own plans so the girls can relax and make absolute fools of themselves in peace.

Whenever my mother's friends joke about marrying me off, I scoff and laugh and remind them that anyone unfortunate enough to end up with me as a wife needs to be forewarned that there will be no returns and no exchanges, to which the ladies fall over each other in hysterics.

"So tell us honestly, Aaida, you nota lika any boi in university," Marika asks, her eyes wide and eager to learn about my love life. Sometimes I think the ladies try to live vicariously through my adventures. However, they realise my adventures are few and far between, and I am more of a loner than they choose to believe.

I laugh at Marika and hold up two crossed fingers so everyone can see them clearly before stating "Scout's honour, when I like a boy, you will be the *last* to know."

Marika's eyes are eagerly expanding as I talk, until I drop the word "last" and she frowns, looks up to the ceiling thoughtfully, then looks back down and advises me I'm cheeky enough to almost get away with that one.

I love my mother's friends. In them, I feel like I've found a whole family unit, a band of aunts who have stood as sisters by my mother through thick and thin, and who have also played a pivotal role in my life as I grew into adulthood. As a toddler, they all took turns babysitting me so mother could work. On the days my mother couldn't drop me off or pick me up from school due to work commitments, it was always one or the other of the ladies who picked me up. At the times I was sick, as mother nursed me back to health, they would visit and drop off soups and condiments and all manner of sweets to make me feel better. And when I returned from Lebanon, broken hearted and shattered, it was these same ladies who rallied around me and brought me out of my murderous mood.

"It's not right to grow too old without a life partner," Jannat advises me now. And I realise, with so many of them commenting on my personal life today, I must be doing something wrong. They've never been like this before.

"I'm not so old," I remark.

"The older you get, the fussier also," she tells me, looking around the room. "You get to a point where you're comfortable in your independence, and then no man will live up to your expectations."

"Why are you all so interested in my love life today?" I ask, grabbing a red apple and tossing it in the air. I swear, I still act as though I should have been born a boy.

"*Habibti*," Najla says, coming to my side to squeeze my shoulder. "We just want you to be happy. And we worry about you-ever since you came back from Lebanon, you've been so sad."

I wince at the mention of Lebanon. Everyone knew not to talk about "he who shall not be named". It was far too painful. After that heartbreak, I had come back to Australia, switched off my feelings, and hidden them in the back of a locked box in the deepest recesses of my mind. I didn't want to talk about that chapter of my life; did not want to dwell on what was and what could've been. I merely wanted to live out the rest of my life enjoying it without the fear or threat of constant heart-ache over something that once hurt me.

"I'm getting there," I tell Najla, looking up at her. I know she means well, but my stare dares her to bring up the subject again. I almost see her shrink away in fear.

"What's wrong with Zein?" my mother asks, as she cores another zucchini.

I watch her carefully, trying to gauge where her mind's at. I know mother doesn't care either way if I get married now or later, and wonder if she's asking only because the ladies are here and the subject open and that's what's giving her the courage to do so.

"What about him?" I ask, thinking about Amna's nephew. He is a tall, studious looking boy with an engineering degree who holds some sort of government job. Nice enough, but he reminded me too much of my other cousin who shall also not be named, Aziz. I wondered if all males who worked desk jobs in an office were dull. Zein just wasn't the sort of man I pictured spending the rest of my life with, and although I was grateful for the introduction (we had become firm friends), he wasn't the sort of marriage material that I was after, and I was quick to learn that I wasn't his type either. So that more or less made us even.

"He's a nice enough boy," I tell her.

"And...?" Marika asks, putting her hand behind her ear to mimic a megaphone and turning the side of her face toward me to indicate she was waiting for the gossip.

"And...he's just not for me," I reply, without further explanation. "Anyway, I think I'll leave you ladies to further meddle in my life while I'm *not* here," I laugh, taking a bite of my apple as I walk away.

"We marry you before year is over," Marika promises, as I leave the room.

AUJENE

We have suitors lining up to ask for Aaida's hand in marriage. She is in her mid-20's, and unfortunately, even til now, culture and custom dictate what is right and what is wrong when it comes to affairs of the heart. Although commonsense has gained traction in the Lebanese community by the turn of the new century, there is still a stigma surrounding girls who have reached a specific age and are still not married. It's unfortunate, but that's the way it is.

Aaida finished school and went to university to further her studies, and I had hoped that she would meet a young decent boy of her choosing during those years, and break the stereotypes so often associated with Arab girls. But she never introduced us to any boys, or even ever so much as hinted at the possibility. While she was journeying back and forth to Lebanon, I understood that she was waiting for her time to happen with Khaled, but following the incident and everything that happened after that, I knew she had closed that door. I did worry, however, that the hurt and turmoil over her separation from Khaled had left her with no desire to meet someone and settle down.

We are traditionalists at heart, and I see no harm in accepting suitors into our home. Many young people, too busy with work or their studies, don't have time to go out, socialise and meet somebody. So allowing people into our home by way of introduction to our daughter is another way of doing things. And I have a real surging fear that Aaida is so traumatised by what happened to her that she has tossed the notion of ever finding love completely out of her head.

My friends mean well, I know they do. But they constantly

worry about Aaida also. They are the single constant in her life from a very young age, and she defers to them all as her aunts and loves them to death. But they too, have concerns about Aaida's mental fragility and whether or not she has been traumatised beyond the point of repair. So when they, her only local family for more than two decades, voice their concerns, I am quick to address them and start to accept a few male suitors and their families for coffee.

"You need to be patient with her," Jihad says, coming around to stand before me as I lean over a garden bed. I stop what I'm doing, looking up at him. When Jihad speaks, all I want to do is watch him and listen. He is the voice of reason to my concern when it comes to Aaida. "I thought we decided to let Aaida make her own decisions, on her own terms and in her own time."

I look down at the the pile of weeds accumulating near my feet. Sometimes it's so easy to forget the past and fall into bad habits which threaten to erode the progress we've made toward a better life. I don't want to prove anything. I have nothing to prove. But there's a solid unreasonable fear residing within my brain that Aaida will end up on her own long after Jihad and I are gone. She has her fears, none of them healthy. She was attacked. Her father's rejection. Her father's attitude towards me. Turan's death. Khaled exiling her.

"What's wrong with giving her a little nudge?" I ask. "A reminder that she belongs to the world of the living."

"Give her time, Aujene. Everything happens the way it's meant to, when it's meant to. Let the chips fall where they may."

"There's a family coming tonight. A local doctor. Should I cancel them?" I ask.

"No. It's rude to do so. If nothing else, we will meet a new family," he says.

"I worry about her," I whisper, standing to meet his solid frame. He lifts my chin to meet my gaze and pushes my hair back from my face. Then he adjusts my hat so the sun doesn't penetrate my skin. Jihad is always looking after me, noticing things that I wouldn't otherwise notice.

"I know you do. But just let her be until she's ready. All in good time, Aujene, all in good time."

JIHAD

It's traumatising watching Aaida conform to something she is not.

She is a good, respectful girl, and would never say no to her mother, even though she has expressed her desire not to meet anyone and not be be married any time soon. Sometimes I wonder at the wisdom of a girl who has seen so much in her short life then turned around and made a life of helping others heal from their own traumas. She is brilliant at what she does, always offering the right dose to set people back on the right track. And she has chosen work in that field in moderation, preferring to offer more time at the shelters instead. She doesn't tell us much about her work there, because obviously there are many safety, security and privacy issues at play, but when she does, her eyes light up and you can see how invested she is in helping others and how rewarding she considers her work to be.

When the doctor attends for his visit, we open the door to a good looking, well rounded individual who is perhaps a few years older than Aaida. She couldn't be the least bit interested in him, and I can see this is just another formality for her. I have extracted a promise from Aujene to give the visits a rest after this one, and look forward to seeing Aaida comfortable in her skin again without the anxiety of another suitor knocking on our door looming over her head. The girl has already been through enough.

The doctor has come with his mother, a nice enough woman, but I can see immediately that she is that mother that can't see past her son's accomplishments. Every sentence she utters starts with "My son" or "Khalil". Aujene and the mother are having their little conversation, learning about each others' respective families, and I watch the doctor carefully as he interacts with Aaida. She is making an effort, I know she is, but it is when she tells him what she does for a living that his true colours start to show, and a seething anger swells in the pit of my stomach.

"But why would you choose such a career?" he asks, scrunching up his face in confusion. He obviously finds her line of work distasteful.

"What do you mean?" Aaida replies, and I can see she truly doesn't understand his reservations.

"You could have studied medicine, or engineering, or law. Something clean. Why did you choose to do something that confines you to dealing with people's mental trauma?"

I could see the way he emphasised the words "mental trauma" was his way of politely trying to phrase words which otherwise wouldn't have come out of his mouth so delicately.

"This is what I wanted to do," she tells him.

"I don't think it's the right occupation for a girl, dealing with the dregs of society. It's a good thing I make enough money that you won't have to work."

That is the precise moment that Aaida switches off and leaves the conversation. He already has her future mapped out for her. She looks right through him, her eyes glazed, her mind elsewhere. I feel her pain as acutely as though I were the one being dealt this blow. And she didn't even want to be here in the first place.

Here is another pompous, arrogant fool who thinks he's better than my daughter and wants to tell her what to do. He couldn't even engage her in conversation long enough to get past coffee. And so I rudely throw my head back and let out a massive yawn then look at my watch and say in a voice loud enough for everyone to hear; "Oh wow, is that the time! I hadn't realised how late it was!"

Aaida looks at me gratefully. Aujene views me with a frown and some degree of suspicion. And the doctor and his good mother take their leave with a promise to call the next day.

"We can't do that again," I tell Aujene after we see them out and she closes the door. "No more suitors. No more coffee."

She looks at me in confusion, a silent question in her gaze.

"You're not going to find the right match for our daughter in someone who's a mama's boy, that's all I can say."

AAIDA

I spend most of what free time I have working at a women's shelter in the suburbs. There are not enough of these centres to accomodate the women who come to us, fleeing violence and abuse. This centre is full to overflowing, and no matter how much we do, there is always so much more to be done.Some come with children, some without, and it's heartbreaking hearing their stories and seeing the terror in their eyes.

I spoon soup into a bowl and place it on a tray for Maha, who has a small child, about 3 years old, clinging to her side in fear, his thumb firmly stuck in his mouth. The little boy has cherubic features and his sandy blond hair sits matted against his head.

"How is he today?" I ask, looking down at the little boy, who never seems to smile. Anwar looks up at me when I speak, blinking rapidly before he looks down at his feet again. Whatever this child has been through has stunted his growth both emotionally and psychologically, and I can't help but condemn a society that allows children to experience such horrors.

"Restless," Maha tells me, rolling her eyes. "Sometimes I wonder whether this is harder on me or him."

I give her a sympathetic smile and she moves along, allowing the next person in line to move up to the counter.

I watch as Maha glides to the side, careful not to drop the tray as her son continues to cling to her. She is cagey and fragile as she places a piece of bread on the tray, then continues to glide slowly toward a table, barely lifting her feet off the ground. Her son is dragging her down, and she is forced to slow her movements to accomodate him.

She's a Middle Eastern woman in her late 20's, although I'm not sure where she is from specifically. I think I've noticed her more than any other woman at the shelter because we're from similar backgrounds, and you don't see many Middle Eastern women at the shelter. I know abuse and domestic violence happen across the board, regardless of race, religion or socioeconomic background, however there's still a massive stigma in the Arab community around what constitutes domestic abuse, leaving most women fearful for their lives when it comes to stepping forward and reporting violence.

There is a flurry of movement at the door to the dining hall, and I look up as a man bursts forward, screaming obscenities and brandishing a knife. I see the moment, as though in slow motion, when he knocks over two female staff members as he continues his forceful assault on the centre, crazed beyond all reason. My hand freezes in mid air before I drop the spoon and it clatters into the pot of soup with a thunderous clunk.

There are strict security and privacy measures in place to prevent the general public knowing the locations of these shelters, but even then, their existence is not a well kept secret. I've heard that husbands and fathers have tried to breach the centre before in search of their families. Most situations passed rather uneventfully, with the women in question quickly relocated elsewhere for their own safety, but I myself have never been present for a breach.

I scramble to take stock of the dining room full of women and children; with a weapon involved, I can already see that this situation could escalate very very quickly and someone could easily get hurt if the situation is not handled swiftly.

It is obvious the intruder is looking for someone, and just as I realise this, I see his eyes connect with Maha's and I hear the loud clanging of her tray as it falls to the ground. Her face is frozen in horror, and her son, now sucking his thumb rapidly, pees his pants, warm urine staining the floor at his feet.

Maha clutches the boy closer to her, then thinks better of it and pushes him behind her as he tries to hold onto her for dear life. She leans down and tells him to run, she is so close still that I can hear her. But the boy merely stumbles a step back then stops, sucking on his thumb rapidly as the man advances on his mother.

In an instant, I have the ladle in my hand and I'm heading toward a shocked Maha, whose face has blanched white. She has gone into shock and the man is gaining speed as he flies across the room towards her, his knife held high. I don't know who he is, but I can see from the rage on his face that he intends to inflict maximum damage.

I don't know what I'm thinking, I'm just acting. There is no way I will let this man hurt this woman. I reach Maha at the same time he does and my hand strikes his knife wielding arm, momentarily scattering him, before he pushes me back and heads toward his target again. For a moment, I lose my balance, then regain footing as he raises his arm and brings it down toward Maha, striking her shoulder. The knife juts out of her body, and I can see him struggling to remove it so he can strike her again, but within an instant, I have raised the ladle again and swipe it against his head, thankful that he isn't expecting my hit. He is momentarily dazed, stumbling backward, but I have not disarmed him enough for him to retreat, so I take another swing and hit him in the side of his neck, winding him.

In the distance, I hear the wail of sirens as police cars approach. I am grateful that someone has obviously had the presence of mind to call them, as I don't think I can hold him back much longer.

I look at Maha, who winces with pain as she looks at the knife stuck in her shoulder, then back at me. I silently order her to run, hoping to hell she is able to put at least a little distance between her and the intruder.

Other staff members have stepped forward trying to fight him off, while the patrons of the centre, already battered and bruised by a lifetime of abuse, have shied away, their fear frozen in stone as they watch on in shock, unsure what to do.

I lift the ladle again, ready to take another swing at him, when the Director steps up behind the intruder and plunges a needle into his neck, rendering him helpless. I look up in shock, unsure how ethical it was to use this tactic for sedation, but just as quickly shrug off this question as the intruder goes floating to the ground.

"Just a mild sedative," the Director explains. "It will wear off in 15 minutes or so."

Later, she explains it's the first time she's ever had to use the sedative. Ordinarily, it would be for those women who arrive at the shelter under extremely difficult circumstances and who need immediate respite from the horror of their lives. But even then, no-one had ever been broken enough to warrant sedation.

When the police arrive, the man is led away in handcuffs and I learn that he is Maha's husband, the reason that she is at the shelter. He's a violent man who has left bruises and cigarette burns up and down her body in an effort to "prevent her from ever being pretty for another man." His words, exactly.

We have a hard time trying to remove Maha's son from her to get her to the hospital, but eventually, with some coaxing, he joins a group of other children in an arts and crafts class and his mother is wheeled into the waiting ambulance. The police want to take statements from all the witnesses, and the Director steps up and reminds them that the occupants of the shelter arrive on our doors traumatised, and this is just another situation which has added to the horrors they have experienced. She asks for a reprieve to debrief, and promises full co-operation if they return in a couple of hours; the police reluctantly leave after the Director threatens to make a call to the Police Commissioner, who I know she knows on a first name basis because of all the mutual community work they are both committed to.

I'm asked to go to the hospital to check on Maha, and someone else tries to locate her next of kin to advise the situation.

Beneath all the trauma and abuse, I can see that Maha is a very beautiful woman who ended up in a very bad situation with a very bad person. Over steaming hot cups of instant coffee, we sit in the cafeteria a few days after she is released from the hospital and she starts to tell me about her life. Her hands shake as she holds the mug to her lips and my heart breaks as she recounts the story of how she managed to end up at the shelter. Her story is so heartbreaking, I feel like my head will explode as she reveals the most gruesome yet intimate details of her life.

"My husband Hicham died in a car accident when Anwar was a one year old. We were very happy, but our time together was limited. My family pleaded with me to return home so they could support us, but I refused." She scoffs, ostensibly at her own foolishness. "I wanted to show them that I could make it on my own."

"So you lived on your own with your son," I surmised, and she nods in response.

"I met Elias through work, but I had no idea he was crazy. He was fun and attentive, and doted on Anwar. But 6 months into our marriage, something changed and he became a different person. Possessive, clingy, accusing me of unspeakable things. Eventually, the abuse started. He started hitting me, sometimes burning me with his cigarettes." I winced at her pain as her story unfolded.

"Why didn't you just go back home?"

She looks at me sadly and gives me a semi-smile before she explains.

"Because that would have meant my failure. My family warned me not to marry him, but I didn't listen."

"And now?"

"Well, I'm not that deluded that I won't admit they were right. I never should have married him."

"Hopefully he'll be in jail for a while," I tell her, although I'm not altogether convinced that that's what will happen. Lobbyists have been trying for years to get the laws changed in regards to domestic violence, but the slog forward has been slow to yield results criminalising domestic violence.

"He can rot there for all I care," she tells me, and I'm curious as to why she stayed with him for so long, but remain silent as I watch her sip her coffee.

"What's next for you?" I ask, and she shrugs, obviously lacking direction.

"I have to find somewhere to stay. The last time he assaulted me, he was out the next day."

I nod my head in understanding and move forward in my seat, turning my mug around thoughtfully as I consider my next words.

"Maha, we had to contact your next of kin when you were in the hospital."

She looks up at me sharply but doesn't say anything, and I know she is curious to know who we spoke with and how that conversation went.

"We were able to get a hold of your older brother..."

"Salem?" She gasps, and I can see a flicker of hope as it enters her eyes. I nod my head slowly and wait for her to say something further, but she is quietly waiting on me to continue.

"He wants you to come home," I tell her.

She shakes her head and tells me she doesn't believe that. Salem was the one who was most vocal about her remarriage, advising her to come home instead and move back in with her family, who could support her and her young son until she could get back on her feet.

"He did everything he could to dissuade me from marrying Elias, but I just wouldn't listen. Our last meeting didn't go so well."

"That doesn't mean he doesn't care, Maha. He's offering you an opportunity to go home and start fresh. Maybe being with your family is just the sort of environment that you and your son need to be in."

"I'm afraid," she whispers, tears forming in her eyes. I lean forward and take her hand in mine, manifesting her misery and pain. And in that one action, my hand folding over her small one, I see a woman, once strong and beautiful and carefree, now broken and scared and unsure of herself. How easily one's life could change from having everything to having nothing. How easily you could in one moment have your future mapped out the way you want it, and in the blink of an eye, your plans change and your dreams evaporate. And you somehow lose your way, clinging to the memory of something that is gone, lacking direction as you wade through life aimlessly.

AAIDA

Maha has agreed to go home to her family, and I have agreed to escort her to the home to help her settle in. I don't want to step on anyone's toes; it's a family affair, but my duty of care lies with Maha and Anwar, and ensuring a smooth transition back into their family home.

When we pull up to the address she's given me, I look up at the house and I'm somewhat surprised. I'm not sure why exactly. I know the suburb she gave me is an affluent part of the city, but nothing could have prepared me for the grandeur of the property I am now parked in front of.

It would be wrong of me to stereotype and assume that Maha comes from a low income family, and I don't think that's what it is, because there was definitely something regal and articulate in the way she spoke and held herself, but I think it has more to do with the question of why she chose to stay with someone like Elias when her family is obviously more capable of caring for her.

The house is monolithic in size, taking up a wide block on one of the most expensive streets in the area. Slightly raised on the higher side of the street, it is a huge Victorian home with a wraparound porch and impeccably manicured gardens. The house is set back from the street, 20 or so metres from the public walkway, and there is a man standing in the doorway, maybe late 20's, with his hands in his pockets, waiting as though expecting someone. He raises his hand in greeting as the car comes to a stop and Maha whispers "Salem", as though awe-struck. No sooner has the car come to a stop than she opens her door and is running toward the man, who walks down the stairs to meet her. He embraces her briefly, then scruffs her hair and smiles down at her. Anwar starts to call for his mummy, so I unfasten his seatbelt and hold his hand as we walk toward the siblings.

Salem has Maha in a hug again and he looks at me over the top of her head, then down at Anwar. He breaks from his sister and moves forward deftly, lifting Anwar into the air and twirling him around. I can see the uncle has missed his nephew and smile at the tender moment as Anwar tries to squirm out of his uncle's embrace. The last time he would've seen his uncle, he would have been very young, and would now not know who this man was; this would require some adjustment.

When Salem releases Anwar and sets him down, he turns to me but says nothing until Maha introduces us.

"Thank you for taking care of my sister and bringing her home to us," Salem says.

"Their bags are in the car," I tell him, and turn to Maha, silently asking her if she'll be alright. She looks at me uncertainly, and I know she is still afraid. I put my hand to her arm to reassure her, but I know that will never be enough after what she's been through. She needs to learn to trust people again.

"Kaysar will bring the bags down," Salem says, watching my interaction with his sister carefully. "Won't you come in, mother would really like to meet you."

"Where *is* mother?" Maha asks, turning toward the house. It is odd, I think, that only her brother has come out to greet her.

"I didn't tell her you were coming today, in case you had a change of mind. I didn't want to get her hopes up."

"But where is she?"

Salem sighs and puts his hands on his hips before looking up at his sister. "Mother's not well, Maha. She's at the doctor doing follow ups, but she hasn't been well in a while. That's why it's important for you to be here with her."

"What's wrong with her?"

"Nothing the doctors can't fix," he tells her. "But she does need a good support system around. *I* need the support. *Dad* needs the support. We can only do this as a family."

Maha nods her agreement and says no more as Salem ushers us into the house, insisting I stay for tea, letting it be known if I left without enjoying the family's hospitality, his mother would disown him.

The interior of the house is even more grand than the exterior, beautifully decorated to the highest standard, and the level of cleanliness tells me he has a house proud mother who may be a little on the OCD side. When she bustles into the house holding two bags of groceries, with her husband hot on her heels holding more bags, I can see that her habit of keeping things neat and tidy extends way past any material thing she may have. She is elegantly dressed in a two piece suit made of tweed, and has on low slingback heels. Her portly middle fits snugly under her suit jacket, and she has a cherubic face flushed with two red spots on her cheeks. She doesn't look ill to me, but that's neither here nor there. She has a big smile on her face, and I am quick to realise that this is a permanent fixture upon her face.

The minute the old woman sees she has guests, she is excited, but when her eyes land on Maha, then on her grandson, she drops the bags and crosses the room quickly to embrace them, a look of disbelief on her face.

"My daughter has returned," she gasps, over and over again. "*Alhumdulillah ya rab!* You have answered my *dua!*"

She remains in a state of disbelief for a few minutes, and I watch on with moist eyes, happy that this reunion has gone so well.

I had understood Maha's reservations in coming home. We are Lebanese. We have rules and traditions; our culture overrides everything. In some parts of Lebanon, in some parts of the *world,* even, there are still tribes that uphold their customs so strictly, a woman in Maha's circumstance would have been exiled rather than allowed to return home.

Maha's family, I can see, are one of the rare Lebanese families that have, while retaining their traditions, discarded the ones not in line with the present and those that did not align with their best interests.

I watch now as Maha's father squabbles with her mother in an attempt to get in a hug with his returned daughter, but the old woman is too excited and too overwhelmed to let her daughter go.

"Maha is my only daughter," she tells me, after we are introduced. "You can understand the importance of having my only daughter back, yes?"

"Well, I'm an only child, so I can imagine," I laugh.

She clutches her hand to her chest and gasps, as if I've committed blasphemy.

"An only child?!?" she repeats. "But how is this possible?" To her, it may seem like a travesty, as Lebanese families tend to have many children. An only child denotes a serious problem; one she wishes to dissect. Maha has already told me that they are 6 siblings, and now I learn that she's the only girl amongst them.

"It wasn't written for me to have siblings, *Khalti*," I answer her, and she looks at me somewhat sadly, as though I'm an odd specimen that requires further investigation. But no sooner does her mood sour than she is spritely again, and it's as if a lightbulb has switched on in her head as a warm smile washes over her face and she says to me;

"*Ma'lash binti*, I have enough children to go around…they can be your siblings."

Maha's mother Hala is an excellent cook. She insists that I stay for lunch, which I beg off, but she won't hear of it; she insists I stay and proceeds to whip up an amazing version of *Makloubeh*, a traditional Middle Eastern dish comprising layers of rice, meat and eggplant literally floating in oil. My mouth waters even before I taste the concoction, as I watch in awe as Hala slides a tray over the top of the steaming pot, the proceeds to tip them both over so the mixture falls out in a dome over the tray, presenting the *makloubeh,* so named because the dish is cooked then "tipped over".

There is an ecstatic buzz in my mouth as the flavour of the

spicy rice mixture erupts on my tongue, and I close my eyes in utter bliss as I hum my praises. When I open my eyes again, there is complete silence as the family watches me in awe. My face flushes red in embarrassment as I realise what I must look like sitting with my spoon heaped and ready to enter my mouth again. But just as soon as I am awash in embarrassing discomfort, I am simultaneously set at ease when Hala claps her hands twice and, eyes twinkling with happiness, compliments me on my zest for food and assures me that not enough people appreciate great food anymore.

"People, as it is, don't give thanks for the food they have, let alone appreciating a good dish," she tells me, reaching out her hand to cover my own. I look down at her hand and wonder at her effortless ability to make me feel so comfortable, as though I'm the one that's come home, not her daughter. Although her daughter has been estranged from the family for a few years and Hala has missed out on seeing her grandchild blossom into a toddler, the woman has a will and a strength to carry on and appreciate life and love and food. She has not fallen apart. She has not become bitter. She has merely been waiting for her daughter to return and catch up to *them,* not the other way around. And I couldn't help but respect the hell out of her.

"Eat, binti, *eat,*" Hala urges me. "You don't know how happy it makes me to see people enjoy my food."

"Mother thrives on cooking and enjoys it when people eat her food and that experience changes their life, no matter how momentarily," Salem explains.

"This dish is exceptional," I tell him, before spooning more food into my mouth. I can't help but chew slowly, drowning in bliss as I savour the taste.

Hala chuckles as she starts to eat and looks up from time to time to watch my expression. I know I will be in a food coma by the time I have finished eating, as I can't seem to stop, heaping a second serving onto my plate and adding some cucumber and mint yoghurt salad on the side.

"That was definitely, *hands down,* the best version of

makloubeh I've ever had," I praise Hala as I set my spoon down.

"*Sahtaan, habibti, sahtaan.* It's the least we could do to thank you for taking care of Maha and Anwar," and I watch as she scruffs Anwar's hair, tousling it as he watches her with a wide eyed yet lopsided semi smile on his face. I can see that he is warming up to the old lady, and I'm sure she'll win him over in no time.

When I take my leave after lunch, begging off tea because I really have to get back to work, Hala hugs me close and thanks me once again, making me promise to come and visit again soon. Most families I have resettled always extract a promise from me to visit again, but unfortunately, it's usually a pattern of moving on to the next case and lack of time. The days start to blend and merge and time carries me onward, and there are never enough hours in a day to do all the things I mean to do, no matter how well cemented my intentions may be.

So when I walk down the porch steps to my car, it is with a heavy yet muted sigh as I pretend not to hear what Hala whispers to her husband when she believes I'm out of earshot. *"Ya eyni, shu mahdoumeh w helwa hal ammoura."*

I smile to myself as I interpret her words. *"My word, how cute and beautiful that girl is."*

SALEM

I know the exact time that Maha will arrive at the house, so I'm waiting at the door when a sleek black car slows down in front of the house.

I am surprised when Maha arrives with an Arab lady from the shelter, who I learn later is an advocate standing in for her caseworker Carolyn while she's on leave. I can see, as soon as she steps out of the car, that she is Lebanese. She has that exotic look with her dark hair pulled back into a tight ponytail and the slightly slanted eyes that resemble almonds. She is wearing jeans and a t-shirt with heels and she is a stunner.

After greeting me, Maha introduces the woman as Aaida, her temporary caseworker and friend. I've spoken with several people at the shelter, but never this lady, so I eye her with some curiosity as she leads my nephew by his hand towards the house.

With Maha home, I am overjoyed not for myself, but for the happiness that I know her return will bring my mother and father. She has been gone too long, just over two years, married to a spineless bastard who never deserved her, and she, being vulnerable and needy after her first husband's untimely death, had fallen for Elias' spiel hook, line and sinker.

Of course, I had known where she was the whole time, had even tried on occasion to orchestrate her return home. But I had failed on said occasions, and finally settled on allowing her to make her own mistakes so she could come to her senses. Which eventually, she did. And we couldn't be happier to have her home.

"Are your brothers coming?" she asks later that afternoon as we walk across the grounds, planning where we'll put Anwar's swing set when it arrives.

"They'll drop by tonight. In all honesty, I called them only after lunch. They'll give you some time to settle in and will come for dinner."

"I've missed them," she tells me, and I'm sure she has. Maha grew up an only girl amongst 5 boys and was spoilt rotten. She had never wanted for anything, and each one of us, along with our parents, had treated her like a princess. I tousle her hair and kiss her head as I hug her to me, happy to have her back home.

"We should go back in," she tells me, shortly. "Anwar may be restless."

"He's fine, Maha. Let mum and dad work their magic on the boy."

She smiles and realises I'm right, and I understand her reservation is not that Anwar would have become restless with our parents, but the fact that she herself is probably experiencing detachment issues with her son. I put my hand around her shoulder and guide her back towards the house, understanding more than anything that her return to the family home would require some patience as they adjust to their new lives.

AAIDA

I have occasion to run into Maha again when she turns up at the shelter weeks later to offer her services as a volunteer. The good thing about the work we do is that in helping those less fortunate, we are also building a support network of grateful women who in turn choose to give back to the shelter by helping others. That network, combined with ongoing sponsorships from local businesses ensure the ongoing commitment of our services to those most in need. So when Maha shows up and pledges a huge sum of money from her family trust, we can't afford to turn her away. However, I do have some reservations, not least of which is the trauma she suffered at the shelter when she was assaulted by Elias.

"You're in a position to do anything you dream of doing," I tell her, referring to her family's financial strength and good standing in the community.

"But nothing will satisfy me as much as contributing to the welfare and livelihood of those not in a position to help themselves," she tells me.

She is looking immaculate, as though she left the old Maha buried at the shelter and a new Maha was born in her place. She is dressed well, and has her hair fashionably styled and makeup delicately done. On her face is a smile that I have not previously been privy to, and I can't help but muse at the enormous changes in her.

"How's Anwar?" I ask, and I laugh when she scoffs and swipes her hand in the air theatrically.

"Pfft! He is so smitten with my parents, he no longer even asks about me. No need for childcare when he's surrounded by family who adore him."

"And how are you spending your days?" I ask her.

"Well, I've been catching up with family, and I've reconnected with friends. And I've wasted enough time on meaningless endeavours. I really want to do more to help others, and now I'm in a position to do so."

I look at her thoughtfully. I have no doubt that she is sincere about her intentions towards others. I am just curious to know whether or not she has considered the implications of working in an environment that might stir up old memories, or where Elias may be able to reach her again. Although I know he is in prison still, awaiting his trial for the assault against Maha, I know there is always the possibility that he will get off on the charges that have been raised against him.

"It doesn't bother you to be back here?"

She shrugs nonchalantly and asks me why she would be bothered. "I just switch off," she tells me. "As long as I don't think about it, I'm okay."

She reaches into her bag and removes an envelope, sliding it across the table towards me. When I ask what it is, she tells me to take a look. I do so, extracting a cheque made out to the shelter. I balk at the sum on the document; it is an exorbitant sum of money which most would refer to politely as a "generous contribution". I look up at Maha, hoping against hope that she doesn't assume such a generous offer automatically allows her entry into the arms of the shelter. I believe she reads my thoughts precisely as they are because she answers my unspoken question in the next breath.

"Relax, Aaida," she assures me "this is not a you scratch my back, I'll scratch your back type of scenario. The shelter will receive these funds regardless of their decision to allow me to volunteer here at the centre. This is just a token of my family's appreciation for the good work the shelter does."

I wonder what sort of business her family is in, that they can afford to give away such a large sum without batting an eyelid. Although my family lives comfortably and I have never wanted for anything, we don't have the sort of money that can so easily be donated without feeling the pinch. I silently applaud and appreciate her family's contribution, yet there lingers a gnawing, cloying curiosity as I set the envelope back on the table for the administrators' consideration later.

"I'll make sure the administrators receive the cheque," I tell her. "And I'll mention your desire to contribute to the volunteer program here."

AAIDA

I learn three very valuable lessons when I present the Director with the cheque from Maha. And those lessons are;

-money talks

-the system is overwhelmed and seriously underfunded

-sometimes you have to look the other way to achieve a win for the greater good

Against my better judgement and recommendation, Maha is allowed to offer her help at the shelter. I'm not really sure what is motivating her, since she doesn't need the money and won't be getting paid for her time anyway. However, the shelter is so understaffed and so overwhelmed with intakes, the administration has spread itself thin with resources, and the government isn't too keen on investing more tax payer funds into the centre. So Maha's contributions - her time *and* her money - come at the precise time when they are much needed, and the Director is willing to overcome any reservations she has regarding Maha being in a situation where she has previously been attacked if it means she will be saving others.

Although I have concerns, I continue to put in my hours at the shelter in my down time from the clinic, until it seems more and more like all I am doing is rotating from one centre to another. In the process of trying to save the world, one woman at a time, it seems like I have lost myself.

At times, my path crosses Maha's, and we chat briefly in passing in the corridor as we do our rounds, and I am extremely surprised by the effort and time that Maha is putting in to help these women. Being born into such privilege, I find it hard to reconcile what would motivate Maha to work in such a soul crushing environment, but she seems to thrive in her role, telling me she feels like she has finally come full circle and she's where she was meant to be.

AAIDA

Maha invites me to coffee after we are standing in a hallway chatting away for some 15 minutes. I tell her I've just finished my shift, and she acknowledges this announcement as being perfect; she too has just finished and is free for us to enjoy a coffee at a local cafe. My mind is racing at 100 miles an hour as I try to think of a way to avoid the interaction, and it's as though Maha resides in my head, because she laughs and tells me it's time I took some time out and enjoyed something for myself for a change.

"You can't be a martyr all the time, Aaida," she reminds me. "You're entitled to enjoy yourself. It's just a coffee-how long could it possibly take?"

She convinces me and we make plans to meet at a local cafe in 20 minutes. I drive to the destination and arrive before Maha does, and take a seat under the umbrella of an outdoor table. The coffee shop is almost full, and I realise I have not experienced such an outing in many many months. I have thrown myself into my work and completely ignored the other aspect of my life where I need to relax and unwind.

"Love this place," Maha says, as she glides into the chair opposite me.

"It's quaint."

"I'm glad you came. We have so much to catch up on, it doesn't seem normal that we spend long stretches catching up in the hallways at the centre."

"You're looking very good, Maha. It would seem your time at the shelter has certainly helped you make an enormous change in your life. One for the better."

"I like to think of this next chapter in my life as the one where I am reborn. So everything is fresh and new again.

"And your parents are helping with Anwar?"

"My parents have been a Godsend," she tells me. "The change in Anwar has been extraordinary."

"I'm glad. What about life otherwise?"

"I'm reconnecting with old friends. I'm brushing up on my administration skills so I can help my family grow the business."

Over coffee and almond croissants, Maha tells me all about her family business and I finally learn the fascinating story behind their substantial financial means. Her mother is amazing in the kitchen, and when she and her father migrated to Australia, to pass the time while her children were at school and her husband was at work, Hala would pickle cucumbers and green tomatoes and beetroot-all manner of vegetables. When she offered her pickled goods to a local grocer, they flew off the shelf and soon enough, demand was higher than supply.

"Mother single handedly created a brand. A whole line of jarred delicacies that just grew once she established that brand. It grew to such an extent that father quit his job to help her oversee deliveries and stock control."

"She made the products all on her own?" I asked, wide eyed.

"Well, yes, initially, but then the business got so big, they had to hire others to help. They rented a factory and set it up as a commercial kitchen. They hired staff on recommendation-migrants arriving in Australia after fleeing the war, giving them job security in this strange country they had come to."

My eyes go from being wide eyed to almost star struck as I listen to Maha recount her family's success story. She goes on to tell me more, and I am in awe of her mother as she tells me all the things I didn't know. It's rare that you come across a person who has such a beautiful and eloquent story to tell, and I realise that Hala is truly an unpolished gem in our community.

"How did I sit with your mother and not know all this?" I ask, aghast, and Maha laughs. She gives a hearty chuckle and throws her head back, then raises her hand in greeting to someone across the road. I turn and see her brother Salem crossing the road toward us, his long legs making it seem as though he is taking but two strides to reach us, when he is metres away.

"I hope you don't mind," Maha says, turning back to me. "Salem needs some paperwork from me and I told him where we'd be."

I shake my head slightly but say nothing as I watch Salem approach us. For some reason, I feel an uncomfortable blush surge through my body and up my neck as I sit transfixed, almost suspended, in a trance-like stare-down with her brother. I break the moment and look back at Maha, who I realise has been sitting watching me carefully, a knowing smirk on her face.

"What?" I ask, irritated to no end that something I couldn't explain just transpired.

Maha shrugs as if to say "oh, nothing", then reaches into her bag and takes out an envelope which she sets on the table.

"It's good to see you again," Salem says, as he finally reaches our table and looms above us. For some stupid reason, I rise and stand before him, but I'm not sure if I should stick my hand out or what. It's customary to rise when greeting a person, but it just seems odd doing it here and now.

I have always been awkward in the company of the opposite gender, and for some strange reason I cannot fathom, I'm doubly awkward in Salem's presence now, where I don't think I had been the first time I saw him. I could kick Maha silly when I see her sitting watching the interaction with a knowing grin on her face, making the situation all the more uncomfortable. For me, at least. Not for Salem. He seems as cool as ever as he watches me, ostensibly waiting for me to say something. I nod in acknowledgement, but my tongue is so twisted, I can't say anything as I slip back into my seat and watch the siblings as they exchange a few words and Maha hands Salem the envelope. He is wearing a dark navy suit with the top buttons undone and the tie long discarded, and as he looks down at his sister, I wonder how it came to be that he is so tall and she has such a petite frame.

"By the way," Salem says. He turns back to look at me after he starts to leave "Mother keeps asking about you and was saying the other day she'd really like to see you again," he tells me. "I'll let her know you'll come past on Friday night so she can make *makloubeh*." He delivers his edict; it is a statement, not a question, then turns to walk away briskly, crossing the street and disappearing out of sight.

I watch him go, then let out a breath I didn't know I'd been holding, and turn to look at Maha. Her eyes are dancing with humour, like she holds a secret that only she has the key to.

"What was that?" I ask.

"An invitation."

I look at Maha and she can see that I am irritated. She knows exactly what I am talking about but decides to play coy.

"Why is your brother inviting me to dinner with your mother?" I ask. "Why not you?"

Maha laughs and regards me thoughtfully before she speaks again.

"Salem is a little forceful at the best of times. He would lay his life down for our parents, that's how much of a *merdi* he is. Ever since you complimented my mother on her *makloubeh*, you've become her new favourite person. You're all she talks about. Salem just wants to make her happy. Plus, it's her birthday on Friday and he doesn't know what to get the woman who has everything."

She beams at me and I can't help but soften at her words. Maha is a beautiful soul, and I can see that she comes from a beautiful family. She had the misfortune of falling in love with the wrong person, but now that she is out of that situation, I can so clearly see that she is thriving, and is on the fast track to becoming the person she was always meant to be.

"Say you'll come," she urges.

"It's your mother's birthday, that should be reserved for family."

She shakes her head and picks up her coffee. "We don't really celebrate our birthdays; he just wants to make mother happy."

SALEM

I have to question Maha's motivations in making me run across town to pick up paperwork I was expecting to have on my desk the day before, especially when I approach the coffee shop and see her sitting with Aaida. They are deep in conversation until Maha throws her head back in laughter then sees me and raises her hand in greeting.

I can't help but soften at the sight of my sister laughing and enjoying herself. Her road to recovery has been better than we expected; it was as though she simply brushed herself off and went on with her life. Not that we were complaining, but her resilience just surprised us, as we'd been told victims of domestic assaults usually experienced prolonged trauma which needed intensive therapy. But despite everything she'd been through, the old Maha was starting to shine through, bigger and brighter than ever, and we were happy to have her back.

Aaida rises from her seat when I approach, but says nothing, standing oddly tongue tied as I look at her. When I turn to face my sister, I can almost feel her breathing a sigh of relief as she slides back into her seat and sits quietly in her chair.

I don't know why I do it, but before I leave, I turn back to Aaida and invite her to dinner. No, that's not true. I don't invite her. I tell her. Not giving her a choice. Dick move, I know. But I'm told I can be a little intense like that at times. She sits looking at me dumbfounded, before I turn and walk away. I know she probably won't come to the dinner on Friday. She's probably so freaked out she'll most likely start to avoid Maha at the centre, so it's a huge surprise when I open the door on Friday night and find her standing there on our doorstep.

For a moment, it is me who stands tongue tied as I look at her, transfixed by her presence. Her hair is pulled back in a high ponytail atop her head, and she is wearing minimal makeup, but her eyes framed in dark *kohl,* are mesmerising. I hold the door open and allow her entry at the same time that Anwar comes bounding through the house and hurtles into her arms. Aaida grabs the boy and twirls him around, then settles him against her chest, his head of curls neatly tucked under her chin as she closes her eyes and breathes him in.

"How's my little champ doing?" She asks, as she sets him down. The child takes her hand and drags her through the house to the living room, where he announces that his friend is here.

I watch as Aaida greets my parents, her hand across her chest respectfully as she nods at my father, and then she has my mother in an embrace as she pecks her cheeks.

"If only you knew all the lovely things Maha and I were discussing about you the other day!" Aaida says to my mother, and I see my mother's eyes twinkle as she perks up at the thought of sharing some stories tonight. My mother is a master storyteller. She loves sharing stories of her life with others, and from what I know of Aaida and the work she does, she is an interested listener. My father, he is the strong yet quiet type. He is a reflector, but not much of a talker, opting only to talk when absolutely necessary.

Maha comes bounding into the room and greets Aaida warmly, and as I look on, I'm glad for this friendship that has formed between the two women; there is no denying that Aaida has had a positive influence over my sister and has contributed immensely to Maha's recovery.

"Let's eat!" My mother says, clapping her hands together. I know she is excited for tonight's dinner and basking in the compliments she'll receive from our guest.

Tonight, mother has made *makloubeh, shorbet addas, and kibbeh nayeh.* She watches in awe as Aaida eats with zest, savouring each and every bite of her food. Her eyes flutter in satisfaction with each morsel of food, and it's as though she's found heaven here on earth. My mother doesn't need words from Aaida. Just watching the expression on her face as she eats tells her everything she needs to know. Aaida is so overwhelmed with her culinary experience that it is a while before she realises everyone has stopped eating and is watching her. She lowers her spoon down in embarrassment and swallows, then apologises that she is eating so fast.

"Not at all, my dear," my father who only speaks out of necessity says, and I look at him, surprised that he is the first one to speak, no less about something so inconsequential. He must really like Aaida. "You go ahead and eat and enjoy your food."

"Sometimes we forget that we've had mother's cooking all our lives," Maha explains. "Watching other people enjoy it so much reminds us not to take her cooking for granted."

"I second that," I add.

"This is truly amazing, next level. I can't even put a name to how good it is," Aaida remarks, turning to my mother. "Why did you never open a restaurant?"

"That's a whole other story we'll leave for another day. Enjoy your food now," and my mother raises a spoonful of rich lentil soup to her lips.

Very early on in their marriage, my parents opted not to have a wide circle of friends, and decided instead to dedicate their lives to each other, to the family, and to growing the family business. They have acquaintances, who they see on occasion. And they are very involved in community projects, albeit behind the scenes. But their private lives have remained just that. Private and special. With no interference from the outside world, which I believe has helped my parents' endurance.

We are fortunate enough to have a beautiful manicured garden on expansive grounds that would seem like a dreamland to most. Once a month, a gardener spends three days pruning and shearing and shaping the foliage so we have a beautiful space in which to entertain. Most of our entertaining is done between our families; we siblings and our partners and children gather around the fire pit or the pool in warmer weather, and eat and laugh and make a lifetime of memories.

Aaida is one of the few "outsiders" who has been provided access to our sanctuary, and again she is awe struck by the sheer beauty that surrounds our home. We are not a family of boasters. We do not throw the weight of our name or brand around, and we do not live excessively, even though we are able to. Humble is a word I would use to describe our family. However, Aaida's reaction to the gardens enthrals us-what we see as normal is to others extraordinary, and she is a sight to behold as she walks around in awe, admiring the various trees and shrubs and impeccably landscaped flowerbeds.

"You have a beautiful home," she tells my mother, as she settles into a wrought iron chair under the pergola. Maha brings her a throw to ward off the chill, and I sit in comfortable silence at a table a few metres away looking up at the night sky. This is my practise every night after dinner; I sit outside in quiet solitude and go over all the events of my day and ask myself what I could have done differently. Tonight, I share my evening with others, and instead of drowning them out as I am so good at doing, I find myself perking my ears up at the sound of Aaida's voice, clinging to every word that comes out of her mouth. I learn about Aaida as though I am reading a book; her life is a mosaic of rich experiences that most people would take a lifetime to live.

She tells my mother that her parents are divorced, and both have remarried. I am expected to be judgemental like the rest of our society, but I can't be, because my own sister is a widow and a divorcee. I'm glad that my mother doesn't flinch at Aaida's revelation; til now, in this day and age, a divorced Muslim woman is frowned upon in our community. My mother asks her how she gets along with her step parents, and she glows when she speaks of her stepfather, but a sullen sadness overcomes her when she reveals she has never met her stepmother.

"But you have been to Lebanon many times, yes?" my mother asks, trying to understand how she would not have met her stepmother. "Isn't that where your father lives?"

"Mother," Maha says softly, placing her hand over my mother's own. I lower my eyes from the starlit sky and turn to look at the three women huddled by the fire pit. Aaida's face is aglow with the flames of the fire, and I can clearly see the distinct etch of disappointment on her face as she shakes her head and tells my mother she doesn't have any contact with her father. My breath catches at her pain, and my mother, God bless her soul for being as insightful as she is, claps her hands together and turns to Maha and says "Maha, where is the Turkish delight?!? Make sure it's the premium label!"

The moment is instantly diffused as Maha hurries to get the Turkish delight and my mother points out a shooting star to Aaida.

"*Yallah*, make a wish, quickly!" My mother urges her.

"Aunty, isn't that just a fib adults tell to keep young kids dreaming?" Aaida laughs, forgetting her sorrow. I laugh internally as I wonder at my mother's ability to so easily bring a person out of the demons in their mind.

"*Khalas*, Aaida, just close your eyes and make a wish!" And my mother clasps Aaida's hand in her own and squeezes her eyes shut to make a wish, forcing Aaida to follow suit. They are like two young girls sharing a secret, and I'm amazed at the bond that has so easily formed between these two women who are divided by generations.

When the moment passes and they open their eyes, my mother does not let go of Aaida's hands, but she turns to the young woman eagerly and asks "What did you wish for?"

Aaida laughs and waggles her finger at my mother conspiratorially, reminding her that if she tells her what she wished for, her wish won't come true.

I raise my chin in query and look at my sister as she walks back up the path toward the house after seeing Aaida off. Her friend hooks a U-turn and drives away, her lights illuminating the dark as she travels down the quiet street. It's almost 1am, and although I have qualms about her driving home alone in the dead of night, she has promised to lock her car doors and stop for no-one on the 20 minute journey to her home.

When my sister reaches the doorway, I regard her curiously and she looks up at me with a devilish grin on her face, almost as though she knows what's coming next. Mother and father are long gone, their weary bones retired to the comfort of their bedroom after a long day, and after mother had excused herself close to 10:30pm, leaving me outside with the girls, I had also excused myself and gone to my study to do some work. Although they were not loud enough to disturb the peace, my study was close enough for me to hear their giggles and sighs as they exchanged a healthy banter whilst enjoying endless cups of coffee. As the night wound down and I heard them emerge from outside into the relative quiet of the house, I met them at the door as Aaida apologised for staying so late and took her leave.

"There's just one thing I want to know," I ask Maha, as she reaches me, her hands swinging at her sides gloriously. She is happy. Content. It has taken so little time for her to bond to Aaida, who has taken the mantle of the sister Maha never had.

"What's that?" She asks.

"Did you orchestrate my meeting you at the coffee shop deliberately so I would run into Aaida again?"

Her eyes twinkle in that sisterly manner she has when she's trying to suppress letting the cat out of the bag.

"Maybe," she simpers.

"So you craftily planned this whole evening."

"No Salem, I planned the meeting at the coffee shop. *You* invited her to dinner." She puts her finger to the side of her mouth and taps it there thoughtfully, gazing off for a moment. "Actually, it wasn't an invitation," she reminds me "it was you going all caveman and *telling* her to come for dinner."

"What are you up to, Maha?" I ask, squinting my eyes at her, as though in doing so, I'd be able to squeeze her secrets out of her.

"Whatever I'm up to," she starts, standing on the tip of her toes to peck my forehead "It will only happen if God wills it." And she walks off with a flourish, leaving me standing in the doorway realising her words had elicited more questions than they had answered.

AAIDA

It is just past 11pm when I drop Maha off at home after the movies. The floodlights come on as soon as my car parks in front of the house, and the front door swings open to reveal Salem standing there in the doorway.

"He waited up for you?" I ask incredulouly, waving towards Salem in acknowledgement while I remain seated in the car.

"He's just being overly protective," Maha tells me, as she shuts the passenger side door and leans in through the window to thank me again for the movie.

There's a sense of belonging burning within me as I drive away. My house is a 20 minute drive away, give or take a couple of minutes depending on traffic. I consider all the things I've missed out on in life, not least of which is a functioning family unit. My father not only rejected me, but he also deprived my mother and I the opportunity of having a big family.

I have now met all of Maha's family, and they are amazing people. They have taken me into their home and sequestered me neatly under their wings, treating me like they do their own sister until I have felt myself whole again. I wonder what kind of hold Elias had over Maha to be able to steal her away from the beautiful life she has with her family, but then relegate the thought of him to the back of my mind; if Maha is able to tuck away that part of her life and put it down to making a stupid mistake, who was I to question her choices?

In a way, I envy Maha her large family. The siblings hovering over her. Salem's attentiveness and support towards her. Her doting parents. For although my mother has doted on me my whole life, it has not been the same as having brothers and sisters to squabble with and know that there is someone else there to depend on. We have been lucky, my mother and I, to never really need anyone past each other, but extended family goes way past need and more into the district of want.

Salem is the sibling I have come in contact with the most, and he is always there in the background to offer his wisdom should I need it. At 32, he still lives with his parents, and although this might seem a little strange in the Western world, amongst Arab families it's normal for a man to remain with his parents until he marries and moves into his own home. In this case, Salem is the eldest, so he'd be the one most responsible for his parents and their care as they age. Maha tells me she doesn't think Salem will ever leave her parents on their own, and adds that she doesn't think she'll ever leave the house again either. There is a certain comfort in living in such close proximity to your parents, she tells me, adding the house is big enough to accomodate multiple families.

Through my interactions with the family, I come to learn a lot about them, and the more I learn, the more enamoured I become of the matriarch that has stitched this family together, and continued to reinforce the seams constantly with nurturing and love. Hala and her quiet husband have created a dynasty most people would be envious of, then guided their children to take the reins and work side by side to expand their brand and product line. I can't say I know many people that would have the business acumen to accomplish such a feat, but Hala and Sajed came to Australia with nothing but the clothes on their backs, without a whiff of English in their vocabulary, and created magic.

In a rare nostalgic moment one night after dinner, Hala lays bare her history, and I am emotional as I listen to her heart warming story. I don't know anyone that is more worthy of the success that she has been awarded.

Salem sits in a nearby chair-I learn it's a nightly ritual for him to sit outside and stargaze after dinner. He has his own special chair, where he sits off to the side in solitude. He needs that, Maha tells me. He needs to declutter and unpack all the baggage he crams into his mind on a daily basis. But recently, his chair has inched closer and closer to where we women sit; it's still the same chair he always sits in, but he has taken to lifting and dragging it a few feet closer to us, then sitting and facing the gathering, as though he is an interested bystander to these congregations. He rarely-if ever-offers up any dialogue, but I know he sits and listens attentively to the conversation, his mind a swirl of more information he insists on ingesting.

"But what made you come to Australia?" I ask Hala, when I learn that she and her husband migrated to Australia in the 60's. The majority of Lebanese families migrated after the mid-70's, when conflict in the small port nation was rife. When the civil war erupted in 1975, there was a flurry of immigrants making their way out of the country to avoid persecution and ultimately the death and destruction that eventually followed.

She looks through the large glass sliding door separating the home from the garden and smiles when she sees her husband sitting by the fireplace looking at her with a contemplative look. He is too far way to hear what we are talking about, but just the way he looks up to stare at her at the same time that she looks at him tells me I'm about to hear an extraordinary story. I follow the interaction with my eyes, mesmerised by the invisible thread of love that flows from one side of the house to the other. Here is a remarkable story of two people who obviously love each other deeply.

"I met Sajed quite by accident," she tells me, her breath puffing out a cloud of fog in the cold. "My mother was his mother's seamstress. On one occasion, my mother fell ill but had to deliver a dress to the woman for a ball, so I was sent in her stead to deliver the dress and make any alterations required on the spot."

"You sew, as well?" I breathe in disbelief. There was nothing this woman couldn't do. Hala shakes her head and holds up a finger to stop me; I know she is thinking. She is transported back to that moment all those years ago, and she has taken me with her. Her story plays out like a movie reel before my very eyes.

"I don't like sewing, but I know the basics. Mother insisted we all learn to do it, and so I had the fundamentals." Hala pauses and sips her coffee, then sets her cup down. I follow each and every one of her movements eagerly, as though time is moving in slow motion, and all I see is this woman before me, recounting her story.

"I had never been to the house, so I didn't know what to expect, but when I arrived with the dress draped over my arm, Sajed opened the door for me and there passed endless seconds where he just held the door open and said nothing, and I in turn replied with nothing." We laugh at the same time, and I can so clearly see a youthful Sajed holding the door knob and staring, a non-talker even back then.

"I don't know what happened that day, Aaida. But when you hear stories of a zap of electricity when two people fall in love, know that it is true. You may not know it at the time, but the feeling is there. It's whether or not people choose to evolve their feelings that leads to a union."

"And you two did?" I ask, looking at her then pointing my chin casually in her husband's direction.

"Oh boy, did we!" She exclaims, giving a low, tuneless whistle. "We fell insanely in love from the moment we set eyes on one another. But his family was well-to-do. Actually, that's not the right word. His family was obscenely rich. *My* parents were working class people-my mother was a seamstress, and my father was a builder. So his family was against the marriage from the get-go."

I wave my hand around to indicate our surroundings, the house and the children, and the grandkids, a life well lived. "But you *did* get married," I point out.

"We eloped," she tells me, and I think I hear a heavy metallic tink as my jaw hits the floor. Of all the things she could have told me, this was definitely not what I was expecting. Not that it was a ridiculous notion, but Hala and Sajed just seemed so refined and normal, there was no way I could have predicted that their lives had started out by their running away and getting married against their parents' wishes.

I hear a chuckle and turn to see that Salem is laughing at my surprise. When he sees the irritated look that crosses my face, he purses his lips and looks away innocently. Maha sits quietly listening, enjoying the interaction and the storytelling, even though I know she's probably heard this story a million times before.

"Logically, there was nothing to stop us from marrying," Hala tells me. "Except that we came from two different worlds. It's the same old story-rich versus poor. Sajed argued with his family constantly, but they would not budge."

I shake my head in disbelief; it's so sad that when two people love one another, something as inconsequential as money keeps them apart.

"Sajed had-has-an uncle; his father's brother. Quite a religious man, too. He stood up for us and argued in our favour for marriage, explaining there was no reasonable excuse for us not to be married. When that failed also, his uncle arranged the paperwork for our migration. We married in secret the night before we departed the country. And that was how we came to be in Australia."

"It gets better," Maha says, opening her mouth to speak for the first time that night.

"We came to Australia with barely the clothes on our backs," Hala tells me. "When his parents realised what we had done, they disowned Sajed. We had to start from the bottom up, just like everyone else." She looks into the house lovingly and I follow her gaze. Sajed is watching his wife carefully; almost as if he knows the story she is telling, and the years melt away as I see them both standing together after they have arrived in Australia with no-where to go.

"It was very different back then," she tells me. "There was no structured process for dealing with migrants. Sure, they let us in, but there was next to no government support for those who arrived. You had to rely on the good graces of people who were here before you to settle in. And we knew no-one here… Australia was simply the first country to accept our application, and so we ended up at the end of the world." She smiles as she reminisces, then continues on with her story.

"Sajed's uncle had given us some money to get started, so we found accomodation in a boarding house until we found work. Sajed worked in a factory, and I found that my mother's instructions for me to learn to sew didn't go to waste. For a while, I bled my fingers dry doing alterations by hand until I was able to buy a sewing machine. At night, we both attended classes to learn English."

"I listen intently until Hala pats my hand and tells me it's time for her to turn in. I'm a little disappointed; I could talk for hours about history and the past, but realise she needs her rest, and watch her as she rises to walk inside to her husband. I watch her go and smile as he takes her hand and leads her through the house.

"What they have," Maha muses, "many people spend a lifetime searching for." I nod in agreement as I turn back to her and rise to take my leave.

SALEM

Aaida becomes a permanent fixture in our home. She is instrumental in helping Maha regain her balance and find her way. Anwar has taken to calling her aunt Aaida instead of "my friend". And my parents are absolutely smitten with her.

When my brothers meet her, one by one, they fall a little in love with her. Those that are married are met with an elbow to the ribs from their wives, but truth be told, even those are playful, as even my sisters in law have taken to Aaida as though she's a long lost sister. I realise that, as an only child, she has probably never had the luxury of being surrounded by family. She walked into our lives and fit right in as though she had been there the whole time.

"What's not to love?" My mother asks, after Aaida picks Maha up so they can go and watch a movie one Friday night after the family has had dinner. "Somebody, tell me why the girl is still single! *Rah enjelet bas faker bi qisithaa.*"

"She's very beautiful," one of my sisters in law remarks.

"Intelligent and funny. Very well-mannered," my mother adds.

"*Ma hada fi yhet fiha 3eli,*" my father says, and we all turn to face him. My father, a man of so few words, sings Aaida's praises incessantly. And when the conversation turns to the girl, he is always the first to add his impressions. He has never been like this before, and I know this is all Aaida's doing; she has enchanted the whole family. A family which is not easily impressed by anything or anyone.

It is only when my brother Brahim's wife Leyana speaks up that something stutters deep in my soul at her words.

"*Wallah, btaerfou*, " she says thoughtfully, as if a lightbulb has just gone off in her head. "My brother Hilal is still single and looking. She would make an amazing wife and sister in law!"

My mother's face blanches as she turns to Leyana, but she doesn't say anything. She simply turns back to face forward, sits all the way back in her seat and straightens her back. Mother is astute like that; she always says "If you don't have something nice to say, then say nothing" and I guess this is one of those moments when she could choose to say plenty or decide to hold her tongue. I don't know what her issue is though with what Leyana says, as she comes from a good background and there would probably be no cause for concern if Aaida is to become part of their extended family.

I stop myself short as the thought strikes me and look up at the ceiling to stave the overwhelming fear of loss that washes over me. Aaida has become a part of our family, I realise. A welcome part. If she were to marry, we would lose her presence. No matter how close she and Maha got, once she married, Aaida's time would be dedicated to her new family and within no time, she would slip away quietly into her new life and we would become but a distant memory to one another. The thought of this causes my throat to constrict and my heart to beat rapidly. I look forward to seeing Aaida. I am attentive to every conversation raised where her name is mentioned, wanting to devour every last bit of information about her in order to learn more about the mysterious stranger who flew into our lives like a comet, wreaking havoc on all our hearts. The thought of losing that causes my soul to stumble and fall, and I raise my hand to my chest and rub slowly at my bruised heart.

My father notices and turns to me, nodding toward my hand.

"Just a little indigestion," I tell him, letting my sweaty hand fall to my thigh, where it settles. I continue to listen to the conversation unfold, and it lingers for several minutes on Aaida as my family continues to describe her in the highest complimentary ways possible. My mother and father are very fond of Aaida, maybe too fond. I don't know how it would affect them to lose her, but I can't imagine it would be a good thing, even though they would be the first to wish her well.

"*Sahih*, Salem," my brother Kaysar pipes up. "It's been a while since we've had a family celebration. When are you going to get married?"

They all turn to look at me, and I imagine I look like a stunned mullet at the sudden change in conversation, and I sit gaping at them, lost for words.

"Salem will tell us when he's ready to get married," my mother chimes in, sparing me from having to answer their questioning looks.

"If you really want to celebrate something," I tell my younger brother, leaning forward to kick his foot playfully, "lets celebrate *you* getting married."

Kaysar pokes his tongue out at me and shakes his head in laughter. He has never displayed any inclination to get married, and it is so obvious that he will be the perennial bachelor, moving from one project to another as he fills his time with work goals rather than girls.

AAIDA

Hala summons me to the family home on a Saturday on the pretense of me taste testing a new line for her. I say "pretense" because I have the oddest feeling that she just wants me there so I can gush over her food. In all honesty, I could eat her food all day and night and gush just as long, it's that good.

The weekends are my time to relax and unwind and leave the week that was behind. I'll catch up with a friend or two for coffee, shop with my mother, or just hang out at home with my parents and enjoy a nice quiet bbq out in the sun with them. I spend time with Maha generally on weekdays after work, so this is the first weekend, or even the first daytime trip I've made to the house since that first time when I delivered Maha back into the fold of her family's arms.

"Come early," Hala says, and I ask her to define what she constitutes to be early. In my books, 7am is early. But I'm not pulling a 7am on a Saturday morning.

"*Ya3ni, shi* 9," she tells me.

"And how long do you think we'll need?" I ask her, scratching pen to paper as I jot her into my diary.

"*Yeee, la3 binti.* This might go all day. I have a lot for you to test. You'll need to be here all day."

I laugh and tell her Saturday is my day to catch up with chores that have been building up throughout the week and errands I can no longer put off. She relents and tells me she'll take me for as long as I can stay, and I tick the 9am entry in my diary and set it aside.

That weekend, I spend the entire Saturday at Hala's house. I had only planned to be there for a couple of hours, but Hala ropes me in with her delicacies and starts to regale me with stories of her past. I am so entertained, I lose track of all time and remain firmly planted in my seat well past midday.

Hala is a gem, an icon to modern history as she weaves tale after tale of her life in Australia. It is not lost on me that she rarely mentions her birth country, choosing instead to live in the present. Over tea and home made jam, she tells me more about her early life when she and Sajed first arrived in Australia. I am an avid listener, hungry for more memories.

"So Sajed and I," she says, in between a mouthful of heavily layered jam scones. Her mouth is full to overflowing, and she frowns then holds up a finger to indicate she needs a moment and takes a gulp of her tea. "Sugar!" She stammers, realising the tea is too hot. I watch her quietly, giving her time to get over the initial shock of burning her tongue.

I love that everything in this house is homemade. Everything in this home, I correct mentally, for it is a home, not a house. Everything about it screams of love and warmth and family. This is a home. It is an anchor.

"We didn't know anyone when we came here," Hala starts up again. "The taxi-driver was nice enough to take us to a boarding house in Neutral Bay. You know, where all the houses are scrunched up against each other and you can't sigh without your neighbour hearing you."

I laugh and marvel at her accurate description.

"We were lucky though, it was close to the water so our leisure time, what little of it we had, we would walk down and watch the water as it lapped at the bay and the seagulls flew ahead. We would talk about our hopes and dreams, Sajed and I, and marvel at this beautiful country which had extended its arms to us. Sajed found work as a factory hand, and I did a few sewing jobs here and there. At night, we would attend English classes then collapse from exhaustion after we made it home."

I listen intently, not cutting her off to ask any questions, for fear that she would lose her train of thought.

"We stayed at the boarding house maybe 3 months or so. Then

we moved to a small house in Bankstown. It was so small, two bedrooms, and the toilet was outside." She pauses to roll her eyes. "You know, I never did understand why they built houses that way." I don't stop her to explain that outhouses existed because there was insufficient plumbing in homes and toilets tended to get smelly. Instead, I remark "it's a long move, from Neutral Bay to Bankstown," and she nods in agreement.

"It was. But there were newer homes in that area, at affordable prices. There was a swell of incoming migrants heading that way regardless. Did you know that Redfern was once a hub for the Lebanese community?"

I rear my head back in shock and she nods her head knowingly and looks at me out of the corner of her eye, as though she has a secret to share.

"A lot of the earlier Lebanese settled in Redfern and opened warehouses and factories there. They employed others and for the most part, they flourished. Then in the 50's, the government decided it wanted to clean the area of the slums and redevelop the suburb, especially where a lot of the old businesses had been located."

"I've never heard this before," I tell her in disbelief.

"By the time the government got through with repurposing the land, not much was left of our heritage there. The time the Lebanese spent in Redfern is like a wrinkle in time that most people have forgotten."

I listened on in interest, so intent was I on learning from this woman with her amazingly rich history.

"So it came to pass that we moved to Bankstown and I started pickling vegetables and fruits. It was slow getting started, but it gave us a steady income and something to keep me busy while I raised our children. But when it took off, boy, did it take off!" She rolls her eyes to the sky and blows out a breath, and I can't help but be infected by this woman's exuberance.

"Yes, it took off into the stratosphere!" I hear someone yell from inside, just as Sajed comes walking out of the glass doors to the garden, followed by Salem, who looks surprised to see me and raises his eyebrows but says nothing. It is a little out of context for him to see me at his house on a Saturday during the day, and I feel a little awkward, as though I am intruding.

"I should go" I say, rising after they greet us.

"Nonsense!" Sajed is firm when he speaks, and Salem whips his head quickly to his dad, his mouth fixed in a gaping "o". "It's lunch time; you'll not leave until we've eaten together!" I'm not sure what Salem is more surprised about-his father's tone or his insistence that I not leave.

"*Na'am Aaida, khalikhi,*" Hala pleads, pulling me back down into my seat by the hand. I sort of fall into my seat abruptly as I argue with the couple that I really must leave and attend to some errands. But neither will hear a word of it as the matter is settled and Hala announces we'll have a bbq.

"Aaida likes her Saturday bbq," she states, matter of factly, and I'm not sure how she knows this, but I can only imagine that Maha has been at it again.

"Where's Maha?" Salem asks, whipping his head around the garden, as though merely saying her name will conjure her appearance.

"*Wlek, hal binit!*" Hala gasps, and it's the first time I detect that she is a little exasperated with her daughter. "I told her Aaida was coming, but she had already made plans to take Anwar to see his grandparents for the weekend."

"*Ma'3alaysh,* Hala, she'll come when she comes. Let's get lunch ready."

Sajed lifts Hala's hand delicately and leads her toward the house. She stops at the large glass sliding doors and turns back, regarding Salem and I with dewy old eyes. "*Yallah,* are you kids coming?"

HALA

For all my plotting and planning, things are working out better than even I had anticipated. When I tried to talk Aaida into spending the day at ours, it was honestly out of a real desire to spend more time with her. The added bonus would have been if she and Salem just so happened to "accidentally" bump into each other when he came home in the late afternoon. I was so sure that if the both of them just looked past their insecurities, they would get along so well. They were so perfectly matched, I couldn't wait for the day the lightbulb would go on in their heads and they would realise what I had known all along. Even Sajed, who never involved himself in such affairs, was rooting for a union between Aaida and Salem. Even a whiff of interest. But both were so respectful of boundaries, neither dared even allow their mind wander towards that possibility.

So when Sajed and Salem come home early-unusually early-I am surprised but ecstatic. And I'm overjoyed when Sajed completes my work and convinces Aaida to stay for lunch.

I've craftily assigned Salem to the salad and Aaida is helping me skewer the meat while Sajed lights up the bbq. I have always prided myself on teaching the boys to be handy around the house, even in the kitchen. Even when other Lebanese families frowned upon a man partaking in such a domesticated, feminine role, I ensured the boys knew how to do anything and everything and helped around the house so the burden would never fall on any one person. Traits which I know my daughters in law appreciated beyond words.

Salem surprises me when he is the first to speak and asks Aaida a question. That wasn't my doing. All on his own, he starts a conversation with her, and I take great care to keep my mouth shut and listen to the resonance in both their voices to gauge a measure of their emotions.

"So what do you prefer with your barbecued meat?" Salem asks, chopping the lettuce. "Salad, tabouli or fattoush?"

When there is only silence, I turn to face Aaida and see that she has scrunched her face up in distaste. Salem too has stopped chopping and is watching her. It's a comical setting as we wait with bated breath, wondering what has disappointed her so much. "Fattoush?" she asks. "Fattoush? Who eats fattoush with meat??"

Salem laughs and resumes chopping as she says "Salad all the way for me. Tabouli is for chicken. But fattoush is a no go zone with bbq."

"And your dips?" he asks.

"Hommus and baba ghannouj. What's a bbq without dip, right?" and she smiles up at him. It's disarming how beautiful she is when she smiles that genuine smile of hers. I see Salem's lips tip upward out of the corner of my eye, and I know he is smiling back at her. Progress.

"Mother makes a mean baba ghannouj," he tells her, but I think she already knows this.

SAJED

Most would attribute our family's success to me. After all, I'm the man of the house, and my family comes from money, so the foundation is there. This is what those around us know. What most people don't know is that our fortune is based on a concept that Hala founded. I was just along for the ride.

Hala wanted to keep busy while I was at work and the kids were at school, so she came up with an idea that she implemented from our tiny home in Bankstown- but that idea soon gave birth to a whole range of products, until she became so overwhelmed with orders, I quit my job to work alongside my wife. My family's rejection perhaps played a role in her perseverance and drive to succeed; she wanted to prove that social class should not be taken too seriously when you introduced marriage into the equation.

She proved her point. And how. She built her dream and she just kept chipping away at the market until her pickled goods were front row, left right and centre in supermarkets and grocery stores all over Australia. The beauty of my wife's ideas was that she thought outside the box- where she had started with products targeted specifically at an Arab market, she was soon to realise there was a wider market to break into and branched out into condiments that appealed to every other taste and ethnicity known to man.

I served as her right hand; I know most people would scoff at this, but Hala was the brains behind our business and I did the heavy lifting. But I attribute our success to her and her alone, and I'm man enough to admit she is the rock and the glue that held everything together. She is still the same down to earth girl I married. In her eyes, we were- are- a partnership, and she considers us a team of equals. I couldn't love her more if I tried.

As our family grew, so too did our business. When it was time to move into a bigger home, I came across our current home quite by accident. The agent mentioned a new home that was about to hit the market, but it was out of our area of choice. What attracted me was the huge amount of land the house was built on. It helped too that the house was magnificent, large enough to accomodate our growing family comfortably. I bought the house that afternoon without Hala having seen it and we've been here ever since.

I'm reflecting on our amazing life and our beautiful home when Hala emerges from the house carrying a tray of skewered meat and a great big smile on her face. Hala's interest in Aaida has developed into a full blown obsession, and I know she's angling for a union between the young girl and our eldest son Salem. Aaida would make a wonderful addition to our family, although I don't know that she's interested in marriage at this point in her life.

Hala sets the meat down and falls into my lap, sitting sideways and winding her hands around my neck. She is happy and her happiness is infectious. We have had a good life, she and I, and I can't wait for the next chapter of our story to be written as we go from one strength to another.

When Aaida and Salem emerge from the house, Hala and I have our foreheads tipped together and we're laughing over something Hala has just said. Aaida blushes, and Salem scoffs and rolls his eyes when he sees us. His expression wordlessly says "ah, they're at it again!" before he claps his hands together and tell us it's time to eat.

AAIDA

Salem asks all the right questions to set me at ease. Although I've been coming to their home for a few months now, there has never been occasion for he and I to have a full fledged conversation on our own. What would we even talk about? But now as I stand skewering meat and he stands beside me making what looks to be an awesome salad, there is an easy, casual air surrounding us and we fall into a comfortable dance as our hands move in symphony. He is wearing a shirt with the sleeves rolled up, and I can't help but notice the lines in his forearms as his hands work their way through cutting an array of vegetables.

"You put capsicum in your salad?" I ask, looking at the red pepper as it slides into the bowl. He stops mid air and turns to me. "Yes. You don't like it?" and he starts to pick it out with tongs.

"I've never had it in my salad. Leave it, I'd like to try."

I've never really looked at Salem. Like looked looked. It's always been a sort of side eye, or looking anywhere else but at him on the rare occasion when he spoke to me. But now I look up at him, and he's smiling, and I'm dazzled by the warmth of his smile. I notice there is a permanent furrow in his forehead, and his hair, parted to the left, at times falls into his eyes when he lowers his head. He and Maha look so much alike, with their brown hair and hazel eyes and similar features. They even share the same chiselled cheekbones and dimples in the cheeks. And they are both beautiful.

By the time we make our way outside to Sajed and Hala, both of whom did not return to the kitchen after Hala went outside, we have slipped into friendly banter and I'm more relaxed than

I have been previously in Salem's company. Hala and Sajed have their heads close together as they talk and laugh in their own secret language that no-one else understands. It's cute, but I find myself blushing nonetheless as we approach them; I am still an outsider and I'm not entirely used to seeing such shows of affection amongst others.

"Time for you kids to settle down, keep your hands to yourselves, and eat!" Salem laughs, as his parents pull apart and look toward us. Their smiles alone, their happiness, their own special language of love, tells a story of a couple so entwined with each other, they are like newlyweds more than 30 years into their marriage.

SALEM

Aaida is very tight lipped about her family. We know she is an only child, her birth parents are divorced and both have remarried, and she no longer has any contact with her father. No matter how I try to navigate the conversation, she always manages to sidestep and avoid the subject of family altogether. I know there is some dark history there, most notably where her father is concerned, and she is a good listener and loves a great story, but when it comes to her, she is not so forthcoming with information regarding her life.

Although I think it may be a little odd, I do understand that there may be some pain there that's been festering for years that she has been unable to let go of. She's been to Lebanon, that much I know. She went every year for 4 or 5 consecutive years, then abruptly stopped going and now doesn't even acknowledge Lebanon anymore. I know her father lives there, and I wonder if on her many trips back home, something happened between them to put her off going back altogether.

I know she's not involved with anyone-what little free time she has left after shifting between two clinics is always either spent with us or her mother and step-father. Who we haven't had the pleasure of meeting yet. But tonight, mother has decided it's time we meet her family. She tells me she would like to meet the woman who single handedly raised such a perfect daughter. I know this is part of it, but lately, I've felt something more brewing on my mother's mind. She drops little hints about how lovely Aaida is (this, I know), how she would make a wonderful wife to some fortunate man one day (for some reason, the thought of her married and leaving us scratches my heart), and how she is going to be the perfect mother raising perfect children (I have no doubt about this either).

By the same token, I'm not being honest with myself if I don't admit that Aaida crosses my mind more times in a day than anyone else. I'm not an emotional man-I think and feel in logic, not emotions, but these heart palpitations are getting worse and worse as the days wear on. I look forward to seeing her, and when she leaves, I stand in the doorway with Maha and watch her drive away, and it's as though she's put my soul in the passenger seat of her car and taken it with her. Maha always looks at me with a knowing eye, purses her lips then shakes her head sombrely. I don't ask her what that's about. In a way, subconsciously, I already know, but I won't admit it. Still, logic dictates.

Things only get worse when Aaida's parents walk through the front door, because they're perfect. I refer to them as her parents, because that's the way Aaida refers to them, and if you didn't know it, you'd definitely think that her step-father is her birth father by the way he addresses and treats her. Neither of them bats an eyelid at the grandeur of the house, which I can see we're all impressed with, but her mother remarks what a lovely home we have, and my mother beams brightly.

Aaida's parents are remarkable people, and I can see this from the moment they step into the house. Her mother, Aujene, is a beautiful, regal woman with an air of refinement. I can see where Aaida gets her dark hair and petite features from. Jihad sticks his hand out to greet my father and introduces himself as her father, and he may as well be with the way he so obviously dotes on her. They are a beautiful couple, complementing each other perfectly, and I can see there is an easy, happily uncomplicated relationship between the three of them by the way they interact with one another.

I watch on as everyone gets settled and the conversations mount with my parents and Aaida's parents, and the girls. Mother has kept this gathering intimate, so none of my other siblings are in attendance, but I think that is in most part because mother wanted to keep things casual and relaxed. I wonder if it's even right for me to be here when my siblings aren't, but then I recall my mother reminding me to keep Friday night free for this dinner. I know she's plotting something, but I'm not sure what, although I might have a vague idea.

There is a lull in the conversation between Jihad and my father, he of little words, and Aaida's father turns to me and asks me about my work. We chat for a while before my mother announces dinner and we make our way to the dining room. Everyone has fallen into a comfortable zone and we eat and chatter over dinner like we are eating with old friends. I watch the interaction between all parties; everyone seems to be having a great time, and Aaida and Maha are like twins with constant conversations interspersed with laughter. The way these two girls have integrated with one another is unbelievable.

"I can't tell you enough times how amazed we are by Aaida," my mother says to Aaida's mother, and I momentarily forget how to chew my food as I watch my mother speak with the other woman. "She came to us at just the right time, and she's been invaluable to Maha.

Aujene nods her head, smiles and sips her water before she speaks. When she does, her eyes wander in Aaida's direction before she addresses my mother.

"I'm glad Aaida's found a friend she enjoys sharing her time with so she's not always working so hard," and at this, everyone laughs.

"They're like two peas in a pod," my mother remarks. "And I'm glad they have each other. Just know that Aaida is part of our family and will always be welcome. *Mashaa Allah,* how well you've raised her!"

Aujene turns smiling to Jihad and in that single glance, I see a wealth of commitment and love, even though I know they have not been together for many years. But it's so obvious to everyone in that room that Jihad's entry into their lives probably helped heal whatever trauma Aaida suffered from.

"And it helps that she loves my food!" my mother adds quickly, and everyone is stitched in laughter as they help themselves to more food.

After dinner, we all gather outside in the garden, and my chair somehow manages to find it's way into the circle gathered around the fire pit as everyone shares stories well into the night. I look at Aaida as she and Maha sit huddled next to each other, like two little girls sharing a secret then giggling about it. The glow of the fire throws light against Aaida's face, and I watch her turn this way and then that, before she throws her head back and laughs at something Maha says, then leans down to whisper something into my sister's ear. She is a truly beautiful girl with a remarkable personality, and I feel the squeeze in my chest that is becoming more and more frequent. I blink back the pain of the tightness and catch Jihad's eye, before looking away quickly, somewhat ashamed that he's caught me staring at his daughter.

"Perfect girl, perfect family, perfect everything. I cannot find one little thing that is bad about her," my mother says, after we have bid Aaida's family farewell for the night.

"Why are you trying to?" My sister pipes up, although not rudely.

"Your mother didn't mean that in a bad way," my father explains, and we all turn at the sound of his voice. My father so rarely speaks, sometimes we forget he's even in the room. But when he *does* speak, we all listen. Hungrily. Waiting for him to impart a few rare words of wisdom. He looks up from the cigar box he's handling and sees that we are all watching him, waiting for him to continue. He sets the box down quietly and I notice how we all lean in eagerly waiting.

"I don't involve myself in your personal lives," he starts, looking at my sister and I, and my mother's eyebrows shoot up. I think she knows what's coming. "But this needs to be said." He stands straighter and I automatically assume the same position. "Son," he says, somewhat firmly, putting his right hand to my left shoulder and squeezing firmly "If you don't marry that girl soon, someone else will." And with that, my father walks out of the room, leaving us all to follow him with our eyes.

HALA

Tradition would have you believe that I have done things in reverse.

In Arab custom, when a family wants to enquire about a girl's hand in marriage, it is incumbent upon the male's family to visit the female's family to get to know them.

I did things a little differently because I don't pander to what is considered "the norm." If I were that person who did the normal, proper thing, I wouldn't have come this far in life.

According to some Arab cultures, I have broken an unspoken rule and probably should be exiled.

Yes, there are traditions and customs, a lot of which we abide by, but what's wrong with doing things a little differently as long as we're not doing something that would be considered immoral or would stir the wrath of God?

What I love about Aaida's family is that they are exactly like us. Normal, down to earth people who buck tradition and understand that sometimes things happen a little differently. Any other family with a young daughter of marriageable age would not have stepped foot into a house with a young single son without the male's family visiting their house first. Not Aaida's family. They're as forward thinking as they come, and I'm sure they did not come to my dinner with the intention of marrying their daughter to our son, because I realise later they did not even know we had a son! Aaida had told them so little about us, all they really knew was that Aaida had a friend named Maha who she spent all her time with.

So when they return the favour and invite us for dinner, I know with everything in me that this family is awesome enough to play a role in our lives. Salem's brows knit together when I tell him and he asks if he has to attend.

"Of course you must attend, Salem. Aaida's mother specifically asked that both you and Maha attend."

Aaida's family lives in a modest single story home about 20 minutes from our own home. Although it appears to be a matchbox in comparison to our home, it is a quaint and charming little craftsman bungalow that I can see has a lot of historic appeal. The home is immaculately kept, and I can see that Aujene is house-proud with the perfectly delicate furnishings and the beautifully kept gardens. Whilst it may look small on the outside, the inside is spacious and comfortable, and we take our seats in the living room and fall into comfortable chatter as Aujene puts the finishing touches to her dinner.

"Are you sure you wouldn't like any help?" I ask, and Aujene smiles at me widely as I enter the kitchen. I know exactly what she is thinking; she is extremely pleased that I am comfortable enough to leave my spot and join her in the kitchen, rolling my sleeves up as I walk toward her.

"Everything's done," she beams, "but I could use the company as I add the final touches."

In Aujene, I have finally met my culinary match. The woman can cook up a storm! She has made *Wara eneb and kibbeh nayeh*, and Aaida has contributed by creating a perfect vegetarian pasta dish with rocket, cherry tomatoes, kalamata olives and parmesan cheese. Aujene impresses me by advising that most of the vegetables used in tonight's dishes have come from her garden, and I stand wide eyed as I admire the quality of her produce sitting in a basket on the bench top.

"Come, I'll show you!" she insists, and we exit through a door in the kitchen and down a narrow path that opens to a backyard with perfectly manicured lawns and all matter of vegetation growing in every unused corner of the land. There's radish and parsley and silverbeet and mint, tomatoes and cucumbers, lettuce and chilli and eggplant. There are so many vegetables, I don't know where to look; it's like she has created a mini market in her own back yard. And right in the middle of her beautiful grounds is an aged green apple tree that spreads its shade and is a wonder to behold.

"You grow all this yourself?" I ask her, marvelling at the perfectly formed leaves and healthy lustre of her vegetables.

Aujene nods her head and bites her lip, then smiles. "I've always loved the earth. Gardening is my therapy."

"But my dear, you have enough vegetables here to feed an army!" I cry, wondering what she could possibly do with all the vegetables when there are only three mouths to feed.

"I *do* feed the army!" She says, then shrugs nonchalantly and corrects herself. "Not the army, but the bulk of it is donated to soup kitchens and charities."

Aujene stuns me. She is beautiful and smart and articulate, and works tirelessly for the benefit of others. She raised a beautiful daughter and keeps a wonderful home. She is a rarity, and I look at her with rapturous wonder as my mind imagines all the amazing things we could accomplish together.

"Come, my dear," I say, holding out my arm for her to tuck her own within. "We have so much to talk about!"

SALEM

I watch the interaction between our two families throughout the night. I have been in Aaida's company many times, albeit as a lucky bystander looking in at her relationship with my sister. But tonight, I am mesmerised. Not by her sheer beauty, no. I am spellbound by the way she holds herself, the way she interacts with my family the same way she interacts with her own, the absolute ease with which she moves between us heaping fruit and sweets on our plates. Even my father, usually so reserved and introverted, has laughed and smiled and cracked a few jokes, referring to Maha and Aaida collectively as *"banaati"* , his daughters.

When Aujene smiles and remarks she didn't know he had more than one daughter, a sheepish smile invades his face and he juts his chin out in Aaida's direction by way of explanation. Enough said.

"Aaida, *Allah ywafikha*, has become an extension of us," he explains. "Seeing her is like that feeling you get when you're coming home."

Aaida blushes and lowers her head, and a stray strand of her hair falls over her eyes. She scrapes a long slim finger through the strand and pins it deftly behind her ear. When she looks up again, her eye catches mine and we both look away quickly, but not before Jihad, sitting back in his chair quietly, spies the exchange and raises his eyebrows in question. I shake my head slightly, as though to dispel any misgivings he may have, then kick myself at my foolishness. There's nothing going on between Aaida and I, so why would I feel the need to assuage his feelings where she is concerned? I quickly understand where that glance has taken Jihad when my father excuses himself to pray and he asks me to walk with him.

"Let me introduce you to some rare organic plants," he tells me, as we walk slowly toward the rear of the garden. We walk side by side, the night stars winking their light over us as Jihad moves us into a private alcove.

"You're a guest in my house, so I won't insult you by asking what that was about," he starts, referring to the exchange between Aaida and I. He holds up his hand to silence me when I move to open my mouth in my defence. "Just know that even though not biologically, I am her father in every other way. And I will kill anyone that hurts her. If you have any intentions towards my daughter, do it the right way and do it soon. Don't come through the window."

And it is then I understand the full magnitude of the ache in my chest, as I realise Jihad and I are in the same predicament. I myself would kill anyone who sought to hurt Aaida. So why would I choose to be that person that corrupts her soul by tainting and tarnishing it? A swell of unease settles over me as I look up at the night sky and take in an exasperated breath. I could kick myself for not seeing it earlier, but I finally understand what everyone around me has been trying to tell me without actually coming out and saying it. That ache in my chest is the void I feel at the thought of losing Aaida. That lack of concentration I've been suffering from has arisen because my thoughts are consumed with her. That pain in my heart, so heavy and full of burden, is because I've fallen in love with the girl, something as unexpected as it is unplanned.

"Now, talk," Jihad says, raising his chin as he commands me to put forth my case.

"I have no ill intentions toward your daughter," I tell him.

"I have no doubt," Jihad says. "That's why I'm giving you the nudge you need."

And with that, he turns and walks back down the path toward the house and I'm left looking after him as I turn his words over in my head. I was born in Australia and although my heritage is Lebanese and I understand the virtues of tradition, I'm not as well versed as say someone like Jihad who has been born and raised adhering to customs his whole life. I believe, although I'm not entirely sure, that Jihad has just given me his blessing and literally told me to get a move on where his daughter is concerned.

My mother is quick to invite Aaida over for dinner again soon after we have visited Aaida's family home. She goes so far as to tell Aaida that she shouldn't have to invite her; this is her home and she is her daughter, and she is welcome any time.

Aaida, as always, consumes my mother's food as though it's her last meal, with a healthy zest for food and life and all it encompasses. There is, however, a reserved air about her as she sits with us at the table that I have not previously detected in her.

When dinner is done and we retire to the garden for our usual ritual, I bring my chair wholly into the circle created by the girls and sit with them. Aaida gives me a confused look then quickly rights her expression, while Maha raises her eyebrows and smirks, but says nothing. My mother reaches over and taps her hand over mine, as though she is welcoming me into their inner circle. The girls chit chat and mother and I touch on some work related product issues before she turns to Aaida and draws her into the conversation.

"*Sahih*, Aaida," my mother says, "there's a new almond date dip I'd like you to test for me." Aside from eating and loving mother's food, Aaida has been my mother's greatest asset when it comes to taste testing new products. She has proven herself a worthy food critic, and her expression alone tells you everything you need to know about how she feels about a particular product.

Maha leaves us to retrieve the biscuits and dip at the same time that father ducks his head out the great glass sliding doors and asks mother to retrieve something for him. I watch her go then realise Aaida and I are alone. She squints into the night sky, furrowing her eyebrows before turning to me and laughing.

"I believe your family has been elaborately plotting this moment so that we are left alone."

"Not so elaborate," I tell her. "I'm sure this whole scenario didn't take them more than two minutes to concoct," and she laughs heartily as she imagines my family members devising their little plot.

"Does that mean there's no almond date dip?" she asks, feigning disappointment.

"Oh, there's definitely almond date dip. It'll be here any minute now."

Aaida smiles and looks down at the grass beyond our feet, deep in thought. She is still a mystery to me. A beautiful mystery. I know the important bits, but I also know there is so much history there that has yet to be told. I know that Aaida will be an interesting subject to unpick, and I look forward to the day when she trusts me enough to start revealing her secrets to me.

"So what's the plan?" she asks.

I shake my head, indicating I don't understand what she's referring to, and she mentions the dip again, asking whether or not we'll be releasing just one or a range.

"I think mother wants to test the waters with one dip," I tell her.

"Almond date sounds nice, but you know what I'd like to try?"

She's never volunteered information about her likes and dislikes before, and I perk up, giving her my undivided attention.

"Almond fig," she tells me. "The combination sounds divine. And almond orange. With a nice crusty rustic bread."

The look on her face as she imagines the combinations causes my heart to stutter. She describes food with such joy, it's as though the delicacy is already teasing her tongue.

"Come tomorrow and these will be ready for you to taste test," I tell her, and I know, without saying anything more, that she will be here. If not for the food, then for the command lacing through my words. Aaida needs to be commanded. She makes enough hard decisions during the day without having to make any more after hours.

AAIDA

Who knew that almond could be such a versatile nut?

Hala releases not one, not three, but six new dips in a new line she explicitly allows only Maha and I to advise on. Under the family label, she brands the dips "Two Sisters", in dedication of our joint efforts, and sets up a trust fund, pledging 10% of all profits to aid and assist victims of domestic abuse.

The dips, ranging in amazing jaw dropping flavours, are so popular they fly off the shelves until the production line is backed up and can't meet demand. Hala, ever the savvy businesswoman and humanitarian, makes a move so amazing, I can't believe no-one thought of it before. She opens a second production company for the dips and proceeds to hire women from the shelter in an effort to empower them and give them a sense of purpose in life.

I cannot believe her generosity. And the more she gives to the community, the more she is blessed with incomparable wealth and abundance.

"Ultimately, I'd like to be hiring women from interstate who need to be relocated," she tells me. "I know a lot of these women would like to leave, but lack of funding and resources, maybe even fear, doesn't allow them to. We're in a position to resettle women who would otherwise not be in a position to leave the comfort of what they know."

I look at Hala, awestruck beyond all measure at her words. It is 4 months since the dinner at my parent's house, and I have been working non-stop around the clock at the shelter as well as at the plant to help Hala launch her range of dips. Within that time, I've worked closely with Salem and Maha, as well as their other siblings, who still manage the other income streams pertaining to the family business.

"This could be our biggest seller yet," Salem says, flipping between pages attached to a clipboard.

"Well, that's good to hear," Hala tells him. "It's always nice to know a product isn't going to flop and sink."

I laugh at Hala's words and wonder how she could ever believe one of her creations would fail. The woman has built an empire out of pickling and jarring and packaging delicacies that a time poor population loves, and even well into her 50's, there doesn't seem to be any slowing down for her.

"Aaida, I need you to talk to your mother for me. She's being stubborn again," Hala says, as she looks down at the clipboard that Salem has handed her.

"What is it this time?" I ask her, laughing.

"I need her here in the factory overseeing quality control. I don't know why she is so resistant in coming to work for me."

"It's not you, Hala. Mother just enjoys the simple things in life. She wants to give her time to her charity work, grow her garden, live the quiet life."

"So do I," she quips. We all want the quiet life. But now is not the time. What if I could just get her in here for a few hours two or three days a week? Do you think she'd agree to that?"

"Well, you could ask."

"I don't want to push her."

"Then don't. Offer her the flexible timetable until you are able to find someone else. Maybe get her to do the hiring so you know you're getting someone you can rely on?"

"And now to the most pressing matter," she says, looking up at Salem and I as we stood side by side, her tone serious. "When are you two kids getting married?"

Salem is my safety net.

By that, I mean he's strong and dependable and comfort all in one. He's stability.

I never have to worry about anything I say or do-or don't- with Salem. He accepts me as I am, with all my faults and moods and sadness.

Do I love him? Of course I love him. It may have taken me a while to get there, but I understand this was due to my reluctance to let anyone else into my inner orbit after Khaled. Weary. I was weary. I had to be sure. But with Salem, there are a few things that are a given;

He would never hurt me.

He would never reject or desert me.

He's willing to accept me as I am, regardless of past hurts or trauma.

He is an amazing son, a brilliant brother, and a kick ass lawyer.

He is going to be an awesome father and a loving, attentive husband.

And I know all this because he loves me more than life itself.

AAIDA

Our first big argument comes even before we're married. I don't want a big, elaborate wedding, and Salem is worried that one day I'll regret this decision and is insisting on a wedding. With 800 guests, no less.

"I don't even know 800 people-where would we get 800 people from?" I ask, somewhat irritated. I don't want a wedding, I don't like formalities, and all the thought and effort that would go into planning such an event is making my head spin.

"We have that many guests," he advises me. "They would all want to be there to wish us well."

I throw my hands up in the air in exasperation and blow at a strand of hair that has fallen in my eyes, before I go in search of my mother in law.

"*Bas*, Aaida, you should have a wedding. Money is no object. You can choose *whatever* you want." She and my father in law are over the moon that Salem and I are getting married.

"It's a waste, *mart 3ami*. And I don't want the formality of a wedding."

She taps her finger to her chin thoughtfully and looks toward her husband sitting in his recliner by the fireplace. He nods once, an approval, a sort of mutual agreement that only they understand. I'm still amazed by the secret language that they share with one another with merely a glance.

"*Khalas*, you don't want a wedding? There will be *no wedding*," she enunciates, in a tone of finality.

Salem walks into the room just as she announces this and I victoriously poke my tongue out at him like a child. He laughs and grabs me around the hips with one hand, twirling me until I am giggling.

"It's a good thing I'd do anything for you, Aaida. Otherwise I wouldn't take this loss lying down."

We opt for an intimate family dinner in the grounds of my in-law's home with both families, a handful of close friends from either side, and me wearing a simple yet elegant white gown. I am happy. For the first time in a long time, I am happy and complete as Salem and I sign the marriage certificate before the Shaikh, who goes on to deliver a short sermon about the rights of spouses, in an off handed attempt to remind everyone to treat their partners well.

My mother and Jihad, the biggest supporters of this union, are beaming as they mingle amongst friends and enjoy the evening. A handful of mother's friends are in attendance with their spouses, and everything is perfect as I take this leap of faith into the unknown.

I have already moved my things into the house, where Salem and I hope to make our home and raise our children close to their grandparents. Hala and Sajed, I know, would not have put up a fight had I opted for my own home, but leaving the decision up to me, I had chosen the comfort of their companionship in their twilight years, which made the couple extremely happy.

"*Yallah, ya 3arous,*" Maha whispers to me, as the night winds down and guests start to leave. "The car is waiting. You should get changed." My beautiful sister in law wears a dress in burgundy lace that sets off her light brown hair and hazel eyes. She is stunning. And she is my best friend. She advises me it's time to leave and head to the airport for our honeymoon flight to Fiji. I have never left my mother for any measure of time, so its with a heavy heart that I embrace her, this one final goodbye before I embark on this new journey in my life with my new husband.

PART 3 : 2010 - 2020

SALEM

Nada. Khairouz. Malek. Dalal.

Aaida has given me four children. Each one more beautiful than the next. And she has given me the greatest gift of all. Herself.

Nada was named by my mother. Tradition says the eldest born son is to name his children after his mother and father. Aaida wanted to keep with tradition and name our first born Hala, but mother would not hear of it.

"You'll do no such thing!" my mother announces when Aaida hands her the bundle and advises the newborn's name.

"Then you name her," Aaida offers. "If you won't let me name her after you, I want you to choose her name."

My mother had looked at Aaida with soft eyes, the edges glistening with tears. She loved Aaida like she did her own daughter, but this selfless act now cemented Aaida's place in my mother's heart. Aaida could do no wrong, and mother named our first born Nada.

With the birth of Nada, I saw a marked change in Aaida. She was near perfect before, but now she wordlessly commanded respect wherever she went, and I had developed a somewhat unhealthy obsession with my wife as she tethered herself to our new child. She stopped working at the shelter. She resigned at the clinic. And she went about raising our daughter with a gusto unparalleled to anything I'd even encountered before. There was no mention of day cares or pre-schools. Aaida voluntarily sacrificed the professional life she'd built for herself to raise Nada; to nurture and guide her, to teach her the basics of the English language, to be her mother and her friend. She was so invested in Nada, I realised being a mother was what she had needed all along-to love and be loved unconditionally and without the fear of rejection.

She did the same with each and every one of our children, giving them the love and attention and time they needed whilst building us a perfectly beautiful life. And when they went to school, it was Aaida who packed their lunches and did the school runs. Aaida who picked up any child who had fallen ill at school. Aaida who bounced them back and forth during soccer and netball practise. She never missed a beat. She gave our children their due, and in turn, we received four beautiful, well-mannered children who we could be proud of.

I am constantly astounded by Aaida. When I think there's no way that she can elevate herself in my eyes, she throws a spanner in the works and surprises the hell out of me. Even when the kids have grown and are in school, she does not go back to counselling. When I ask her whether or not she misses it, she regards me coolly and asks if I want her to go back to work.

"Hell, no," I tell her. "I'm just wondering if you miss it."

She looks out the large sliding glass windows thoughtfully then turns back to me before she answers.

"Counselling is mentally draining," she tells me. "I'd rather be a mother and nurture what I have here at home than be out trying to save the rest of the world while my family falls apart."

I get it. I understand exactly where she's coming from, and I see that she has thought long and hard about the choices she's made and what she's had to give up. Coming from a woman who worked herself to the bone before she had children to build the foundation of a professional life, it means a lot to me that she's given up her hard work to be present for our children. She has made the ultimate sacrifice, foregoing a career that was on the rise to be a mother, and I love her all the more for it.

"I have been thinking, though," she tells me, a twinkle in her eye.

"About what?"

"The children are older now, and they don't need me as much.

Perhaps I could take on a minor role in production." She watches for my reaction then quickly adds "while they're at school only- I'd still drop them off and pick them up."

"I have no doubt you can manage as many projects as your heart desires," I tell her, pecking her on the cheek. "But you know you don't ever have to work."

"I know that," she says, and is quick to correct me by saying "but I do need something to help pass the time."

"I can think of many things we can do together to pass the time," I announce, smiling mischievously as I lift her light frame and fling her over my shoulder.

AAIDA

My parent's marriage was over before it ever started.

It was a forced marriage, one in which my mother had no choice but to follow her father's instructions. When she sits and tells me, in pieces, the fractured mosaic of her life story, my heart trembles. Not in fear. But in anger.

My grandfather, *Allah yerhamou*, had 6 girls and was labelled *"Abu El Banaat"*, a moniker which served to mock his name and his standing in the village. My grandfather Amjad had been a man with a vain streak who had eternally sought to gain credence in societal circles. But he had so many factors working against him, not least of which were his 6 daughters. Eventually, he realised only one thing was attainable to him in order to lift his status amongst the other men in the village.

Travel.

Travel to a far away country.

It was what everyone worked toward in the day.

Travel equalled status. It made you wise and worldly, and you could always come back and talk of things others could only dream about, giving you a leg up in society. He believed it was his only hope in securing his long awaited standing amongst the men of the village.

And his only option lay in giving his daughter Aujene to Samer, who was the most ambitious suitor when it came to travel. My grandfather was sure that Samer would attain his wish to travel, and eventually, the whole extended family would be in a position to follow suit and travel also to Australia.

But my grandfather didn't plan well. His treatment of my mother had worsened over time, until they were subsequently estranged, which meant there'd be no travelling for anyone other than Samer and Aujene.

When my mother tells me about her miscarriage, my hand flies to my mouth, clamped shut in shock and horror as I watch her eyes glaze when she relates her story. There are no words for me to explain the feeling that envelopes me, and I swear if my grandfather were still alive, I'd probably kill him myself.

I cannot fathom what my mother has been through. I cannot stomach the pain she must have felt, the empty loneliness of a loveless marriage and the migration to a country where she didn't know a soul, nor did she speak the language. What must it have been like? To wander around and hear people speak in another tongue, never knowing what was being said. Not knowing how to communicate with others, having to struggle twice as hard as everyone else to prove herself. Her hair was different, her eyes and colouring so far removed from those of the Anglos with their fair skin and hair and blue eyes.

I recalled when I was a child she had a friend named Meghan, her one and only native Australian friend, and most likely one she never would have had if it had not been for Meghan living next door to us. I recall Meghan's husband, Wayne, and the way he would growl at me every time my path crossed his. He was a racist who was intolerant of change or any kind of cultural diversity, spending his days in a drunken stupor, his voice penetrating the walls between our house and theirs when he would get worked up over Meghan visiting our home. One day Meghan simply disappeared from our lives-she was there and then she was not, and it was many many years later, when I was much older, that my mother revealed to me that Meghan had been a victim of domestic violence and had orchestrated her own disappearance and moved to Queensland in order to get away from her abusive husband.

"We were both victims of domestic abuse," my mother told me, as she sat relaying Meghan's story.

I nodded my head to the side in question, silently asking for an explanation.

"She was physically and verbally abused. I don't know how the woman did it for so long."

"Most women never leave," I remind my mother. "It's a miracle that she got out when she did."

"Father never hit you," I say, and it's a question more than a statement. I don't recall a time from my childhood when my father was violent towards us. But I do know that my grandfather beat her multiple times, and one time it was so bad, it resulted in the miscarriage of her first child. That was the last time she saw her father, she tells me. When she woke up in the hospital, she refused to see him; she migrated to Australia without ever having spoken to him again and he went to his deathbed without her forgiveness.

Mother goes on to tell me that while father never hit her, he was emotionally abusive and controlling, deciding what she should wear, how she should style her hair. Making derogatory remarks about her friends. There were many opportunities that opened for her that father wouldn't allow her to accept; it was a never ending cycle in which he sought to repress her independence. There were the instances where he would push her up against the wall menacingly, or grab her arm too hard, but the most damaging had been his lack of empathy towards either myself or my mother, she reveals. And as I consider this, agreeing with her, I understand all that much better how hard it must have been for my mother to live with a man devoid of any emotion. If it had been damaging for me, how hard must it have been for my mother, to be stuck with someone like that, and know that there was no way out for her.

"Your father was not a pleasant man to be married to," she tells me.

"Yet, you finally got out."

She hums her acknowledgment that indeed, that is what happened, and looks off to a corner of the room. I know she is back there in the past, wrestling with her demons. There is so much she has not told me. So much that she cannot bring herself to tell me. Even knowing that my father is dead to me, she is still such an amazing woman that she would never willingly speak ill of him.

AAIDA

History is that thing that happens which we can never get back. It isn't always a bad thing. It teaches us who we are. Where we come from. And it's destined to repeat itself.

Sometimes I wondered what made people keep secrets.

Was it to protect the one you love?

Was it the shame of what happened and the fear of being judged?

Or was it simply that the thing that happened was so traumatic, you unconsciously push it to the back of your mind to forget, shifting from the status of secret and into memory loss.

I can tell you with a certain amount of clarity that that's what happened to my mother. For the longest time, she simply pushed the most painful memories of her life to a shaft in the back of her head and there she left them, forgetting they existed until my memories started triggering within me a series of images and dreams that warranted explanation.

That was when my mother came clean. But she definitely had to be reminded. My memories unearthed her long held lockbox of memories, unleashing a pandora's box of events so horrifying, I started to view my mother as somewhat of a martyr.

Her memories explained so much about the person I'd become. So much of why I was the way I was. But it was only when I was in my 40's that the truth began to come out.

My mother cleanses her soul by telling me things I should have known years ago.

I'm now 40, and I've gone my whole life existing in a sort of trance like fugue state.

She is reluctant to tell, and it is obvious the memories cause her deep pain. But eventually, she starts to tell me all about the boat trip from Beirut to Cyprus.

The leaky overcrowded boat. The dreadful weather. The change in wind conditions. All of these factors coupled together, forcing the boat to roll against the water as though a tidal wave had sprung forth from the depths of the sea, extending its arms and snatching the souls of those unfortunate enough to go overboard and sink to the bottom of the ocean.

19 lives lost at sea. 19 souls that were beings for a momentary breath of time, then extinguished by the hand of fate that lurked beneath the dark murky waters.

One of those souls had been my 8 month old brother, asleep in a crib that slid off the deck of the boat and into the sea, one of the first to go overboard. I had gone overboard also, but miraculously, had been hauled out of the deep dark sea by a young boy, a would be doctor who performed CPR on me until I spurted back to life.

I was one of the lucky few that went into the water and came back out again.

My mother's tears as she relays the story causes my heart to splinter into a million fragmented pieces as I sit quietly listening to her purge her secrets, the heat coursing through my body expanding to such an extent I thought my head would explode.

"After that, I clung to you for dear life. You were all I had left in the world. Not even your father...your father was never mine to begin with."

She tells me that everything that came before me was irrelevant. Everything that happened on that boat was traumatic enough as it was without having to live it day in and day out, so she had set the whole ordeal to the back of her mind and moved on. Australia was meant to be a fresh start.

"Your brother was only 8 months old," she tells me. "I was still nursing him. The pain of that loss was so immense, I thought the heartbreak would kill me."

I touch her hand softly and urge her on. I know she's never spoken of this with anyone. And maybe that's been part of the problem. The fact that she had unresolved trauma and wasn't able to take comfort in anyone.

"You were the only thing that kept me going. Even your father, it felt like he just shrugged it off and went on with life like nothing had happened. I was devastated. The pain of that loss was so acute. Milk leaked from my breasts for many weeks afterward, and I would find myself in the embarrassing situation of walking down the street with a stained shirt. I didn't know how to explain what happened."

I shook my head helplessly and looked away momentarily, biting my lip to hold back the tears that threatened to flow. If this was causing me *that* much pain, I shuddered to think how much heartache my mother still felt over this experience.

"I lost so much on that boat," my mother whispers. "Just by getting on that boat, I lost my family. It would be 15 years before I saw them again. I lost my son. I almost lost you. And I lost my soul-I lost it on that journey when it sunk to the bottom of the sea."

SALEM

When Aaida tells me she wants to take a trip to Lebanon with her mother, I regard her with some curiosity. She has never left me or the children, and now she wants to take a trip with her mother. Which I'm not fussed about, but it is so far out of character for her to leave us, I wonder if there's more going on than she's telling me.

"It's just for two weeks," she tells me.

"Is there something I need to know?" I ask her.

She shakes her head and folds a loose strand of hair behind her ear. She is still the most beautiful woman I have ever seen. After almost 20 years of marriage, I am still deeply in love with her. And I know all about her past.

When she first told me about her cousin Khaled, the way she spoke of him, it was so obvious they had been in love with each another and it seemed obvious to everyone that they would end up together. But one event, one tragic event, pushed them into the darkness and nothing ever brought them back from it.

This all came about when we first got married and Aaida got very sick and was suffering from an infection that left her in a state of delirium for the better part of a week. She was pregnant with our first child, and I stayed by her side the whole time, holding a wet cloth to her forehead to stem her rising temperature and praying for her speedy recovery. When, in her state, she started mumbling and kept repeating the name "Khaled" over and over again, I can't say I wasn't disappointed. I was. And I was more than curious. But there would be time for that conversation later. Right now, I had to concentrate on my wife's health and ensuring she got better as quickly as possible.

When Aaida was well again and everything was back to normal, we sat at the dining table having lunch together, and I put my fork down towards the end of our meal and watched my wife quietly. She still wasn't 100% recovered, and this was apparent in both her lack of appetite and energy. Morning sickness had also set in, and she was finding it hard to keep anything down.

"How are you feeling?" I asked.

She looked up at me, then pushed her plate away, before telling me she was tired.

"Do you want to sleep?"

She shook her head and exhaled. She was sick of sleeping. She just wanted to feel normal again.

"I want to ask you something," I told her, and she watched me cautiously, waiting, as though expecting *something*. "I'll only ask you this once, we'll talk about it, then the matter will die here and we will never mention it again. But I need your honesty."

"You've always had my honesty," she said, frowning at me.

"Who is Khaled?" I asked.

She blanched, then let out a deep breath she probably didn't even know she'd been holding in. And that's when she told me all about her cousin Khaled. There is a far away look in her eyes, as though she is back there, in her birth country, reliving the events which eventually led her back here and straight into my arms.

"Do you still love him?" I ask, my fists clenched together and my chin resting on them. I am a man of logic, and I could understand it if she still harboured feelings for him, but I'd be lying if I said the fear of her telling me she was still in love with him didn't squeeze the breath out of me. At the same time, I wondered about the foolish man who had once held Aaida's heart in his hand like a bird then set it free.

She shakes her head, then looks up at the ceiling and rights herself in her chair. "I love him in the sense that he was once an important part of my life," she explained. "But that's over now. I'm married to you and you're the only one that occupies the space in my heart and my mind."

And that was the last time that Khaled's name was ever muttered in our home.

If I were a lesser man, I'd be very worried about her going back. But I'm safe and secure in the knowledge that Aaida loves me and our family. If anything, she probably needs to make this trip to get the closure she needs. And she'll be with her mother, so she's in safe hands.

"Are you sure you don't want me to come with you?" I ask, and she shakes her head, reminding me again that she'll only be gone for two weeks, and she has so much to pack into those two weeks with her aunts.

I wonder if she'll take time out to visit with her father. I've heard he's sick, and I wonder if this fact has softened Aaida towards him. I know the subject of her father is a sore point for Aaida, and she rarely, if ever, brings him up. But to keep the peace now, I don't bring him up. Instead, I rise, stand behind her chair and pull it back, lifting her hand so she rises. "Let's get you to bed, princess."

AAIDA

Beirut has changed.

The people have changed.

The driver that takes us from Beirut to Tripoli (he'll only go as far as Tripoli, he warns us) is a pot-bellied, beady eyed little man who doesn't shut up the whole 3 hour drive towards Tripoli. He tells us all about modern Beirut, as though it is our first time visiting. He explains the lack of electricity, the garbage strewn in the streets, the poverty in many areas of the country. He just won't shut up. And I don't correct him and tell him we're well versed in all matters Lebanon.

Once in Tripoli, he tries to take advantage of us by asking an exorbitant amount of money for having brought us this far. I would have willingly paid him the $400 to keep his mouth shut on the drive, but having sat through that torture, there was no way he was getting one dollar more than the customary $100US fare that is charged.

Pretty soon, as we're standing on the sidewalk arguing with the driver, a small circle of onlookers has formed, and it grows and grows, holding up foot traffic until a parking attendant arrives to quell the crowds. The parking attendant is aghast at what the taxi driver is claiming his fare to be. The milling crowd, a down-trodden population who have been taken advantage of by their own government and every other Arab country under the sun, will not stand for guests in their country to be treated this way and a melee erupts as a group of men jostle the driver's car and proceed to inflict damage. The attendant, knowing very well the taxi driver will end up with no car if this continues, pops the boot and removes our bags before he shoves the driver in the car, throws his $100 fare at him and commands him to drive.

I am proud of my Lebanese brothers and sisters. Proud that they rose and took control of one situation in which they could make a change, no matter how small that situation was. Another driver steps forward and offers to drive us the 35 minutes to Tul Ghosn. The thing about the Lebanese; their hospitality knows no bounds. Well, most Lebanese, anyway.

In Tul Ghosn, the taxi driver won't take our money, and apologises profusely for the behaviour of the driver from Beirut. He makes us promise to enjoy our trip as payment for his services and is on his way before we are able to offer him tea.

I look down the long winding road in reflection. So much has changed. Yet nothing has changed. Instead of Aunt Samiya, its Meray, my aunt Kawkab's daughter, who peeks her head over the balcony and sees us standing by the front door. She lets out a yelp and almost falls over the railings in surprise. Before I know it, I can hear her clapping down the stairs like a bulldozer and she flings the front door open and grabs me to her, hugging me in a tight embrace. She enfolds my mother in her arms as we exchange salutations and it is then that I hear the shuffling of my tayta Tala's feet. She has one hand against the wall to steady herself as she walks toward us, telling us she hears familiar voices.

My mother falls at her mother's feet, kissing them, kissing the ground her mother walks on, so overwhelmed with gratitude that she was able to make this trip to see her mother again.

Tayta Tala breaks my heart. She went blind early in life, and though she had a good network of family supporting her, it was just one more burden to carry after everything she'd already been through. My grandmother holds our faces between her hands as her fingers roam over the ridges and patterns of our skin, smiling, her eyes blurry with tears. She is so happy we're here. She has extended family surrounding her, but she's always extremely grateful and happy with the visits from "her Australian girls"

"I can't believe you're really here," she keeps saying over

and over again, then admonishes us for not telling her we were coming so she could prepare a spread for us and have a welcoming committee waiting for our arrival.

"*Ma'laysh tayta,* we're here now," I whisper sing into her hair as I hold her close and feel the wetness of her tears fall against the side of my face. I breathe her in, her scent burrowing deep within the space reserved for my soul. "We're here now, that's all that matters."

AAIDA

Khaled is the first of my cousins to come and visit us. I haven't seen him in 20 years. Yet it's as though it was only yesterday that I last saw him and he was teaching me how to shoot and how to pray and how to ride a horse. When I see him, the years melt away and I almost-almost-fall into his embrace with the yearning need to recall something of my youth.

He still looks the same, although older, and his eyes still crinkle at the edges when he smiles. His stormy grey eyes hold a wealth of history within them, and I am transported to the past, where we had once held the world in our hands.

We sit and talk for a while, and we exchange stories. He tells me about his life, and I tell him about mine. There is a gaping void looming above our heads with the unspoken words of a past history. Do we just ignore the elephant in the room? That the last time we saw one another, he was banishing me and I was literally holding my head in pain and screaming that I wouldn't leave him. Do we avoid the missing years in between then and now and simply pretend that nothing happened?

When he asks me why I came back, I tell him it's because mother wanted to visit. Due to work commitments, Jihad couldn't make this trip, so instead, I brought her. I also wanted to see my tayta Tala, who was getting on in life, and make sure that she was okay.

So many things were left unsaid, so much history unresolved, but as I looked at Khaled, my one and only first true love, nostalgia thrumming through my veins, I understood that the yearning that enveloped me was one that wished to connect to my youth. People had a tendency to romanticise their youth.

Maybe that's the way they prefer to remember their lives.

I tell him all bout my husband and my children. He tells me he has 3 children also. I've heard that he's doing very well for himself, although his marriage doesn't seem to be a happy one. I understand why he married Soraya, but I feel sorry for him because I know that ultimately, he sacrificed himself and any chance of a happy future when he married her.

After he leaves, I settle into my seat on the swing and look out at the valley. Not much has changed, except the addition of more houses scattered along the meadows. In a few years, this beautiful, organic view would be gone as the landscape changed, giving way to new builds. One day, this would all be gone, and life in Tul Ghosn as it had once been would cease to exist. Already, we were seeing that with the mass exodus of families toward the city. Houses stood empty or were rented out as the village saw growth and could no longer accomodate the needs of a modernised population. Families wanted easy access to universities for their children. Land farming had ceased to become the main source of income for most in the village as parcels of land were sold off to the highest bidder and new houses sprouted up in their place. A few orange and olive groves still remained, though even these were not tended to as they once had been.

I think of tayta Tala, alone in this old house, now too big to accomodate only her. She would live out her days alone in this home, refusing to leave.

"Others have not been so lucky," she tells me, her wrinkled hand waving through the air theatrically. "They have been displaced from their homes, forced to flee with only a few meagre belongings. I am lucky enough to live here in peace; not to be forced to make that compromise. Why would I leave?"

"I worry about you, *tayta,*" I tell her, thinking of all the times I had begged her to migrate to Australia to be with us, only to have her shoot down that plan.

"Why would I leave my way of life, *ya binti*?" she asks. "I'm old and frail, there's no way I could adapt to a new environment at my age. Besides, this is where I go to cling to my memories," she smiles, enjoying the view with me.

"I want you to meet my children, your great grandchildren."

"Then you bring them here. There is plenty of room for everyone. We were a family of 8 squeezed into two rooms, I'm sure we can manage."

Tayta Tala is my heart and my world. The thought of her one day not being here leaves me with a choking feeling. We're all going to die one day, I know that, but tayta is the bridge between the past and the present. The one constant in all our lives.

"Don't you worry about me," she says, as though reading my mind. What tayta lacks in sight, she more than makes up for in insight. "Samiya's children are always here to check up on me. As are my daughters. And my grand children. And Khaled..." she pauses and regards me thoughtfully, then starts again "...God bless his heart, he is always checking in on me to make sure I have everything I could possibly need."

Tayta Tala is the only one not afraid to speak Khaled's name in my presence. She is the only one in my family who will say it like it is. That's what I've always loved about her - she possesses a certain type of wisdom that ensures she knows exactly what to say and when to say it.

"He never got over you, you know," she tells me.

"He married his cousin Soraya. He chose her over me."

My grandmother clucks her tongue and tsks, lifting her chin in a backward nod to signify her disagreement. "Don't let your ego cloud your thoughts, Aaida. He only married her when you refused to come back and he realised he would never see you again. She has always been his second choice, and she knows that."

I knew that what tayta said was true. It just still hurt, although the pain had diminished over the years and I was now comfortably settled into my life with Salem and our children.

"Twenty years ago, when I thought about my future, this is not what I had envisioned for myself," I tell her. Her eyes soften as she looks towards me.

"Are you not happy in your life?" She asks me.

"Contrary, I'm very happy. It's just not how I imagined my life to be. When I thought about my future, Khaled was always in that picture."

"Just goes to show, Aaida. You plan, I plan, and God is the best of planners."

KHALED

Aaida is more amazing than I remember her. When I first lay eyes on her again, after some 20 years, my heart stutters and I am transported back to the past. A past that refuses to leave me alone.

I've tried to make a home with Soraya, but the ghost of Aaida has shadowed us in everything we do. No fault of Aaida's. Not even my fault, really, but Soraya just could not seem to let the memory of Aaida go quietly without a fight.

She sits and tells me all about her life in Australia, that she has 3 girls and a boy and has given up her career to make a home for them. She is a proud mother, and I can see that she is happy. It makes me happy that she is happy. Too much time has passed for me to hold on to any ill-feeling toward her, and while I am still fond of her, I know my heart no longer belongs to her and her heart no longer belongs to me. Once upon a time, we were, and now we're not. We're two cousins with a shared history meeting up after many many years and exchanging updates on where we are in life. Still, I am a man after all, and I can admit that she is still beguiling to this day.

Soraya was rude enough to decline coming with me on this visit. For someone who is jealous of Aaida, I don't understand how she wouldn't want to come and keep her eye on us when we met after all these years, but that's neither here or there. I will ensure she comes to visit my cousin before she leaves, if only to let Aaida know that she holds no ill will toward her.

When I rise to leave, Aaida rises too and thanks me for coming to visit her. My visit means the world to her; I know this without her having to say it. And I know this visit was all about us. Not her, not me. But us. This is the closure we needed, to finally know that we're okay and we've both moved on and neither of us harbours any resentment toward the other.

AAIDA

I have reached some measure of closure during this trip.

Soraya comes to visit me after I have been in Lebanon for more than two weeks. She begged off attending a lunch invitation when aunt Farida invited us to her home, but now she sits in the garden with me at tayta's house, although I can clearly see that she's not here by choice. I could literally kill Khaled for putting her through this, but I understand why it had to happen.

Her reception to me is somewhat lukewarm, and I can see that, even after all these years, she is still weary of me, and I can safely say she maybe even despises me. I just want to shake her and tell her it's been twenty years. People don't just pick up where they left off, especially when both sides have forged lives themselves and now have families and other responsibilities.

Any attempt I make at conversation with her is answered in short one or two word sentences, and I can see her reluctance to be sitting here with me. She is still beautiful, Soraya, with her golden brown waves peeking out from under her scarf and her honey coloured eyes framed by dark lashes. However, there is something ugly about her. She wears a scowl and rarely smiles. Her attitude leaves much to be desired, and I can't imagine that she and Khaled have much to talk about with her lacklustre personality.

To break any lingering tension, aunt Farida is also in attendance, sipping her tea quietly as she watches the unfolding drama unravel with interest. This, I know, was Khaled's doing; he had correctly predicted there would be some resistance from his wife in meeting me, so he had brought his mother along to safeguard the visit, hoping that Soraya would put her jealousies to bed once and for all so they could finally live in peace.

I am nothing if not courteous, smiling at Soraya as she takes another sip of her *ahwi*. She holds her cup aloft with her pinky jutting out, aiming for regal, but instead comes off as trying too hard to mould herself into something she is not. She continues to resist me verbally at every question I ask, yet I remain calm and collected as I continue to try to break the ice.

Aunt Farida is fascinated by the interaction, and I can see her watching us carefully in between snatches of conversation with my mother and great aunt Samiya. Aunt Farida, I know, has never been Soraya's biggest fan, at times cursing the woman because she has brought such misery to Khaled's life.

"It's not right that my son feels he needs to spend so much time away from home in order to avoid his wife," she tells my mother during one conversation when they don't realise I am at the kitchen window a few metres behind them as they sit outside enjoying a rare day of sunshine. I try to move my legs, but as though of their own accord, they are cemented to the ground and I stand glued to my spot, listening.

"I thought Soraya *wanted* to marry Khaled," my mother replies.

"Of course she wanted to marry Khaled!" Farida scoffs. "Every girl wanted to marry Khaled! But she believes what she wanted and what she got were two different things."

"*Kheir, ekhti,* is there something wrong with Khaled?" My mother asks.

There is a long silence, and I wonder if they have stopped talking because they know I am standing right there. Although I cannot see them sitting beyond the window, I can hear them as aunt Farida sighs heavily then explains.

"In her mind, Soraya always sees Aaida. Poor Aaida lost so much when she left Lebanon, none of it her fault, and still she pays the price for the past. For some reason, Soraya cannot let go of the thought of Aaida being in Khaled's mind and heart."

"*Shu, ya3ni,* does he talk about her often?" The tone of my mother's voice tells me she's confused and uncertain what is happening between Khaled and Soraya, and what my role, either direct or indirect, is in their relationship.

"*Wlek, la3!!*" Farida argues, a little forcefully. "Once he got married, he never so much as uttered Aaida's name on his lips."

"Then WHAT?!?" My mother shrieks, a little exasperated.

"*Wlek, whatee sawtik, ekhti!*" My aunt Farida admonishes my mother and tells her to lower her voice.

"I just want to understand what my daughter has to do with all this. Has she been talking to him this whole time and I didn't know?"

"*Wlek, la3 ekhti. Sma3eeni.* It's all in Soraya's head. She tells me he doesn't look at her the way he looked at Aaida, he doesn't talk to her as they did. He doesn't love her the way he still loves Aaida. But it's all in her mind and she can't let go of his past, even knowing that Aaida has moved on and they no longer have any connection to one another."

"*Yiii, hayda marad,*" my mother says "you should get Aaida to talk to her. She's good at talking people out of their head."

I have heard, through numerous conversations played out in my presence, that their marriage has not been a happy one, although it hasn't been for lack of trying. Khaled has given her everything she needs and wants, and has invested his soul into making his marriage work, but Soraya's apparent immaturity and inability to let go of the past has hung like a vaporous cloud above their heads.

I understand that this is through no doing of my own, but can't help but feel sorry for her. Khaled was what she always wanted, but once she married him, she realised she never really had him. She finally understood that she would always take a backseat to the memory of me, even though Khaled had tried for years to dispel these thoughts from her mind.

"*Aaaa, ya!*" My great aunt Samiya finally pipes up, irritation evident in her tone. There is a lull in conversation. She has aged but she hasn't. In the twenty years I've been away, a multitude of lines have appeared on her face, wrinkles etched on her skin like the ridges of valleys as time caught up to her. Her back is slightly stooped and she seems much shorter than I remember her, but this could be my mind playing tricks on me.

The one thing that hasn't changed about aunt Samiya is her unfiltered way of throwing things into the ring. If she has something to say, she will say it, no matter who gets hurt.

Holding nothing back, she turns to Soraya and looks at her with a lack of empathy. I can almost see the steam rising from aunt Samiya's head, and I know, I know, that she has been holding something in for a long long time and there is about to be an explosion. Aunt Farida tugs her sleeve to prevent the tirade, but aunt Samiya merely shrugs her off, lifts her cup of replenished *ahwi* to her lips, and downs it in one swallow, as though looking for her liquid courage. I can see she is somewhat doubting the wisdom of what she is about to do, but she forges on, undoubtedly realising she has nothing to lose. Maybe something to gain.

"The woman has been sitting here for the better part of an hour trying to make conversation with you, and all you can say is *"la3, mniha, ma ba3ref, ya rayt"*. I can count on two hands the words you've uttered today."

Soraya's face turns a deep crimson and I almost feel sorry for her. Almost. But she brought it on herself. Aunt Farida's mouth is open in a silent "o", then promptly shut again when my mother nudges her and wordlessly, using their own form of eye language, tells her to keep her mouth shut.

"*Ya3ni, shu baddik?*" Aunt Samiya continues. "He married you, didn't he? He gave you a home, and children. He respects you. The man has given you *more than you deserve* for all the misery you've put him through.

"*Layki, Soraya,*" and aunt Samiya holds up a long spindly finger and wags it in Soraya's direction in warning. "I'm going to tell you what no-one else will! The man married you, not her!" And she points in my direction, and there is a venomous lurch in her tone as she refers to me. A lot of people were disappointed that Khaled didn't marry me, but *naseeb* is *naseeb*. "He left her and he married you. Concentrate on that. Concentrate on building your home, a loving home, and let the man live in peace. Give Aaida the respect she deserves; she did nothing wrong. And move on with your life with your husband. Stop fixating on the past."

Soraya lifts her chin, somewhat defiantly, and I can see that she has no intention of listening to aunt Samiya or taking her advice. Everyone realises this also, and aunt Samiya's ire is fuelled by Soraya's nonchalance as she crosses her arms across her chest and turns her face toward the wadi, choosing not to entertain any further conversation. I wonder what it is about her, that she sits on her high and mighty throne, believing herself untouchable, while her corrupt mind vindicates her delusions.

"*Layki, wlee,*" aunt Samiya shrieks like a banshee, this time moving forward in her chair to ensure that she is being heard loud and clear. I don't think there's a person within a 3 mile radius that does not hear her. She has a point to make, and she intends to get her point across by any means necessary. "*Soraya!*" She screeches, and the woman turns back to her with a mix of fear and surprise on her face. She is not used to people addressing her this way, I realise, and I wonder how soft Khaled has been with her. He has always been the calm, patient type. "*Wallahi,* I am warning you. Don't think you are above what other women have gone through. If you keep up this attitude and this behaviour toward your husband, I guarantee you, he will take a second wife. And let it be known that I will be the first one dancing at his wedding!"

AUJENE

I call Jihad to ask his advice, as I do with all family matters concerning us, and he in turn advises me to do whatever I feel is necessary to get my own closure. Was he worried about me? I don't think so. He knew, and I knew, that I was not the same woman I had been some 25 years ago. I was a different person, a stronger person, and I could do this.

Aaida refuses to come with me, but I am determined to do this. So I wake up early in the morning, even before she is up, and I make my way on foot through the village until I reach a huge wooden gate. I pull on the handle, the gate swings open and I enter into a courtyard and look toward the house beyond. Samer has built his family a beautiful house, and on either side of the house, more houses for his sons to live in once they are married. I know this is the house, because I've driven past the gate numerous times and people still like to point out the most extravagant villa in the village.

I knock on the front door and wait for someone to open. It's not too early that the household wouldn't yet be awake, and I am waiting for a mere few seconds before the great door lurches open and I am looking at a foreign woman who I presume to be the maid. I announce myself and she shows me into a waiting room and brings me *ahwi*.

"Ahla! Ahla! Ahla, Em Aaida."

I am greeted by an unfamiliar yet boisterous voice and I rise to face the door as a woman, barely a few years younger than me, comes into the room, rolling down the sleeves of her *abaya* as she does. She clutches my hands in her own and looks into my face, smiling, and welcomes me again. It is obvious she knows exactly who I am, even though we've never met. And she doesn't seem in the least bit concerned to finally be meeting me.

I know I should feel something as I look at the woman who replaced me in my ex-husband's life, but I feel nothing. No emotion, no animosity. Nothing. It's like two strangers meeting for the first time, who will probably never meet again.

"I'm sorry to be visiting under such circumstances," I tell the woman, as we take our seats and she pours more ahwi. She scoffs and welcomes me again into her home.

"I heard that Samer...Abu Emad," I correct "is ill and wanted to come and check on him."

"Of course, Em Aaida, that is your right," she tells me and I don't know whether or not to be irritated that she keeps calling me Em Aaida. I feel as though she may be taking a dig at me for not having a boy, and this is her way of twisting the knife in my gut. But she's too nice and too civil to be that evil person, and I put my reservations aside as we rise and she shows me to Samer's room.

I almost don't recognise him, and this is apparent in the sharp gasp I emit when I see him. He is sitting up in the bed with an oxygen mask wrapped around his mouth, the only movement that of his eyes as they widen then follow me as I cross the room towards him. His wife lowers the mask and turns to me, letting me know he can't speak much, and asking me to limit his exertion.

"I will leave you alone for a few minutes," she says, indicating a button by the side of the bed if I required anything.

Samer has aged so much, he's almost unrecognisable. His wiry frame is sunken into the bed, and he is a relic of his former self as the cancer takes hold of him. His hair has taken on a stringy texture, the colour of salt and pepper matted to his thinning scalp.

"I just came to check up on you," I tell him, looking at him sadly. No matter what our history was, the man still deserved to die with some dignity and grace and above all, forgiveness. He moves his lips to form words, but for a long time, nothing comes out.

"It's okay, you don't need to say anything. I just wanted to stop by and check up on you before we leave again."

His eyes go wide and he tries again to speak, but I know he's probably finding it hard to do so. I want to make this short so he doesn't overexert himself, so I say what I came to say.

"I want you to know that I forgive you," I start. "I forgive you, Samer, and I'm sorry if I ever wronged you."

I aim for a tight smile at him, then turn to take my leave. I am almost at the door when I hear, low but surely, something that makes me turn back to him, unsure if I heard right. But when I am facing him, he repeats the word, and I'm sure of what I'm hearing. It may be a little distorted because he's not well, but Samer definitely said "Ada". It was probably all he was capable of. I turned back and regarded him with soft, moist eyes. It was ironic that he had to be at death's door before he asked about his firstborn.

"She's well," I tell him. "She's married with three girls and a boy."

He looks at me, as if questioning why she didn't come, and in that moment, I feel so sorry for him, something stabs at my heart.

"She would've come if she could, but she was unable to make this trip to Lebanon with me," I lie. If I could offer him one last consolation, it would be that his daughter was too far away to visit, not that she didn't want to.

FARIDA

When I look at my niece Aaida, I am taken back in time, to a place many many years ago, where youth resided and happiness whispered unfiltered through the air. She is here but for a short while, with my sister Aujene, visiting in what I believe may be her last trip for a long time. She managed to stay away for twenty years; what's to stop her staying away for another twenty?

She's found happiness, I am told. With the perfect Lebanese man who worships the ground she walks on. I don't begrudge her that. No. After the last time she left Lebanon, crying her heart out because my son was sending her away, I had, with all my heart, wished only the best for her. Even if that was at my expense. Even if that was at Khaled's expense. And even though she wouldn't return his calls, he was the first to marry. And his cousin Soraya, of all people!

I look at her wistfully as she stands on the hill above the olive grove, her hair flowing behind her like a halo. She is still so beautiful and youthful, the only noticeable change in her the curve of her hips after childbirth, which only gives her an even more feminine aura. I watch her now as she looks out over the valleys and the peaks, her face awash with memories, and I wonder what she is thinking as she turns in a semi circle.

"She's looking at the land her grandfather owned which I pointed out to her many years ago," my sister Moraya says, as though reading my mind. "She remembers every plot I indicated."

"Do you think she'll ever be back?" I ask, and I am suddenly consumed by an overwhelming sadness. Aaida is the loss we never really got over. It just feels like we never really had closure with her, and things ended not exactly the way that anyone had planned.

"I don't know, *ekhti*," Moraya tells me. "She has her own life to live now. She has a husband, children to consider."

"*Akh,* ya Moraya, where did the years ago?" I ask, somewhat sadly.

"This is life, *ekhti.* You know this better than anyone. Nothing comes to pass but that it has already been written."

KHALED

When I've thought about Aaida over the years, it's been with a yearning for a time past that I knew without a doubt I could never get back. After the incident that claimed my brother Turan, my life quickly went downhill as I made a series of choices, most of them mistakes, that could never be reversed.

The first mistake I made was sending Aaida away. That was the one decision I made that I would live to regret til my dying day. The loss of Aaida had been too great a sacrifice, and I had paid for it dearly. She had haunted my days and nights, her face embedded in my memory so vividly, at times I thought I would go mad at her absence. When the painful weight of her memory became too much to bear, I made my second mistake, another which I would live to regret.

In a feeble attempt to designate Aaida to the history books, I took Soraya as my wife. She was my cousin, and had it not been for Aaida's entry into my life, she would have been the likely choice as dictated by nomadic custom. First born of one brother would marry the first born of another. That's just the way it was. And though I had worked tirelessly to break the shackles of our outdated ancestral traditions, I myself had fallen into that trap and married the woman who society dictated I should marry, not the woman I was madly in love with.

For all her yearning and pining for me, which I was not immune to over the years, Soraya betrayed herself with her bitterness. I tried my hardest to make her happy, but she held on, as though clinging to a lifeline, to the memory of Aaida, quietly dragging my Australian cousin into our home. I could have so easily put Aaida out of mind, and in part, that was why I married Soraya. But my wife just kept dragging up the past, over and over and over again, until the memory of Aaida was sitting at our dining table and sleeping in our bed. Soraya's constant reminders only brought Aaida to the forefront of my mind, ensuring I never forgot her, no matter how hard I tried.

In a way, I pitied myself. For more than 20 years, I have lived with a woman who knew no happiness, no love, no warmth. She is not maternal in the least bit toward our children. She is not loving and caring as a wife should be toward her husband. And instead of building a kingdom, she works tirelessly to tear down her home. She is filled with so much misery that she brings only misery to everyone around her.

Seeing Aaida on this, her latest trip, 20 years after I sent her away, has given me time to reflect. She seems happy. She *is* happy. When I ask her, she tells me all about her husband and her children, what she's done in the time she's been away, and the way she's lived her life. When she speaks, she holds up an invisible mirror and shows me what my life could have been like. There is a thick lump in my throat that I can't swallow past. I am happy for Aaida, happy that she's found tremendous happiness in her life, and found her footing after so much heart ache.

Aaida's trip has brought with it clear revelations that I understand I could benefit from. Aaida did not let my actions defeat her. When I sent her away, she was in a very bad place, but she rose above that. She opted not to wallow in the past and went on with her life. She met someone and made the most of what was right there before her, ultimately falling in love with a man who I hear has put her on a mantle and treats her like a queen. Aaida deserves nothing less. She deserves so much more. She deserved better than what I did to her. Yet here she is, forgiving the past and talking to me as though that ugly thing that happened never had. She is the greater person, and her humility has humbled me, giving me so much to consider.

I've sent Soraya to meet with Aaida, hoping that my wife can finally put her jealousies to rest and let us live out the remainder of our lives in peace. When she returns, her lips are pursed and she is furious. My mother follows her quickly into the house and shakes her head in defeat. I can see it did not go well. I kiss my mother's forehead and thank her, and she holds my left arm lovingly and looks up at me with sadness in her eyes. I hate myself for causing her such disappointment. Even if I hadn't married Aaida, Soraya would not have been my mother's first choice for me. And she had been right. There was something not right about Soraya, and I had spent many years trying to decipher the mechanics of her brain, but there was obviously something wrong with her. Even my grandmother Farah, God rest her soul, had warned me to her dying breath that Soraya (her own granddaughter) was cursed and would never make me happy.

"*Ya ebni, ya Khaled,*" she had wheezed. "We are all here on this earth but fleetingly. You deserve some happiness. Don't let that *3aerbi* (Scorpion) strip you of the most basic of human rights. You are light, and you deserve to walk in the light. Her bitterness will lead you into the dark."

When I enter the bedroom, Soraya is sitting on the bed looking out the window. "How did it go?" I ask her.

"Another humiliation in a long string of humiliations," Soraya mutters bitterly. I sigh and ask her what happened. If anything, I have always been patient with Soraya and always given her the opportunity to speak her voice. Even when what she spouts is rubbish, I have never sought to suppress her opinion. I listen wordlessly, then counter her words with commonsense.

"What happened?" she scoffs, shrugging a shoulder as if to say "What *didn't* happen?"

"Tell me," I say, but it comes out almost a whisper.

"I just want to know when it will all end!" she screams, rising to face me and grabbing the side of her head and pulling at her hair. She has started with her madness again.

"When what will end?"

"AAIDA! When will *that woman* leave us to live in peace?!?"

"Soraya, what are you talking about?" I ask, walking toward her and forcing her to lower her hands from her head. She snatches her hands away from me and points a stern finger in my direction.

"You still love her!" she accuses. "You *all* still love her. Everyone ganged up on me and defended her, and you should have seen the condescending way she was talking to me! And your pitiful aunt Samiya couldn't stop. She *wouldn't* stop! Blaming me for everything, when it's been that cursed woman living in your heart and your mind this whole time!"

I listen to Soraya but say nothing. My silence only seems to agitate her as her mind somehow betrays her and tells her that my silence makes me complicit in her misery. I stuff my hands in my pockets and let her rant on until eventually, she is thumping her fists into my chest when she gets no reaction. I have been here a thousand times or more. It is the same scenario playing over and over again, without change, and my mind asks how much misery can one person actually hold? Soraya breeds misery. She will never be happy. She thrives on pain and anguish and the perception that she is the "wronged one." This hasn't changed in 20 years, and I come to the realisation that it will never change. My grandmother's words play over in my mind. She died last year, about the same time that a fragile dam within me started to erode.

"Where are you going?" She asks, as I turn and start to walk away. I have never walked away from her, regardless of the circumstances. I have always heard her out, then tried my hardest to calm her down. Right now, I realise that I don't care to do so. I know I made a mistake marrying Soraya, but there's no reason to compound that mistake by perpetuating it.

I half turn when I am across the room and regard her carefully. I can't be a coward about this. I turn and face her completely, and she is silent as she waits for me to say something. I have veered off the usual script and she is uncertain what happens next.

"Have you finished?" I ask her softly.

She says nothing but lifts her chin and juts it out defiantly in that way she has of telling me she'll be finished when she's finished.

"I want to make one thing clear," I tell her, and again I realise that I'm talking to her as though I'm talking to a child. Maybe this has been the issue all along, that I have not been forceful enough with my words and I haven't drawn boundaries that she was not to cross. But after more than 20 years of marriage, I think it's a little late for that. "Aaida left 20 years ago and I married you. I have never so much as uttered her name; you're the one that keeps bringing her up..."

Before I can go any further, she screams out, for all the world to hear "You were in love with her! You still are!"

"She's married," I remind her. I'm still the level-headed one in this room. "I'm married. We lead two very seperate lives and all we are to each other now is cousins."

"That *sharmouta* would leave her husband in a heartbeat if..."

Three things happen all at once and Soraya does not get a chance to finish her sentence.

My deceased grandmother's words *"her bitterness will lead you into the dark"* rings in my ears.

I realise there have been no boundaries drawn in our marriage, yet Soraya has just crossed a very steep one.

Then I slap her. Hard.

I have never in my life laid a hand on a woman. I'm surprised just as much as she is, but my fury over-rides everything. At the end of the day, Soraya has just called my cousin-my COUSIN-a whore, and that's unacceptable. I shouldn't have let my anger get the better of me, and I never should have hit her, there's no excusing my behaviour, but I can't undo what has come to pass.

Soraya gasps and raises her hand to her rapidly reddening cheek. She looks at me in disbelief. Never did she think things would escalate to the point where I would lay a hand on her, but I've reached my threshold.

Soraya is the architect of her own demise.

The next day, I order her into the car and drive the short distance to the cleric's office, where I declare my divorce from her. She is stunned, almost spell-bound by the ease with which

I have tossed her aside, and I know that's not what she was expecting. The thing about having so much power is it gets you places. No sooner have I divorced her than I know the Shaikh is already lodging the paperwork. There'll be no feet dragging on this one. I lay out Soraya's future as it will look to her, holding up my hand when she tries to open her mouth and say something. The look in my eyes must tell her everything she needs to know, because she thinks better of arguing and shrinks back. She has finally found her place.

She will live in the family home, surrounded by her grown children, while I will retreat to my parent's home. She will receive a generous monthly allowance and all her household needs will be met. I'm allowing her to retain the maid and the car. She looks down at her lap sadly but says nothing. She's trying to pass for remorseful, but if I know anything about Soraya, it's that she doesn't have a sorry bone in her body.

When we return to the village, no longer husband and wife, I take my keys out, removing the key to the front door and placing it on the console. I tell her to get the maid to pack my things and send them next door to my parent's house. The unfortunate irony here is that I will still see her on a regular basis; there's no escaping that in a village as tight as ours, and the home I've built right next door to my parents.

I tell her not to contact me unless it's regarding the children, and turn to walk away.

"You never defended me the way you defended her," she whispered as I walked away. I stop and pause, then turn back and face her. I owe her this at least - my truth.

"You never gave us the chance to be anything worth fighting for, Soraya. From the moment I married you, Aaida has been that invisible third person in our bed. And you put her there, all on your own."

I turn and walk away. I don't want to entertain any more of Soraya's madness. I don't want to crack open the window that will rehash 20 years of misery. What's past is past, and I refuse to drown in a sea of self-pity of someone else's making.

A heavy burden lifts from my shoulders as I get into my car and start down the road out of Dhar Khamra and onto the road to Tul Ghosn. This was the road well travelled as it linked between our two villages and led me to Aaida. I smile nostalgically at the memory of us. Aaida is already gone, but her memory lingers. And if there's one person who can set my soul at ease and grant me respite from my aching heart, it would be

my grandmother Tala with her words of wisdom and her lockbox of memories.

THE END

TRANSLATIONS

In order to better understand the text, especially for those from non-Arabic speaking backgrounds, the following words which appear in the book have been translated for your convenience. They are listed here in order of appearance. Please note phrases are translated as per the context in which they appear; use of these words/phrases have been italicised throughout the book.

Tayta: grandmother
Dhar: courtyard
Ijjit Aaida!Ejjitee ya binti?: Aaida has come! You came, my dear?
Bint elmtalkha: daughter of the divorced woman
Ekhti: sister
Ahwi: Lebanese coffee
Allah Yerhamou: may he rest in peace
3ayb: morally wrong
Amou: affectionate term for father in law
Abu El Banaat: father of the girls
Astagfirullah: seek forgiveness in God
Wajib: honour
La'a ya Abu Firas: No, Mr Firas
Walaw: contrary
Kifak Inta?: how are you? (masculine)
Haseeri: large straw picnic mat
Karam: grove
Wlee, skiti!: you, shut your mouth!
Khalas!: enough
Laysh bas jibe seerto?: why did you only mention him?
Kousa: zucchini
Hayk lash: that's why

Ba'daan: however
Hissee!: shut up!
Rouki binti: relax, my child (feminine)
Sharrira: troublemaker
Khalas, ekhti: enough, sister
Ma'laysh ibni: it's okay, my child (masculine)
Binti: my daughter
Ya amar: my dear
Chai: tea
Habibti: darling
Khalty: aunty
Marhaba: hello
Kifik?: how are you (feminine)
Hala: welcome
Ya zgheeri: young girl (used as a term of endearment)
Emshee: walk
Dabke: Middle Eastern dance comprising of stomping of the feet
Barzi: the traditional throne on which a bride and groom sit on their wedding day
Na'am: yes
Masebha: rosary beads
Kibbe a'raas: dish of crushed wheat and meat stuffed with mince meat, spices and nuts, then fried
Salam Khaled, habibi: hello my dear Khaled
Wallahi: I swear
Yallah, ma belashtou?: come on, haven't you started yet?
3an jaad?: seriously?
Ya3ni?: is it?
Kifik ya helwi?: how are you, beautiful?
Kifak ya ebni?: how are you, my son?
Astagfirullah, ebni: Seek forgiveness in God, my child (masculine)
Ya bint: oh daughter (as an introduction to persuading a girl to do something)
Jhaaz: bride's glory box
Tabal: celebratory drums
Zalghouta: ululation

El mtalka: the divorced woman
Salamaat: greetings
Yallah: come on
Ma'laysh tayta: it's okay, grandmother
Ya ayni ala hal bint: this girl is wonderful
Masha'Allah, la quwata illah billah: there is no power nor strength except by Allah the Almighty
Boomeh; buzzkill
Kheir?: what's up?
Abu: father of (in Arabic, adults are addressed as "Abu"meaning "father of so & so")
Mart Akhi: sister in law
Inna lillahi wa inna ilayi iraji'oon: verily we belong to Allah and verily to him we do return
Akhi: my brother
Nour: light
Bkhatrak ya ibn khalty el aziz: goodbye, dear beloved cousin
Ya binti: my child (feminine)
Sahlab: a middle eastern creamy milk and cinnamon drink
Kheir, shu fi?: ok, what's up?
Alhumdulillah ya rab: All praise and thanks be to God
Dua: prayer
Ma'lash binti: it's okay, dear child (feminine)
Makloubeh: a spicy middle eastern dish of layered eggplant, meat and rice
Sahtaan habibti, sahtaan: great health to you, my dear, great health
Ya eying shu mahdoumeh w helwa hal ammoura: by God, how cute and beautiful is this girl
Merdi: respectful of his parent's wishes
Shorbet addas: lentil soup
Kibbeh nayeh: spiced raw meat with bulgur, onion, chilli and basil
Rah enjelet bas faker bi qisithaa: I'm going to have a stroke not knowing the answer
Ma hada fi yhet fija 3eli: no one can find anything wrong with her
Wallah, btaerfou?: I swear, you know?

Sahih: that's right
Ya3ni shi 9: so, about 9
Yee, la3 binti: Hmmm, no my dear child
Na'am Aaida,Khaliki: yes, Aaida-stay
Week, hal binit!: oh my God,this girl!
Mashaa Allah: God bless
Wara eneb: stuffed grape leaves cooked on a low heat over two days
Banaati: my girls
Allah ywafikha: may God protect and keep her
Bas: but
Mart 3ami: mother in law
Yallah, ya 3arous: come on, dear bride
Shu, ya3ni?: What do you mean?
Wlek, la3: a resounding no
Wlek, what sawtik, ehkti: lower your voice, sister
Wlek.la3 ekhti. Sma3eeni: no sister, listen
Yiii, hayda marad: oh, that's an illness
La3, mniha,ma ba3ref, ya rayt: no, good, I don't know, if only
Ya3ni, shu baddik?: So, what do you want?
Layki, Soraya: look, Soraya
Naseeb: fate, destiny
Lay, wee!: look, you!
Ahla, Em Aaida: welcome, mother of Aaida
Akh: oh
Ya ebni, ya Khaled: oh my son, oh Khaled
3aerbi: scorpion